PALAIS ROYALE

A NOVEL

Amy L. Clark

Ferry Street Books
Indianapolis, IN

an imprint of Engine Books
enginebooks.org

10 9 8 7 6 5 4 3 2 1

ISBN: 978-1-938126-48-2

Library of Congress Control Number: 2020950375

Palais

Royale

CHAPTER ONE

On the way out of town, Evey asked Sebastian to list off everything he could do in less than three minutes. She said the list itself could take as long as needed.

"Roll a cigarette," he said. Sebastian was driving and Evey was watching a class of Head Start children, each gripping a handle tied to one long rope, make their way to the playground. "Play chopsticks on the piano," Sebastian said. "What about you?"

Evey watched out the passenger-side window as Sebastian navigated the car around a long curve, past a funeral home and a coffee shop called Eggspectations, toward the highway.

"Wait, no." Sebastian said, "Tell me the make and model of every car you remember ever riding in. In reverse chronological order."

"That's not the same," said Evey. She had hoped that this game would take up much more time, would get them out of Somerville at least, and maybe even past the Kowloon Club on 93 north. She had hoped that they could talk about this, about some made-up moment or gesture, all the way into New Hampshire, if not across the Maine border. She said, "And anyway, you didn't finish. There must be other things. Brush your teeth, say the Hail Mary…"

They had reached the highway, and Sebastian picked up

speed on the onramp. All the windows in the car were rolled down because of a probable carbon-monoxide leak directly into the cabin that they hadn't had the time or the money to get fixed before they left for Sebastian's brother's funeral in Maine.

"Hold my breath until I pass out," Sebastian said as he pulled into the stream of traffic, but the wind was rushing past the windows and his voice was carried away.

"What?" asked Evey.

"WHAT?" Sebastian yelled.

"I ASKED YOU WHAT YOU SAID." They were at full highway speed now.

"HOLD MY BREATH," Sebastian answered as a Saab passed them on the right in the breakdown lane.

"YOU CAN'T HOLD YOUR BREATH FOR THREE MINUTES," Evey yelled. They were behind a tractor-trailer.

"UNTIL I PASS OUT." Sebastian changed lanes. "MAKE RAMEN NOODLES."

"WHAT?"

Evey was enormously grateful that a poisonous off-gas was leaking into her ten-year-old Nissan Sentra, making further conversation impossible. Evey knew she should probably be worried about whether the car was poisoning her, whether she would be able to make rent, whether the strike at Sebastian's work would ever end. But she couldn't. She just couldn't worry about those things along with everything else. This morning, while she had packed a suitcase—a black rolling thing with a busted zipper she had stolen from her ex-husband early one morning five years ago when she crept out of a small, cheerful apartment in the town to which she was now returning—full of folded underwear and balled up socks, tee-shirts and toiletries and her good, black dress, she had envisioned several ways this car trip could go. And none of those visions had been as blissfully uncomplicated as the current reality: the deafening whoosh of wind past the open windows creating a kind of silence between Evey and her husband, buffeting all thought deeper and deeper inward, away from the unfathomable concerns of the next twenty-four hours. Evey could not think about the funeral she was about to attend, because she had never attended the funeral of a young person before, and her imagination simply failed her, or skittered back from the edges of the thoughts she tried to form about what Sebastian's brother's funeral would be like, later that afternoon. Her grief for Sebastian, and about Sebastian's dead brother Matt, felt cold and unreal, as if something clammy was lodged behind her breastbone. Evey thought her sadness and confusion felt like nothing else, but reminded her a little of guilt. Evey could not think of a single thing to say to Sebastian to provide comfort or express the weight of concern that had settled between her collar bones. So far, she had gotten away with little sighs and guttural moans, folding Sebastian's solid body into the O of her own skinny arms, and rubbing his back the way she imagined a mother would make circles on her child's shoulder blades, but Evey was terrified of the moment when she would be called upon to say something to Sebastian or Sebastian's mother about Matt's death.

Evey remembered reading Helen Keller's autobiography when she was a child, filched from her father's sagging shelves in boredom one interminable grade-school summer. What she remembered is that Keller wrote that without language, there could be no thoughts. That before she learned to sign and to understand sign language, she did not experience real cognizance, just a tangle of emotions, one knotted to the next without meaning or context. That was how Evey felt now, as if without the words to say to Sebastian, she could not properly form thoughts about Matt's death at all. And now, in the car, somewhere in the endless loop of feelings Evey understood she was experiencing, a thread of selfish panic poked up. It had been six months since she had visited her hometown, and maybe five years, she thought, since Evey voluntarily crossed state lines for anything other than a short, obligatory, holiday visit. And although Evey knew that this trip home for a funeral was not about her, she could not stop thinking that in Illium, it was always about her. Hers would be the only black face in the funeral crowd, which she suspected would number close to a hundred townspeople. Evey closed her eyes. Without looking at Sebastian, she imagined his blue eyes and the puckers of skin around them when he smiled. Sebastian was a beautiful man. He was a white man, though Evey didn't often think of him this way. But going home brought the situation into acute focus for her. Evey's father was white, Evey's husband Sebastian and his whole family were white. Evey could still name off every person of color who had attended North Illium Regional High School. And she did so now, silently to herself: the fraternal twins Nan and Yuan Wu, Michael and his little brother Bubba McKay, Priya Sharma, and Chee Chung. Evey tried to think of this list as another car game, considered yelling to Sebastian, "list off every person of color you remember from high school," but she couldn't do it. It felt more like inventory than like play. She wondered if this was what adulthood was going to be like: taking stock of the things from her past that she had not noticed at the time. Trying to put together the pieces of her life in order to form for herself a picture of who she was now and how she came to be that way.

Evey thought now that while Sebastian held his foot steady on the accelerator, she was inexorably traveling closer and closer to the town in which she was carried home from the hospital to a waiting nursery, was served her first solid meal, took her first steps. It was where she entered school as the only black (or half-black, Evey hated the distinction) child in town, where her mother died, where she was married for the first time. It was, above all, the place she had run away from when she walked out on her first husband at twenty-two years old.

The day that Sebastian's brother died, Evey had been, as usual on a Tuesday, committing adultery. Evey had her head on a bag of bulk coffee in the office upstairs. The office was really just a loft overlooking the small coffee shop interior: galley kitchen, counter space, seating area, display shelves, front door (locked now at 11:03 at night), and there was no wall, just wrought-iron balusters, like those on Evey's third-floor porch at her apartment one town over in Somerville. Evey had reached up over her head from where she was lying on the floor and gripped, one in each hand, a couple of balusters. The metal bit into her palms as she arched her back in desperate, grim pleasure. Angela slid one hand up Evey's flat stomach, and was kneading the skin there as she licked Evey's clit. Evey's eyes were closed, but she imagined that if she opened them, Angela would have hers rolled up into her head. Evey was starting to pant, starting to lose control.

Wait, Evey thought in the car, glancing over at Sebastian. Stop.
That was what happened. But before that:

"Let yourself go limp," Evey said to Angela that Tuesday night. And then, "No, you're applying too much pressure." It was ten-thirty at night and there were no customers in Great Bean. Angela was leaning over the counter, using the scale on which they weighed bags of wholesale coffee beans in an attempt to weigh her head. Evey was sure she wasn't doing it right. "Move out of the way," she said, placing a hand on each of Angela's hips.
"Hey, save it for sexual-harassment Wednesday," Angela responded. Technically, Evey was Angela's manager—boss, really—and she had instituted "sexual harassment Wednesdays"

as a way to keep the younger employees in line all the other days of the week. By facetiously promising them that they could snap as many bra straps and make as many suggestive jokes as they wanted on Wednesday, as long as the customers weren't looking, she could get them to behave nominally like adults behind the counter the rest of the week. But it was Tuesday, and none of the kids were in the shop. Angela was a part-timer, a graduate student at Emerson, and at twenty-five was about the same age as Evey, and that made her old as far as Great Bean employees went.

Angela moved out of the way, and Evey bent over the counter, gathering her long braids up in her hand. Evey lay her head gently on the coffee scale and let her neck muscles go limp.

"Eight point six!" Angela screamed. "I told you that little freak from *Jerry Maguire* was right!" Evey pictured the little white boy with his earnest glasses saying "the human head weighs eight pounds" in the stupidest movie she had ever seen. Angela, who was studying child psychology, had earlier been lamenting the idiotic way children were portrayed onscreen ("it's like," she had said, "the film version of those kids you see in Byzantine paintings, when artists thought children just looked like tiny adults, so the proportions and features are creepy and all wrong.").

"It's still the stupidest movie I've ever seen," Evey said. The bell above the door to the shop jangled. Angela ran her hand up Evey's back, and Evey unbent herself, pushing away from the countertop. The stereo was playing "Girls, Girls, Girls," too loud. The song had seemed funny and charming when the café had been full of Harvard students dishing about their professors and affecting an irony they had no overt experience to back up. It was downright hilarious to Evey to serve a sweatered sophomore or a blue-shirted young Gillette engineer an Americano while nodding along with a deadpan expression to lines about dancing chicks. But it was after ten at night and Evey had already weighed her head from boredom and she had thought, until this very minute, that she'd make it to the end of her shift at eleven without another customer, and the CD was on its eighth loop of the evening. And honestly, it was enough already.

The customer was a white guy in his middle forties, and he didn't look like a professor or an office worker or somebody's dad. He didn't look like the kind of customer it was easy to hate; he looked rather soft, as if though he wasn't outright fat, if you smacked him across the face you'd have to watch the flab below his chin reverberate.

Evey and Angela faced him across the counter. Angela was doing her ready-to-please act, standing alert and erect, eyes bulging with helpfulness, bouncing on her toes to indicate the alacrity with which she would spring to attention when the customer gave his order. This was another game they played occasionally, to make the time pass. They would act like they thought customers wanted to see them, pretending they lived to serve. Angela was disconcertingly good at it. Evey gave her a sidelong look, trying to make her face read "just stop it," but failing, by the tilt of her eyebrows, to indicate seriousness.

"Coffee. Leave room for cream. To go," Wobbles said.

"Okay, excellent. Right away!" Angela fairly screamed, and ran toward the big urns in the kitchen. "I'm just going to get you that coffee! Good choice!" she sang over her shoulder.

Wobbles looked unperturbed, credulous. He handed Evey a five and stood waiting for his change without affect.

It does not matter, Evey thought for the thousandth time, what we do here. She handed Wobbles his change, bills first, then coins on top. This is what she always thought when she thought about her job: We can do anything, because a customer only sees what he expects. But despite this, when Angela returned with the paper cup, Evey stepped nervously back, noticing that Angela had intentionally neglected to put a paper sleeve on the outside

13

of the cup. Angela handed the hot cup to the customer. He took it, then cupped his free right hand around air, moving it up and down rapidly. "Can I have one of those…" he said.

"Happy endings?" Angela asked, smiling.

"What?"

"I'll get you one!" she said. And returned with a paper sleeve to protect his hand from the heat of the cup.

The man left without comment, and Angela turned her manic grin on Evey. "Can I get you anything?" she asked.

"Enough," said Evey. It was ten minutes before they were supposed to close, but she locked the door anyway. Evey cashed out the drawer of the register and left Angela to load the dishwasher and mop the floor and blow out the steamer, while Evey went upstairs to count down the take. She knew before she went up that after she heard the steam from the milk-steamer die away, Angela would mount the stairs and caress Evey's back while she finished closing the safe, and Evey knew that without saying anything, she would say *yes, yes, let's*. She knew they would have sex and she knew she would want it, knew she had wanted it all night, had looked forward to Tuesday, the day she and Angela worked together alone, all week.

Angela, when Angela was being Angela, not fooling around or prancing at the customers, was deft and insistent; she was forthright. Evey closed her eyes for a second and imagined Angela moving around the kitchen. Some of the kids banged the pots around and kicked the fridge doors shut behind them, but Angela was never careless, was always doing no more or less than exactly what she was doing. She didn't grasp the metal coffee urns or flick the nozzles on them open; she laid her hand down and coaxed coffee into cups. She poured sugar from the big five-pound bags into the shakers in one long movement, without hesitation, and never spilling. She cut lemons for the tea into perfectly equal slices, one falling from the knife after the next. She was the only employee who Evey remembered never needing to use the first aid kit. Moving around the small kitchen with her, Evey often thought of ballet. Evey herself had never been a dancer, and had never been graceful. She was not quite in control of her long limbs at any given moment, but Angela drew the grace out of others, stepping deftly around other employees in the kitchen as if their movements were choreographed. Angela was light on her feet, but she planted them firmly, calling quietly, "behind," when she had something hot or sharp in her hands and needed to move behind Evey or one of the kids. She could adjust to other's movements in a small space before they even knew which way they were going to go themselves. Angela could look at Evey and see exactly what Evey couldn't say, without projecting her own emotion or searching for something she wished were there. And that was what Evey loved in Angela's face, that nothing was reflected there, all was openly acknowledged and taken in without judgment, without, Evey searched for the word, *apparent harm*.

It had just been a Tuesday, special for no reason except that Evey had come to wait for Tuesday each week, to wait for Angela. And later that night, when she got home and learned what had happened, she had wanted to say: I didn't know. It was just a Tuesday.

Sebastian had navigated them almost to the New Hampshire border; they were passing the big liquor store on the left, and Evey tried to force herself to look at him and think of Angela. Just thinking about the mundane moments in the shop with Angela, Evey's ears were burning. She wasn't sure why she could remember every moment of a Tuesday night working at Great Bean. Was it the heightened awareness of love? Was it just that she could telegraph that kind of boredom because it was indicative of something larger and as yet unnamed in her life? She loved her husband very much. It was just that she could not seem to hold that thought in her mind at the same time as the reality she continued to enjoy enacting with Angela once a week. She cared for Angela, and Tuesday nights felt like the only time she had where she wasn't Sebastian's wife. But she hated that she also cared deeply for the good life she had with Sebastian, and that she wasn't stupid or self-centered enough not to know that the two would come into open conflict at some point. The first time it happened, three or so months ago, it had seemed almost okay to Evey, because Angela was not a man, and because the sex they had was service-industry sex, desperate and quick and late at night on inappropriate surfaces, like cutting boards or office floors. Evey had thought of it as a professional hazard, like steam burns and a bad back. Something that she would never allow to interfere with her real life. She still thought of that time between the closing of the store and putting on her coat to walk to the T as a secret, separate time, half-unreal and existing out of the context of the rest of her life.

As soon as Evey got home from work on a Tuesday night, she would take a shower. Before even kissing Sebastian, she would stand under the hot water in their apartment, and rinse off and brush her teeth. While she was in the shower, she often thought of moments from her life with Sebastian; half consciously, images would come to her: Sebastian in jeans and an undershirt, flipping potatoes in a pan at the stove. Sebastian coming home from his job at the Somerville Theater and kissing her with cold lips before taking off his coat. Sebastian sitting beside her at a bar, passionately defending some post-apocalyptic novel she was uninterested in as they both took tequila shots. Sebastian ordering Chinese takeout and having to repeat his name four times into the phone.

But the night that Sebastian found out his brother had died, she had not had time. She had come home to find Sebastian on the floor of their living room, nearly catatonic with grief. His right hand was bleeding, and Evey had ascertained quickly that Sebastian had put his fist through a pane of thin glass in the French doors that led to the dining room. She was shocked at the unreality of the scene and at her own lack of preparation to deal with a real tragedy. She couldn't help thinking at the time that if it had been someone she cared about who had died, Sebastian or her father, who had died, she would not have been able to do something so fittingly dramatic and out of character as to make herself bleed. Once she helped him clean off his hand, it turned out not to be much of a cut. Sebastian swept the glass off their soft wood floor himself.

"Sebastian," she said loudly, taking her eyes off the road and focusing on his clean-shaven neck. "How're you holding up?"

"I'm fine," he said, though she didn't hear him.

"What?"

Louder, "I'm fine. Mom's going to be a wreck."

"Okay." She put her hand on his arm. "We're almost there."

Sebastian nodded.

"I love you," Evey said. She wasn't sure whether he heard her.

The moment Evey and Sebastian pulled up to Sebastian's mother's house, Evey's phone beeped. The sudden stillness of the car as it came to a stop on the crumbling blacktop of the driveway was jarring, and it felt to Evey a bit like vertigo. The last thing she wanted was stillness, quiet, time for a space to open up in her mind into which real thoughts might wander. So it was that she, unbuckling herself, fumbling in her purse for her phone and stepping out of the car all at once, arrived back in Illium.

The house was a small two-story saltbox, white and blunt against the sky, and looking at it felt like someone pressing a thumb into her eye. She turned quickly away from the house, heading for the trunk to retrieve her suitcase while glancing at her phone. She saw a text message from Angela. "You doing OK?" and then another: "Here with Wobbles and The Neck." As Evey trundled her suitcase onto the ground: "All my love." Angela. Evey felt a horrible swoop of happiness in her stomach. Angela checking in on her. Angela making a joke about the customers at the store. Angela sending all her love. Evey hated that it excited her, that she wanted to laugh and to cry out with the joy of being loved by someone who was not here in Illium, who was not mourning, who was evidence that Evey had a life outside of Maine, where it seemed to her that her past lived. That Evey had something to go back to. That the past did not flow in one direction only. She felt guilty at the impropriety of that stab of joy on a day like this, but she nestled the feeling of happy belonging to the city and to someone else down inside of her anyway, as she turned the sound off on her phone and placed it back in her handbag.

Sebastian's mother was in the kitchen when they entered, standing at the stove and staring at a patch of wallpaper just above it. Evey expected Sebastian to go to his mother, put his arms around her when they walked in, but he stood beside her like a shadow on the linoleum. "Elizabeth?" Evey asked. And Sebastian's mother turned to them. Elizabeth was a substantial woman, and she did not wear grief well. Sadness could be heroic or poignant on skinny woman, Evey thought. It could seem mysterious in someone who was hollowed out, but Sebastian's mother's grief, like everything else about her, was matter of fact. She looked lumpy and wrung-out, like a dishtowel thrown damply into a hamper. She was barefoot and wearing jeans and a men's button-down shirt, half buttoned. She tried to smile at them, but clearly gave up the effort half-way through and just stood. Evey felt the suitcases dangling from her arms like giant, outsized hands stuck on the end of loose, skinny wrists. She willed Sebastian to go to his mother, willed herself to be the kind of person who was easily demonstrative, or at least who knew how to arrange the features on her own face properly in a moment like this. But it was all a failure, and she said in a strangled voice, "I'll go put the bags down," and turned toward the living room. Once there, she panicked. There was no guest room in the saltbox, which Sebastian's mother had often referred to as "the cracker box," as a gentle dig at her New England neighbors and in reference to her own questionable sanity in moving her youngest child to Maine. There was only Elizabeth's bedroom and Matt's bedroom. Where, thought Evey, would they sleep that night? It was horrible, the idea of Matt's room upstairs. Evey imagined Matt had closed the door behind him on his way out of the house for the last time. Evey imagined it would still smell like Sebastian's brother. She thought for a moment of fleeing to her own father's house—just two miles away—for the night, but she knew she could not leave her husband, could not run away from this. She put the suitcases down helplessly beside the couch and sank down onto it, defeated.

The funeral was to be at one in the afternoon, and after a decent interval on the couch, Evey returned to the kitchen to tell Sebastian she was going to take a shower. Elizabeth and Sebastian were more at ease with each other in the kitchen, now, sitting at the table and talking quietly to each other, and Sebastian merely nodded when Evey slipped out again and up the stairs, carrying her whole suitcase into the bathroom with her.

She made the water as hot as it would go, and stood facing the stream. Evey had always thought it was perverse that people were expected to dress up for funerals. How could anyone think of death while pulling an infrequently used silk shirt from the closet? Why were we expected to worry about our pantyhose when someone had died?

She toweled herself off then slipped on her dark dress. The steam swirled around her, and she smudged a patch clear on the mirror. Evey withdrew a tube of mascara from her toiletry bag and thickened her eyelashes, carefully painting on the makeup to avoid any clumps. She applied lipstick in a savage smear, and rubbed her lips together. Then, she put both items into her small purse.

"Evey," she heard Elizabeth call to her from the bedroom. "Evey?"

Evey wished she still did drugs. It would be nice to feel desperate and selfish, to rub a little coke on her gums or steal a few moments to pop a handful of pills in her husband's mother's bathroom. But Evey hadn't done drugs like those since high school, and she could only glance at herself in the mirror and then hurry to Elizabeth's bedroom.

"Can you do up the back?" Elizabeth asked without looking.

"Sure," Evey said. Elizabeth was half in an enormous black dress, short sleeved and pleated, made of a stiff, thin fabric. Evey carefully moved the zipper up Elizabeth's back, obscuring with cloth the plump flesh around each vertebrae, the wings of soft tissue covering her shoulder blades, and the curve of her neck. Elizabeth's hair was pinned into a gray bun, and Evey brushed the wisps of hair at her nape. She took the necklace Elizabeth was holding from her hands and placed it around her throat, a chain of tourmaline turtles she recognized as a gift from Matt to his mother last Christmas, and clasped it at the back.

"Thank you." Elizabeth turned to face Evey and pressed her hand. Evey nodded, feeling her throat constrict. "You know," Elizabeth said, "it's different with the youngest one. I often think

I shouldn't have had a second child. Not a second son."

Evey stood very still. She felt her scalp prickle. A mouthful of air caught in her windpipe, a hitch in her terrible, living, regular breathing.

"No," Elizabeth said, her gaze steady, searching Evey's face, "I don't regret Matt. It's not something I can explain, how you love those children. But it's not the same for both of them. The first one is so much a part of you you can't separate his breathing from yours. You never know you can love like that until you have one. You never know." She was starting to cry, and Evey wished she had even so useful a thing as a tissue. "You can't ever do it again. The second one is more precious, because he's more separate from you, more breakable because of it. You can't love him the way you do the first time, so you hold him more fiercely to you, you show your love that way. Don't have another one, Evey, if God gives you a first. Put everything into that one, because then..."—she gasped, and it was a horrible, tearing sound—"then you know where it all goes. You know where your love is. All of it. It's in that one...place." Evey thought Elizabeth looked like a bowl of dough, risen beside the stove, that someone had just punched down. Evey wished she hadn't heard Elizabeth try to explain. She didn't deserve this kind of confidence, wasn't prepared to hear it. It felt as if it were one of the conversations she had overheard her father having on the phone after she had been put to bed as a child and stealthily crept back out to the head of the stairs to listen, to try to understand her father's world, the secret adult things that went on after dark. She didn't want to know these things anymore, wasn't prepared for them, couldn't help Elizabeth, couldn't even help herself. Evey put her long arms around Elizabeth, felt her damp fleshy heat, and wished she could love anything the way Elizabeth loved her children.

•

And then the limousine was in the driveway, and Evey climbed in next to Sebastian and his mother. She held Sebastian's hand as they settled into the back for the short drive to the church, and a look of recognition crossed the driver's face when he glanced at them all in the rearview. Sebastian was in a suit Evey had never seen before, but that she imagined must have been sunk in the back of their bedroom closet, waiting in the dark on a drycleaner's wire hanger for an occasion like this. He was wearing a skinny tie, and Evey looked at him and was overcome with an ocean of affection that seemed only to widen the distance between them, alone in their unfathomable emotions in that moment. She saw for the thousandth time a crescent-shaped scar just below his right eye. She knew he had that scar from a time when a neighbor boy, swinging an old phone Sebastian had found in the barn around by its long looped cord, had accidentally smashed the receiver into the bone there. He could have lost an eye, but as it was, only that small scar remained. Every time Evey saw that mark and remembered Sebastian telling her the story, she wanted nothing more than to go back in time and cradle Sebastian's blonde boyhood head in her lap, and to shake the careless ten-year-old neighbor until he was unconscious.

"Wait," Sebastian said as the car moved backward down the drive. The limo driver, familiar to Evey, paused and gave them a questioning look in the mirror. "I should bring the car," Sebastian said. "We might need it for people on the way to the cemetery."

Evey looked at him, concerned. "Everyone will have their own car, Sebastian. It's okay. Let's just go."

But Sebastian could not sit there in the limo with her and his mother, and it showed in the restless way he withdrew his hand from Evey's. "No, I'm going to bring the car."

"Do you think," Evey started to say, but then, looking at Sebastian's eyes, blue and closed off from her, she stopped. "Okay. We'll catch up with you at the church."

The limo driver left the engine to idle and soundlessly exited the front of the car to hold the door open for Sebastian. Stan, Evey thought. His name was Stan. They were in Mrs. Sanborn's third grade class together, eighteen years ago. Sebastian left the limo, and Evey put her arm around Elizabeth as the door was eased closed, thinking of how tall the playground slide had been that year. Third grade was the first year the children moved into the elementary school—third through sixth grade—behind the public park. They had played a game that year in the spring. Damming up the largest puddles on the high ground of the sand play area with constructions of sticks and mud, then carving long channels all around the playground in a Rube-Goldberg configuration of passages they had made with their winter-boot heels. Along each passage a different child would build a smaller dam and then, just before the end-of-recess bell rang, the bigger boys would jump on the dike at the head of the playground, spilling the water in a great rush out into the canals, flowing toward the sewer grate at the low end of the yard. If the dam you had built, Evey remembered, held when the water got to it, you earned the admiration of your peers and the chance to stomp it back into the earth. The water almost always made it all the way to the grate, and if it didn't they would widen the dug-out canals until it did, working seriously and endlessly, eight-year-olds with a job to do. She marveled now, sitting in the back of the limo, that they had all seemed to work together. That they had created as tiny children such a feat of engineering and teamwork. Evey didn't remember the reaction, or even the presence, of any teacher or playground monitor on those long afternoons. It seemed unreal now.

In the church, Evey sat next to Sebastian, who was rigid and immobile, his hand resting lightly on his mother's arm. Evey had never been inside St. Mary's of the Assumption in Illium before, and it was, to her eye, a strange place. A modernist church, its long windows and gold beveled lines tried to convey both the light, stark uplift of the time in the seventies when it was built and the former majesty of Catholic tradition. It failed at both.

Evey glanced around the church, watching people arrive in subdued twos or by the dozen, young people barely containing their discomfort. Evey's father entered from the back but didn't notice her as he took his spot in a pew, looking quietly upright. Evey wanted to signal him, wave a bare arm above her head to catch his attention. Her father always looked so right, so like he belonged wherever he was and like, whatever was happening, he would make the best of it. He always seemed to fit in Illium in a way Evey never could, and never got a chance to ask her mother if she did. She wanted to make some daughterly gesture of sadness and need, but she stopped herself and watched as her father bowed his head, though Evey had never known him to pray. There were women from the church, men from Matt's landscaping crew wearing dark polo shirts and black pants over work boots, some local lobstermen, teachers from the elementary and high school, Elizabeth's many friends and acquaintances—secretaries from the pediatrician's and stylists from the hairdresser, the property lawyer and almost the entire staff at the YMCA, and young people, Matt's friends, who Evey didn't recognize. Stan, the limo driver, stood at the back of the church, hesitating before taking a seat. There were more than a hundred people in attendance, as Evey had expected there would be. A death in a small town was not uncommon, but the death of a young person—and at twenty-four and still living at home, Matt's was almost a child-death—was something everyone felt they had a part in.

The music started, not swelling from the organ pipes, but tinny and wafting from the speakers of a small CD player near the lectern. The priest asked them all to rise, and suddenly Evey was sobbing. Tears dripped down Sebastian's face and he made no move to acknowledge them. Evey was gasping for breath, and as the priest started the Our Father, she steadied herself to join in. There was no one, she marveled, looking around, who was not crying. And she let herself cry with them all. Something in this room was broken, inside of Evey and in the room itself. The landscaping crew wheeled the coffin, an inexpensive, flimsy wood thing Matt's mom had selected for some unfathomable reason—the cheapest coffin money could buy, Evey was sure—in on a medieval-looking stretcher and left it in the middle of the aisle near the dais. Evey dug her fingernails into the wood of the pew in front of her, and wished she had applied nail polish yesterday. When the pall bearers left the coffin for their seats, Elizabeth cried out, a short ragged shriek that she stifled quickly. Sebastian leaned over to his mother to cover her in an embrace. Evey squeezed Sebastian's shoulder to tell him she was there, and then she sat down.

After the funeral, there was a burial in the cemetery that abutted the church. Sebastian whispered to Evey on the way out, "You don't have to stay." And Evey had wanted to say, *yes I do. Matt is my family. You are my family.* But she couldn't do it. The thought of walking to the grave exhausted her. The thought of tossing dirt onto the coffin threatened to collapse her right there, and she had smiled gratefully at Sebastian, and nodded, and found the limo driver. Sebastian would meet her later, after he brought his mother home, at the bar.

Evey took the seat in the far back of the limo, with a perfect view of the back of Stan's head, half-obscured by his neat little driver's cap.

It was probably right, Evey decided, that she had not gone

to the graveside. Evey knew Sebastian and his mother needed time to be alone after the burial. Though she had been married to Sebastian for two years, she felt now that her presence in the house would be an intrusion on the family in this moment of grief.

She was going to ask Stan to bring her to the Palais Royale. The Palais Royale, where she had spent so many nights before she left town five years ago for Boston. Those nights seemed so far away they were like a secret in her mind now, part of a distant and suppressed time that almost didn't belong to her. Evey had read in a magazine once that stroke victims who had limbs paralyzed by the trauma sometimes didn't recognize that limb as belonging to their own body, though it was attached, immobile at their side. She felt that way now about everything that had happened to her in the years between high school and when she had left Illium. She couldn't integrate her past with the person she knew herself to be, the person who was sitting in a limo driven slowly by a man who she had learned cursive next to in a cheerful public-school classroom. Stan navigated them out of the cemetery at a respectful pace.

When Evey looked at Stan in the rear-view mirror, she had the peculiar feeling that she was looking at a two-dimensional, blurred face with big green eyes staring back at her from Mrs. Sanborn's third-grade class photo. Evey wasn't entirely sure what Stan saw when he looked at her. She had always been only partly aware of the effect she had on people. She wasn't sure she looked like herself, like what she saw in the mirror, to the people of Illium. She wasn't sure that what they saw wasn't different from what, for instance, the people of Boston saw when she walked with Sebastian to a movie, or crossed a busy street against the signal, or stood behind the counter at Great Bean with Angela or the kids. She thought maybe it took the eyes of the people of Illium too long to adjust when they looked at her, so that they never really saw her features, because they were so unaccustomed to the sight of black skin. She didn't really hold it against them.

She just thought that there were probably things that she didn't see in herself, because for so long she had been seen by people who, she thought, didn't know how to look at her.

What Evey remembered about Stan was Stan in the public library, wearing a sweater that was unraveling at the cuffs, and looking sweaty, like even standing still and alone he had just finished playing tag. She remembered that when she was a child, they both used to spend a lot of time at the library after school. They were, she thought now, though she hadn't had the vocabulary at the time, both latchkey kids. And she remembered that she would go straight upstairs upon entering the library, to the adult section, to pick out a weighty novel that she wouldn't fully understand. But though she always felt that she had a right to these books, some secret invitation into the adult world because of these hours unsupervised in the library, she never felt comfortable sitting and reading among the adults, so she would take her tome back downstairs and settle herself into a chair surrounded by picture books to read. From where she had sat with the huge book she had selected, she would peek over the pages and see Stan skulking among the R.L. Stines.

"I was very sorry to hear of your loss," Stan said now, eyeing Evey in the rearview. And immediately, Evey felt herself snap back to the moment. Sitting in the limo, she felt something slip into place, and she summoned up a persona that allowed her some simulacra of who she wanted to be seen as by the people of her hometown, who she had left behind.

CHAPTER TWO

What Stan saw when he looked at Evey in the rearview was exactly what Evey was: a woman so achingly beautiful at twenty-seven that it was not possible to look at her without picking one detail on which to focus. Men were mesmerized by her collarbones, women traced the arch of Evey's bare foot in her sandal, and everyone, *everyone* was fascinated by her eyes, so dark there was no visible distinction between her pupil and her iris.

And Stan was certainly no exception. Stan hadn't seen Evey for four years, and he remembered the last time he glimpsed the hem of her dress, a brilliant green dress she was wearing that day. He wasn't sure what he had thought that day, when they had seen each other in passing. And he wasn't sure what he thought about having Evey in the car with him now. He was experiencing a failure of emotion.

Stan glanced at Evey in the rearview. "I was sorry to hear of your loss," he said. Her features didn't change. She had taken out a pack of cigarettes, extruding one from its box, and was tapping it, filter down, on the armrest. Stan looked quickly back at the road.

"Are funerals a full time thing around here," Evey said, "or do you drive for weddings and other things too?"

"I don't do this," Stan said, not looking in the mirror. "My father owns the limo company. I'm just helping out for today."

Stan did not say that when Sebastian's mother had contacted Altman Livery to say that she would need their help for the funeral service, Stan had told his father he would be the driver today. He did not say that his father was always after him to work for the company full time, help out with the family business. He would not tell Evey that he had always resisted working as a driver, resenting even the quick trips to the jetport for the occasional executive. He did not tell Evey how much he hated the assumption his father had always made that this was what Stan should do: come work for the family business.

Stan was disappointed in himself for never coming up with a better career plan; never creating a better plan for his life in general. He didn't mention to Evey that when he took this job for Matt's funeral, he did so knowing that Evey would be at the funeral, in the car he drove. He had heard from friends in town who used to have beers or go fishing with Matt that Sebastian, who Stan had never met, was married to Evey. Stan doubted that Evey knew that this job was unpaid—Stan's father never accepted money for the funeral of a child, and though Matt was in his twenties, he was still a child to the people of Illium. In dying now, Matt had met some deadline in Stan's father's mind. When his father had told him that this would be a job without payment, Stan had quietly been touched that his father still thought of people only a few years younger than Stan as children. He had pressed his father's hand when he took the keys to the car from him, had donned the uniform of the company in front of the mirror in his bedroom this morning, making sure the buttons were straight and his shirt was unwrinkled.

"The uniform is nice," said Evey. "It suits you."

It was a mean thing to say, a belittling thing to put him in his place, and Stan knew it. But faced with this beautiful person, this person who had lived in the city and met people and worked jobs and had drinks in nice bars and probably read the newspaper in the morning, since leaving Illium, and then now had suffered this great sadness, Stan would have felt small no matter what she said to him. He raised his eyes to look again at her in the rearview, but saw himself instead. Some of his hair, lank and banana-yellow, had flopped out over his forehead from beneath his ridiculous cap.

"What do you do, Stan?" Evey asked.

"I play poker," he said, turning them around a tight right corner.

"Do you get health insurance for that?"

If he hadn't been driving, Stan would have been staring at his shoes. "I make ninety-five-thousand dollars a year playing poker. Online. And at tournaments." Stan stared straight ahead at a Civic in front of him on Main Street that was going a painful fifteen miles an hour. It wasn't entirely true. He worked twenty-four hours a week at the deli of the Stop n' Shop on Route One and played poker most nights and all day on Tuesdays. Once, he had made ninety-five-thousand dollars gross in about a year of competitive play, but right now his bank account had fifteen-hundred dollars in it, and Stan could picture the ATM receipt proving it curled in his wallet, which was getting sweaty between the folds of grey material covering his right buttock. Evey didn't respond. Most people didn't respond when you said you made ninety-five-thousand dollars a year playing poker. Stan wondered what her response would have been if he had described his work at the deli, said: *I like it. Even though it is meaningless, what I do, slicing the cheese thin and setting out all the trays of pre-made tortellini and egg rolls, chicken salad and coleslaw, wearing the cut-proof gloves to operate the meat slicer.* He liked the way it was always a little cold back behind the counter, and the fact that each customer handed him a little torn ticket before he asked them what they would like. He liked taking a break and eating a bag of chips with the guys—twice a day for fifteen minutes, and then half an hour for lunch. Stan wanted to be the one to make pasta salad and the mac n cheese, had been lobbying his manager for this step up. But he couldn't tell Evey all this, because it was *embarassing*, he thought, to find this kind of work reassuring the way he did.

It was a beautiful day. The sun was almost painfully bright, and Stan paused at a crosswalk to let a teenaged couple in shorts and tank tops saunter across. He wished he weren't wearing heavy, stiff black shoes. He wished he were already at the Palais Royale, where Evey had requested he drive her, and he wished that he was not her driver. He wished he were drinking a very cold beer from a tall bottle in the gloom of the Palais, watching the bartender move from side to side as she collected glasses and wiped down the bar top. He wished the sun was going down.

There was something that Stan wasn't telling Evey. He wasn't sure if he had to tell her, if he had to make an announcement of it, or if that was just overly dramatic and he was just being stupid. Stan was friends with James, Evey's ex-husband. Of course they had all gone to school together, occasionally gotten in trouble together as children. But he suspected that there was something potentially damaging about the information that he and James still hung out together. That Evey wouldn't like it, or that Stan wouldn't be able to say it casually. "Don't fuck around," he mumbled to himself. Evey heard nothing.

"Come have a drink with me," Evey said.

"At the Palais?"

"Isn't there a bar in the back of this thing?"

Stan knew every inch of this car. When he was a child, he would climb into the leathery depths of the back of a similar limo with his older brother to play made up games—they were aliens in a sleek space ship, or the brain of a Transfomer that would momentarily turn from a car into a dangerous predator. He drove himself and five friends to the prom in an earlier incarnation of this limo (his father always bought Towncar stretches, new) and had brought it to the car wash and scrubbed the thin carpet when Molly Higgens threw up in back. Evey had been at the prom, with James. Stan remembered Evey being at the prom—but it was James's outfit, rather than Evey's dress, that Stan remembered. James came to the prom in a powder blue tuxedo with a ruffled shirt two decades out of fashion. He wore a blue bowler and carried a cane. And Stan had wished more than anything that night that he had been the kind of person who could pull off that outfit, who could make a joke of the whole event and still be its star. Stan would have worn all orange to the prom just to get Evey to dance with him. He would, at the time, have risked anything—not just his reputation (what little pride he had in those days) but his job at the grocery store, his car (the old Duster he had bought and paid for himself against his father's wishes), his friendships, his family. Stan would have driven off a cliff, would have gone to CVS to buy her tampons, he would have done all her French homework or stood up for her in a group of teenagers on the soccer field after school if she had ever shown any need of defending. Stan once ate part of a soda can in the cafeteria on a dare from James to try to get Evey to notice him.

"There is," Stan said. "But I'm driving."

"Oh, pull over and park," Evey said.

"Where should I park?" Stan straightened up behind the wheel.

"Behind the library."

Stan drove the short distance quietly, moving the big, silent car past the elementary school he and Evey had both attended, past the bank and the drycleaner and a McDonald's that featured a parking lot where kids sat drinking milkshakes and dealing drugs most evenings. He drove down the tree-lined street and pulled into the library lot. He found an old oak to park beneath. When he had eased the car into the spot, he killed the engine and got out. Stan put both feet on the pavement and stood still for a moment. He was blinded by the sun; it was a cacophony of brilliance, bouncing from every surface in the parking lot—cars, and the door handle of the limo, the glossy leaves of the oak, the brick walls of the building itself. Heat was radiating off the blacktop. He blinked once and then moved out of the way of the driver's side door. Closing it behind him, he thought, *Evey.* Walking three steps to her door in the back, each footfall said, *I love you, Evey. No you don't*, he told himself. He grasped the handle, *I love you.* Opened the door, *I love you.* Slid in beside her in the cool dark, *I love you.* She moved out of his way, and he didn't touch her leg.

Stan wanted Evey in a way he couldn't explain. It wasn't something he could have put into words, not even to himself.

Stan remembered the first time he met Evey. She had ridden the bus with him on the first day of kindergarten. She had descended the steps of the bus in the school yard just ahead of him. And his memory of this moment is as if of a photograph. In the photograph, Evey is in front of him, and he can see her only from the waist down. Her brown shorts concealing half her little legs. A pinkish Band-Aid stuck to the place on the back of her ankle just above her heel. She wore, he is certain of it even now, white Keds sneakers on that first day of school. And at her side, swung a plastic lunchbox she had clasped loosely in her left hand. Because it is a child's memory he has lodged in his brain, there is no perspective and no proportion. In his memory, her legs and arms, her hands and lunchbox are not small—they are the same size as his. He knows that if he saw a photograph of that moment now, as an adult, it would be the photograph of a child, but in his memory, she is simply a person. And a person who he wants. Now, Stan wonders if Evey remembers her first day of school. He wonders if this moment had any significance in her life. And if it did, he wants to know if he was a figure in the memory, even on the periphery of her remembered vision. Stan is not sure what he would have done to be able to love Evey when he was in kindergarten, and he wonders what he would be willing to do now.

In the car, he allowed himself only to sit very still and close to her and to try to think about ways of making conversation. "Like I said," he said, "I'm very sorry for your loss." And then, after a minute in which Evey didn't respond, "It must be good to be back in town." *This*, he thought, *is where I tell her that I'm friends with James. This is where I ask her if they're in touch.* Stan knew they weren't in touch. Stan knew that Evey probably didn't know what a disastrous mess James was these days. He felt like he was holding something large and finely balanced, and that it was about to tip out of his hands.

She shifted in her seat, then slumped back and let out a long breath. "I love my husband very much," she said.

Stan looked away. He imagined her saying *I love my husband very much*, but *it's not working out between us.* Or maybe she meant this as a warning. Maybe she meant, *I can see what you want, but you have to know how much I love my husband.* "How did you two meet?" asked Stan. "He never lived in Maine, did he?"

Evey started to say something, her mobile features worked in an effort to shape a sentence that looked to Stan hopeful or cheerful, but maybe also practiced. But she sighed again instead of saying whatever it was she was about to tell him, and slumped back into the seat like a starched shirt that has fallen off its hanger onto the bottom of the closet. "No," she said. "His family moved to Illium when he was in college. Can I smoke in here?"

Stan gripped the door handle. His father never let customers smoke in the cars. "Crack the door open."

"Did you know his brother? Matt?" Evey opened the door and a slice of sunlight fell on the seat next to her leg, unwelcome. She lit the cigarette and inhaled.

"No. He was younger than us. I read about the accident in the paper, and after that it turned out that I knew a lot of people who knew him, but I never met him. His mom goes to our church."

Evey looked surprised. "That was your church we were at?"

Stan nodded. "Do you want a drink? We only have whisky and cognac."

"Either. No, cognac." Evey was wearing a dress that was so black it made her skin look gray. It was such fine silk Stan's fingers felt rough from looking at it.

He filled a glass with too much cognac and handed it to her, then topped one up to the mid-point of the glass for himself. They sat and drank in the weird filtered summer of the back of the limo for a minute. And then Stan started to feel as if the whole affair was decidedly and unnecessarily solemn, like they were observing a moment of silence and it had gone on a moment too long. He almost couldn't sit there anymore.

"Cognac is gross," Evey said.

He sighed with relief. "Yeah. I think only old people drink cognac. But you have to try, you know. It's important to try things."

Evey tapped her cigarette ash out the door.

"I'm not a big fan of whiskey either," Stan said. "I used to think my father put the most disgusting, most adult types of liquor in his cars specifically so I wouldn't sneak in and drink them. In high school we used to mix it with the most horrible stuff. Kool-Aid. Kiwi-Strawberry Snapple." This Town Car was not new, would probably be replaced by Stan's father within the year. And Stan had spent little time in it, but could picture the seams of the upholstery, the neat compartments in the side for bowls of nuts, a trashcan, and yes, four highball glasses and two decanters of liquor, that Stan's father had carefully and mercifully filled to the top last night, after he wiped down the seats with a damp rag and washed and waxed the whole outside.

"You know, Matt was in Iraq." Evey finished her cigarette and tossed the butt out the door. She immediately withdrew another cigarette from her pack, then looked as if she changed her mind, and tapped it against her thigh. "That's part of what's so stupid about the whole thing." She went for the cigarette after all, and the lighter flared. "Anyway, he hated the army. But his uncle told him he should get a tattoo while he was over there, or he would regret it later. Really," Evey said, "he told Matt he would regret not getting a tattoo while he was in Iraq. So he did. He got 'USA' done in red, black and blue. Big block letters with stars and things inside them. He got it on his forearm, just below the crease. That inside of the elbow crease, what do you call that?" Evey inhaled, and then exhaled, pointing smoke out the crack between the door and the frame.

"I don't know. I don't think there's a name for that."

"There must be. Everyone has one."

Stan thought about this for a moment, about whether there was a name for every thing of which everyone had one. He wasn't sure.

Evey took another gulp of cognac. "When he came back from the war and I asked him why he got it there, he said, 'So I can always see it, and how ugly it is.'"

Stan looked at Evey and tried to make his face completely blank, tried to be completely open. This was not difficult for Stan, for two reasons. One, his face was set up that way. It had something to do with his nose, which was so snub it looked as if his mother, in a fit of the zeal that kind of love engenders, had rubbed the end off trying to get a smudge of dirt when he was a child. And two, it was possible to discern in Stan's small, round eyes what Stan had always known to be true: there were many things in the world which he did not understand. This was one of those things, and Stan was open to it, and was also ready let it roll off him if it turned out that it was simply another thing he would never understand in the vast and varied world.

Evey exhaled, threw her burning cigarette out of the car, and closed the door with a click, eliminating the single piercing ray of sunlight that had disturbed the murk of the big back seat. She moved her left hand up toward her face and then let it flutter there uselessly in an aborted gesture. Stan caught her hand with his, without thinking. And he pulled it down to rest on the seat between them, his fingers around hers.

Evey let it lay there for a moment. And it seemed to Stan that they could both feel his body vibrating from his heartbeats, which were much too fast.

Then she leaned over and kissed Stan on the mouth. He didn't stop her, didn't know what to do. He sat very still and didn't lean into the kiss, but opened his lips, just a little. She pulled back and looked at him for a minute. Then she leaned forward again and kissed him so hard her teeth skidded against his.

The neckline of her dress hung loose from her body when she leaned forward, and that was all that needed to happen for Stan to imagine her small, bare breasts. That was all that need to happen for Stan to let go of something inside him and for both of them to notice that it had happened by the bulge in his gray uniform pants. She moved away from him on the car seat and reached down to undo the straps on her shoes. Stan wasn't entirely sure what would happen next, but as she pulled one tiny silver strap from its small buckle, he wished she would bend toward the floor that way forever, he wished he could do nothing more than watch her back and arm and foot and feel this prolonged ache inside him for the rest of his life. When she straightened from the waist, he kissed her on the side of her face, on her neck, as if now that they were in contact again he could not have lived another moment without her skin next to his, knowing that if there were some hesitation one of them would think better of the contact, one of them would think. He licked her neck, thinking of ice cream. "Evey Kiss," he said. When she unzipped her dress, he turned, and from where he sat on the limo seat next to her, placed his hand flatly on her breast, and then ran his palm down her torso to her underwear. Her dress was caught around her ankles. When she lifted her legs to pull the dress off her feet, Stan stopped.

He shrugged out of his uniform jacked and then stopped again. "I have to tell you something, though," he said, not looking at Evey.

"No, you don't. Whatever it is, I don't want to know," Evey said. "Just lay down a minute, without this," she poked one of the buttons of his white shirt out from their holes. He finished the job and lay down in his pants, tight across the crotch, and his undershirt, which was clean.

He started to say, "I really think—"

"Nope." She laid her hand on the side of his face. Stan struggled out of his shirt, and took off his shoes, then she pushed him back on the long seat. He lay back, and she moved so her body was half on top of him, her lips resting on his neck where he had turned his head. She just lay there, very still. He held her hand in his. He could feel how warm she was, and light. Could feel the tautness of her naked skin. He thought nothing, not even about what he had wanted to tell her.

What Stan had been about to tell Evey was that he had an enormous penis. It was, he knew from not-extensive experience, the biggest penis most people had seen. He had a nickname in high school, bestowed on him by the boys who had grown up showering in the locker room with him, staring in awe and repulsion, and making it all into a joke. He remembered the last girl he had gone home with. A girl from Portland he picked up at Rosie's bar one night when the game was on. She told him that watching him put on a condom made her think of the precision needed for surgical procedures. The sex with that girl was fine, and he had loved her plumpness. But it sometimes caused problems, his penis. Not the least of which was the little speech he felt he had to give women before sex, the embarrassed fair warning. Some women laughed, or frowned. They often didn't believe him at first, or thought he was being vain or funny, or that he was strange and possibly dangerous. No one thought he was trying to just be nice, until they actually saw it. It was better if he told them, though. He did not think now of the condom in his pocket, or why he had placed it there on his way to a funeral. He had told himself that morning that it was just because, it was just something he wanted to get into the habit of doing, carrying around a condom, like his wallet went in one pocket and his cell phone in another, like some men carried around pocket knives. He did not let himself think, even now, that it had had something to do with Evey.

"Stan?"

He could feel the vibration in her throat and chest when he spoke, and hoped she'd never stop. "What?"

"Promise me something."

"What?"

"Promise me you won't fuck me."

"Okay. I promise." Stan thrilled to hear the word *fuck*, even spoken in denial of what he wanted. He cherished the sound of it from Evey's mouth, formed by her tongue.

"Okay," she slid her hand down his pants, past the pocket, and around to where his cock was.

"I'm not going to fuck you, Evey."

"Okay. Because, I don't think we should. I mean, or maybe we should. I would—"

"It's okay."

They lay there for a long time, not moving, not talking, just being close. Stan thought this might be what love felt like, but he wasn't sure. Maybe it was what tenderness felt like. Or maybe it was just excitement. He didn't care that he wasn't, it seemed, going to have sex with Evey Kiss in the back of his father's limo, behind tinted windows, in the parking lot of the public library in his home town. He didn't even care that he had almost had sex with her, or that for one moment he had thought that was what would happen next. He didn't care that she was married, or that he had thought about her for what seemed like his whole life. He didn't care about the funeral, or his job, or his apartment in his parent's basement, didn't care about the people he would see later at the Palais Royale and that they were the same people he always saw. He didn't care about James. He didn't care about Evey, or the car. He just lay there, and admired the moment, admired himself and her, and being so still.

The sun was still up, it would be light for hours, but it was getting later. Evey didn't move. Stan tightened all his muscles to keep himself from encouraging her to move, and to keep himself from keeping her there on top of him by some force or gesture.

Evey still did not move, but after a moment, she said: "I'm having an affair."

"What?" Stan was startled, but he forced himself again to remain perfectly still. "You're not having an affair. We didn't do anything. I mean, we didn't cross any significant boundaries." Evey didn't respond, and after a minute, Stan said, "Evey? Evey, it's okay."

"No. No, it's not okay." Evey turned her head so that she was facing him. "It's not you. I'm having an affair with someone else."

"You are?"

"Her name is Angela."

Stan felt a small ecstasy, but he was not entirely sure what excited him. The thought of Evey with another woman? The thought that if she was having an affair, it somehow absolved him of any wrongdoing? The idea that perhaps this meant there was more to come? He tried not to think; he tried just to listen. "Does Sebastian know?"

"Of course he doesn't know. And you don't know either. You have to keep this in an entirely separate part of your brain from the part you normally use. You have to not know this after I tell you about it. In fact, you should put this whole afternoon in that place and keep it there."

"Mmm. Compartmentalizing?" Stan pictured shoving a thought into a cardboard box and sealing it with packing tape.

"Sure. Whatever. Her name is Angela and I work with her."

"Do you love her?"

"That's not the point, Stan."

Stan was not sure what the point was supposed to be.

Evey said, "I don't know why I'm telling you this. I don't know why I'm doing any of this."

"I won't tell anyone."

"No, you won't."

They lay there for awhile longer, not talking. The thought of Evey having an affair was not taped down into submission in Stan's head; it wouldn't stay put no matter how he tried. It buzzed like electricity in his mind. Stan pictured Angela: she was short and dark-skinned, she was painfully thin. No, she was tall, too tall, gangly and awkward. It didn't matter. It wasn't Angela's physicality that was interesting, it was the fact of her, the fact that Stan had a secret of Evey's now. There would be a connection between the two of them. There would exist something close and unspoken, something small of hers that Stan could take care of, cradle, nurture on his own. He could do that for her. And then Evey slowly moved off of him. Stan almost thanked her, but thought better of it. And then he thought perhaps she should thank him. He wasn't, after all, going to say anything to anyone.

When she got up, Stan reached down on the floor without looking, fumbling for his shirt. When he had it, he realized it was now very wrinkled and gave it up, throwing it in a ball onto the front passenger seat. He would put on the uniform jacket when he got back into the driver's seat. He put on his shoes, and then drank more cognac from his glass while Evey got dressed. "You've always done your hair like that," he said as he handed her a drink. Evey's hair was plaited in swooping lines close to her skull, with thin braids that hung down and away from her face in the back. Stan thought that the configuration was amazing, that it showed off the perfect shape of her skull. He wanted to ask her who did that for her. He wanted to know who in her life had the skill and the intimacy to create that for her.

"I had it different for a while."

When she was zipped back up and had her shoes properly on, Stan said, "It's amazing, you know, you look like you were never undressed. Some women need hours in front of a mirror. It's like some people, after they cry, there's not snot or anything on their face, they just recover immediately."

"Yeah, I can do that with crying too," said Evey. "Make it look like it never happened. It's one of my skills. I don't know that it's an honorable one."

"What should we do?" Stan asked, putting down his glass in one of the perfectly sized holders.

"I don't know," Evey was looking out the window. She gulped some cognac. "We should go to the library." She finished her drink while he shrugged into his uniform jacket.

She didn't look like she was kidding, so Stan opened the door. They got out of the limo into the early summer sun, which was beginning to fade just perceptibly now. Everything felt hot and slow until they were inside the library. When they made it inside the front doors, Stan felt strange wearing his uniform in the public library in Illium, with a beautiful woman in a simple, extraordinary dress next to him. Beside the front desk there was a large sign on an easel which read "Story Hour 4:00." Evey grabbed Stan's hand and pulled him into the room to their right.

There were about twenty children sitting cross-legged on the carpeted floor. *Indian-style, we used to call it,* thought Stan. There was a woman on a stool at the front of the room, holding a book and wearing many silver bracelets on her right arm. They clinked together when she opened the book and held it up to her audience. No one looked up when they entered the room. Stan and Evey sat down behind the children, leaning against the far wall of the room. The librarian moved the book around so everyone could see the illustration of the mouse asking for a cookie on the first page.

CHAPTER THREE

In his mother's living room, Sebastian was eating a ham sandwich and thinking about Camus. He thought he remembered that the protagonist of *The Stranger* had caught a lot of shit for eating, or smoking, or maybe it was drinking, while he was sitting with his mother's dead body on the day that she died.

What was it now, he thought, about our culture in this new century that scoffed so wearily at self-sacrifice? The idea of sitting in his mother's house on the day that his brother was buried and *not* eating a ham sandwich was slightly ridiculous to him. Refusing food on a day like this would have seemed melodramatic. Maybe that was it. Self-consciousness, or acting out of a knowledge of what one *should* do, has become the uncool to the point of taboo, he thought. *How disgusting*, he thought, that self-knowledge—examining one's own psyche—is a thing we abhor.

Sebastian was, in fact, guiltily savoring the ham. He and Evey were both vegetarian.

Since his mother had moved to Illium when Sebastian was in college, and after Sebastian's father had left her for good, Sebastian couldn't revert to most of his childhood ways when he came home to see her. She had moved into the nice salt-box they were in now; she called it the "cracker box." Sebastian couldn't come home and sleep in his childhood single bed, surrounded by rock posters or track trophies like other people his age. He had never brought his laundry home. So he reverted to other aspects of his growing-up, and that included eating ham sandwiches and saying the rosary with his mother. He wouldn't tell Evey that he had eaten meat.

His mother, in the armchair beside his, was eating potato salad into which she had mashed up a Vicodin and an Ambien. She had never been able to swallow pills, and Sebastian thought that his knowledge of this childish detail of his mother's life might just be one of the most terrible burdens he had to bear. To his great shame, his mother's weaknesses or needs had always caused him deep consternation.

When Sebastian got the call from his mother, he was walking the picket line outside the Somerville Theater with the rest of the striking projectionists. It was a warm day, and they were all in jeans and tee-shirts. They had been ambling slowly in a circle in front of the entrance for four hours, since the theater opened for the evening business, using the scab labor that Sebastian couldn't really hate—college kids who needed the money and wouldn't look the protestors in they eye when they walked past on their way to their posts at the big platter machines inside. The projectionists knew the law; as long as they kept moving, they couldn't be ordered off the sidewalk. They were chatting with each other, because after so many hours, they couldn't be bothered to shout any slogans, and passing cigarettes and bottles of water among themselves. Sebastian's phone had been set to vibrate and stuffed into the right pocket of his pants. When it went off, he assumed it would be Evey, calling to tell him she'd be home late or asking if he could pick something up from the store on his way home. He fished the phone out of his pocket and glanced at the screen before answering. When he saw that it was his mother, he almost didn't pick up. He hesitated, because his mother was prone to calling him recently with inane updates about the neighborhood (someone's kid he didn't know was diagnosed with leukemia, another neighbor hadn't cut her lawn in three weeks) and Sebastian didn't want to take that call while walking around with five other guys. But his guilt got the better of him, and he answered.

"It's Matt," his mother had said. "It's your brother."

Sebastian didn't remember the rest of the conversation accurately. At that moment he had known something was irretrievable, irreversibly wrong. That something was broken in his life and his mother's life. What Sebastian remembered clearly was that he kept walking, staring at the once-white sneakers of the young man in front of him. He hadn't stopped moving and he hadn't realized he was crying until after hanging up the phone. The guy in front of him had looked back and said, "Sebastian, are you all right?"

"My brother just died," he said. And as soon as he uttered it, it felt like a betrayal of Matt. "My brother just died. I have to go home."

He had walked off the line toward the street that would take him home. The man ahead of him in the picket line had followed him. He looked concerned, and Sebastian was sure in retrospect that the concern was genuine and honest, but at the time he had thought the boy was scrolling through sympathetic catch phrases, trying to find one that fit. "I'm fine," Sebastian had said. "Or I'm not. You should just leave me alone. It's okay. I have to go home." He thought he had seen a fleeting relief on the boy's face as he walked off. He could only imagine now that it was a relief—what do you say? What could you do?

Sebastian had walked home and felt, despite the sunlight, cold. He dialed his mother's phone and got the busy signal. He dialed again. On the fourth try he got through. His mother was not crying, though Sebastian was. She explained that she was still at the hospital. Her brother Jack was coming to pick her up. Jack was going to help her arrange for the funeral. When she said the word "funeral" her voice started to shake. Sebastian didn't want to ask his mother how Matt had died, but he couldn't not know, and after a while, he said, "What happened?"

"He just died," his mother said. "It was at work. He was with Johnson. Something with the truck. He didn't hear it coming, or Johnson was going too fast. He's a mess, Johnson."

When Sebastian got to the apartment, his mother had just finished explaining that Matt had been hit by a truck. Hit by a truck! He tried for several minutes to put his key in the front door lock, but couldn't get it to go. He focused on the word YALE engraved on the brass lock. When he got into the apartment, his mother was telling him she had to go. She was telling him to call Evey, that he shouldn't be alone. Sebastian did not call Evey. He went inside and sat down in the middle of the living room floor. When he hung up the phone, he got up again. He put his right fist through one of the panes in the French door and then sat down again, bleeding.

Sebastian's mother, Elizabeth, shifted in her chair. "This is horrible potato salad," she said quietly. "I don't know why people always think food is such a comfort at times like these." She was staring straight ahead at the large, dark cabinet television. It was silent; it was off. "People tend to think there's something moral about mashed potatoes. It's ridiculous."

Sebastian realized that his mother hadn't looked at him once since the funeral. He looked at her profile, and his grief at his brother's death was overwhelmed by guilt. That he would go on to do complicated, adult things—and his brother would not— was unbearable to him. That he would leave in several days to go back to Boston, and leave his mother alone in her house without her youngest son, was a fact with weight he was uncertain he could carry. "It all feels so unreal," Sebastian heard himself say to his mother.

"Would you like to pray?" she asked. "I keep praying the Hail Mary, because it is a mother's prayer, and it makes me feel more present."

"Praying makes it worse. When I pray, I feel like I'm a completely different person. Like maybe the person praying is someone this could have happened to, but not me."

"That's terrible. How can you say things like that?"

"I don't know. I'm sorry, Mom. I'm going to get a glass of water. Do you want anything from the kitchen?"

Elizabeth did not respond.

Sebastian went into the kitchen and ran the tap until the water was cold. He got a glass from the cupboard and filled it. He drank the whole glass down, standing at the sink and without turning off the faucet. Then he held it under the stream of water to fill it again. He looked away for a moment at the electric clock on the wall, and the weight of the water filling the glass surprised him. He dropped it into the sink and it shattered in the porcelain basin.

"Jesus," said his mother, arriving in the doorway to the kitchen. "Are you okay? What did you do?"

"It's nothing, Mom," he said. "I broke a glass. I'm sorry."

His mother walked slowly across the kitchen floor to where Sebastian was standing at the sink. He thought she was going to put her hand on his shoulder. But she grasped his shirt and pulled him to his knees on the old linoleum. "You pray with me." She said, "Hail Mary, full of grace, the Lord is with thee."

Sebastian started to pray with her. "Blessed art thou among women, and blessed is the fruit of thy womb Jesus." His voice got stronger: "Holy Mary, mother of God, pray for us sinners, now and at the hour of our death."

His mother whispered, "Amen." She started again: "Hail Mary, full of grace." She said the prayer three times in a row, and Sebastian said it with her. After the last Amen, she got off her knees and turned to go back to her chair in the living room. Sebastian didn't know what to do. He slowly rose from where he was kneeling, then went to the refrigerator, and stood in front of it. There was a picture of a pair of red alligator shoes on the door that his mother had cut out from a magazine and taped up many years ago for some reason Sebastian couldn't fathom. He opened the refrigerator door and stood there for a long time.

After a while, Sebastian took a beer from the fridge. It was a Miller, something he would never normally drink. He popped the tab on the can, and walked toward the living room. His mother was asleep in her chair, and seeing her there, Sebastian felt exhausted, like he could sleep for twenty hours. He made his way quietly up the stairs to the bedrooms in the house. At the top of the stairs, he hesitated and then went to his brother Matt's room. The door was closed and he imagined that it had not been opened since Matt had shut it on his way to work the morning that he died. Sebastian eased the door across the lintel.

It was astonishingly bright in Matt's room. Though the curtains had been pulled in the rest of the house, Matt's shades and windows were open, and the full force of the summer sun was streaming across his unmade bed. Sebastian could hear traffic on the street outside the windows. He stepped across the threshold and set his beer down on top of the dresser. He turned around to close the door. He didn't think he could do more than one thing at once, at the moment.

Now that he was in his brother's room, Sebastian felt for the first time that he was at home. Matt had taken this room when their mother bought the house. He was ten years younger than Sebastian, so while Sebastian was in his sophomore year at Tufts, Matt had only been in the fourth grade. He had grown up in this room, and had only ever left when he went into the Army. He had come back from war to this room. Standing there, Sebastian felt like he was at home with the dead. That was how he had thought of Matt's body at the funeral, and after: as the dead man. It was much easier to think that there was a dead man, being sung over in the church, there was a dead man being lowered in his coffin, than it was to think these things were happening to his brother.

Sebastian moved to the dresser, but instead of picking up his beer, he pulled open the topmost drawer. He smiled hysterically at the sight of all of Matt's white athletic socks, rolled into bulging balls. Matt's boxers were all folded in half and rolled from the band to the hem, and Sebastian was momentarily stunned to realize that he had never known that Matt folded his underwear in such a particular way.

Sebastian looked around the room. Matt and he had never been as close as he wished they were. They had only really been children together for a year or two, because of the ten years separating their births. Matt was so little when their father had left, so small, still, when Sebastian had gone to college and their mother had moved Matt to Illium. When Sebastian had come to Illium to visit he had never known quite how to interact with his younger brother. He came home infrequently in any case; Sebastian had moved off the Tufts campus into Medford in his sophomore year (then later to Somerville), and once he had his own apartment, he had only returned to Illium for Thanksgiving and Christmas.

•

Once, Matt had visited Sebastian and Evey in their apartment in Somerville. Matt had been seventeen at the time, and had driven down from Maine and got lost in a mess of side streets out by the U-Serve Storage units. By the time he arrived, it was nine-thirty at night, and Sebastian just handed him a tallboy of Pabst Blue Ribbon. Matt had sat at their kitchen table and eased one work boot off with the toe of the other. They had talked about the drive up –Matt making jokes about the traffic and the impenetrability of the streets, and they had talked about the house in Illium and their mother. As it got later and they had drank more, Sebastian asked Matt a question he knew his mother would want him to ask: "Do you have any idea what you want to do next year? After you graduate?"

"Nope," Matt had said, hunching forward over his beer.

"You could come look at colleges in Boston, you know. We could be close by."

"Not really interested."

"Matt, why? You do so well in school, and you're going to have to do something."

"It's okay, I'm just not interested. I hate the city, for one thing. And I think I need some time off."

"So what are you going to do?" Sebastian insisted. "You have to do something."

"I know it. Don't worry about it."

Sebastian took a deep breath and vowed to let it go. His gaze rested on Matt's shoes, size ten work boots. Sebastian had never owned a pair of work boots in his life. He looked at Matt's backpack, an old Army-surplus pack he had picked up in the Old Port at some point. Sebastian tried to imagine what it contained: homework? A change of clothes? A book Matt was reading? His asthma inhaler would be in there, and his cell phone. But beyond that, Sebastian had no idea what his brother would carry with him, had no idea, he supposed, what kind of person his brother was growing up to be. And it frustrated him and made him sad. "Do you have a girlfriend?" Sebastian asked his brother, looking up into Matt's face.

"Yeah, I do." Matt took another drink.

"How's that going?"

"It's fine, I guess."

"Matt," Sebastian said, "tell me about your life."

"I'm seventeen, Seb. There's nothing to tell."

Turning from Matt's sock drawer, Sebastian noticed a cardboard mask, painted orange with uneven black stripes. The mask was held to a porcelain phrenology head by its sagging elastic band. Sebastian remembered that mask. Matt had been a tiger in a school play in fourth grade. The play had something to do with the jungle, Sebastian thought, though he didn't remember the plot. The performance had been a couple days before Thanksgiving, and Sebastian had returned home for the holiday early to watch his brother. Though Matt had not had a starring role that Sebastian remembered, and his costume had not been one of the best, Matt's participation in the play had won him an unprecedented pride from their mother. What Sebastian remembered was sitting in the creaking folding chairs in the Illium Elementary School gymnasium, feeling afraid for his brother. His mother's excitement at Matt's part in the play made Sebastian wary; he was sure that Matt would forget his lines, or stumble on his way to center stage. But Matt, always oblivious of this type of dread, had performed beautifully.

Oldest children, Sebastian thought, as he sat down on his brother's unmade bed, are never relieved of these feelings. And he was sure they were somehow tied to a feeling of responsibility. When he was a child and had caught a sniffle, his mother used to say to him: *don't you dare get sick*. Then she would pinch his cheeks until they were glowing. He knew now that she said that to show her love for him. What she had meant was that it hurt her when he felt bad for any reason. What she meant was that she refused to even consider that her child could be failed by fate and could be in even temporary pain. But as a child, Sebastian had always thought of it as his responsibility not to get a cold. When he did get a childhood cough or stomach flu, he had experienced it as a failure on his part; he had always felt immense guilt that he couldn't even do this one thing for his mother, he couldn't even keep himself safe. Later, he would think of his brother as his responsibility, however geographically or chronologically far apart they were. The first thing Sebastian had thought when he heard that his brother had died was *thank god it's not my fault.*

Above the headboard of his single bed, Matt had hung a portrait of the 133rd Engineering Battalion in the desert. Three of the soldier's faces had thick, black marker crosses over them. Sebastian wanted to x-out his brother's face too. His brother had not died a combat death, but Sebastian knew that many soldiers didn't die the kind of deaths civilians thought of when they thought of war. Maybe some of the boys in the picture had been shot by an enemy sniper, or died when an IED went off, Sebastian guessed. But it was just as likely that they died in training or in auto crashes. Suddenly he was angry. Matt had hated the army, and had hated the boredom and the casual cruelty they had tried to inculcate in him, had hated chanting "lock and load with your 240 / Mow them little motherfuckers down." Sebastian never heard about exactly what Matt had participated in in Iraq, because Matt never talked about it. Matt's anger when he returned had been mute. That didn't surprise him; the brothers had never spoken on the phone with frequency or at length. But what still surprised and angered Sebastian is that he had never heard why his brother had joined up to begin with; he was not sure he had ever properly asked why. He suspected that Matt was ashamed of his reasons, or that he had been unclear about them himself. Matt had never told Sebastian or their mother that he was thinking about joining the service. He had simply come home from the mall one day and announced with a resigned note in his voice, that he was leaving for basic training in two months. When their mother had called Sebastian, and then put him on the phone with Matt, Matt had sounded exactly like joining the army had been his fate, and he had simply accepted it by talking to a recruiter outside the Orange Julius. Sebastian could never get anything out of him about how this had happened. Matt had never even pretended that in joining up he thought he would not be deployed; there was certainty by then that a war going to start. He had facetiously said that he liked the way "combat engineer" sounded.

Tacked on the wall next to the photograph was a drawing from which Matt's tattoo had been made. It was an ugly tattoo. Sebastian couldn't help thinking that Matt was smarter than people gave him credit for. Their mother seemed to have exhausted all her scholarly ambition on her oldest son. It had been expected that Sebastian would go to a good college, and he had. But when Matt had finished at Illium High School, he had floundered. He had been a good hockey player there, and after graduation, he stayed in his mother's house and got a job with the town rink, driving the Zamboni. Their mother never seemed to mind. In fact, she seemed to like to having her youngest boy close to her. In the spring and summer Matt worked as a landscaper. That job would kill him, eventually. Matt had survived the war, only to be run over by one of those big pickups filled with electric hedge clippers and gas-powered mowers. Either or both Matt and Johnson Anderson, who was driving the truck at the time, were drunk. Sebastian thought that either way, Matt's death was awful but it probably wasn't senseless. This was a time when many young men were coming back from the war and then dying, he thought. It may have been a death for no reason, but it made sense.

Sebastian drank down the rest of his beer and decided to conduct a thorough search of Matt's room. He wasn't sure what he was looking for, but he knew he wanted to be looking. He knelt down and started with a Tupperware storage container under the bed. He found fourteen tee-shirts, rolled in the same manner as the boxer shorts had been, a picture of their absent father standing on a dock jutting into a lake, a small magnifying glass, a cheap silver ring featuring a marijuana leaf made of black stones set on the band, four unused condoms, an unopened tampon, and a letter that Sebastian had written to him and that Matt had always said he never received.

Matt's arrival at basic training had coincided with the start of the second term in the year that Sebastian had decided to go back to Tufts for a master's degree in literature. Sebastian had been twenty-nine, and since his college graduation he had worked as an ice-cream scooper, a seller of used academic books, and a cashier at a gourmet food shop. He was not a good cashier, so he had decided to go back to studying, which he knew he was good at. It was only later, when he got the job at the Somerville Theater while in grad school, that he found out he was also a good part-time projectionist. The war against Iraq was heating up, and Sebastian was taking a class on the literature of atrocity. He was also starting to learn, outside of school, what posture he wanted to take in regard to the war in particular, and the atrocity that was international conflict in general. That his brother was being trained to fight this war had galvanized Sebastian's feelings.

Former President Bush—the first, the father—had come to speak at Tufts, and there was a minor uproar among the more liberal students over the speech. They were particularly pissed off that students in attendance would be hand-selected by the administration, their questions for the question and answer period vetted and censored. Sebastian knew he wouldn't be chosen, and he didn't want to be there. There was an anti-war protest scheduled by the community for the same day, and the organizers had obtained a permit to march to the school auditorium and shout anti-Bush slogans at it from half a mile away. Sebastian wanted to be out there. When he had arrived in Davis Square in Somerville, for the start of the march, he was surprised to see so many police officers. He had been to other anti-war protests, and had seen cops, had even seen kids roughed-up by them a couple times. But these officers had gas masks strapped to their thighs, and their batons were already out. When Sebastian got closer to one of them, he could see that many wore black bands over their badge numbers. The crowd was a couple-hundred people, and they marched peacefully, singing and chanting, and stamping their feet against the frozen blacktop, toward Tufts. Sebastian was near the back of the march when it stopped. He had been bored, and cold, and impatient. He pushed his way to the front, where some students explained to him that the police had blocked their path. This, three miles away from the college campus, would be as far as they were allowed to go, despite their permit, and despite, or because of, their wish to be heard by those attending the former President's speech. The other students and people at the front of the march were young, and they were angry with their government, and they were tired of being told what to do. Sebastian had been with many of them when they had been penned-in by police before. Most of them, including Sebastian, had been in New York City the previous weekend, crushed onto sidewalks up against barriers when the police ran a van through the crowded streets at thirty miles an hour. And most of them, the previous weekend, had chanted "Whose streets? Our streets!" and nonetheless stood on the sidewalks and did not jostle. Sebastian linked arms, elbow to elbow, with a South Korean kid he recognized from his class on African-American literature, and they all stood in a line facing the police across a barrier. Someone started a call and response chant: "Repeat after me. Repeat after me. There's more of us than there are of them. There's more of us than there are of them. There's more of us than there are of them. There's more of us than there are of them. We're going through. We're going through." This part the police got right in the report Sebastian received the next day, when he filed out of court and handed over a hundred dollars in cash in exchange for his freedom and this document, his police report. They said: *At one point People yelled 1, 2, 3, go! and the crowd surged forward.* This was that point. Together they rushed against the police line. It took less than thirty seconds to bring down the barrier and even less time for their arms to be separated. Sebastian didn't know what happened to the people on his right and on his left, never saw his Korean friend after the scuffle, but Sebastian remembered exactly what happened to him in those thirty seconds, as if each second was slowed and stretched. He closed his eyes and threw himself forward. The barricade was down and under his feet. He was up against a plastic shield. He remembered exactly how large the black letters spelling POLICE were, and that they were just under his nose. The officer behind the shield was pushing and he was pushing, and he was amazed that there was give and take, he was not just pushed back, he was almost past him. The officer could have been the one who ended up on the ground. There were people everywhere, and in his peripheral vision he could see the whirl of a police baton being brought down on some protester. Sebastian was pretty sure he never got hit. He was kicked, though. He couldn't hear anything, each second of struggle was silent, as if every bit of Sebastian's energy was concentrated on his muscles, his body up against a shield and a man. And then Sebastian was on the ground. He never knew how he got to the ground, if he fell or was pushed by the crowd or if the police threw him.

On the pavement, Sebastian curled up, balanced on his knees and his shoulders. Someone shouted "stay down!" Sebastian shouted, "No!" then looked back and realized that the person telling him to stay down was handcuffing him. There was an organized effort by the protesters to un-arrest those in the clutches of the police; someone grabbed Sebastian by the shoulder and tried to pull him up, but he was pushed away and Sebastian fell back to his knees. He remembered squirming a little on the ground because he was in pain, and scared, and in handcuffs, and the officer on his left kicked him once, hard, in the ribs and the wind was knocked out of him. He was very still after that. They finished securing the cuffs on Sebastian, kneeling on his back and holding his shoulders to the pavement, although he was not moving. Sebastian never forgot those thick, plastic handcuffs, securing one wrist atop the other.

He was in jail for five and a half hours, and that was when he realized that he would loose his mind if he were ever put in solitary confinement. He started out in a small cell, alone and in the dark. But he was moved because, he was told, the reason it was dark in his cell was that the light doubled as a surveillance camera and it was broken. He remembered a kid, a fifteen-year-old, he had been arrested with, that he caught a glimpse of when they were bringing him to his second cell. The kid was too young to be kept in a cell with adults, so the police had manacled him to a banister. He had been sitting on the stairs, bound at the hands and legs, and he had smiled at Sebastian.

When he got out of jail, and had been sentenced only to pay a hundred dollar fine for being a "disorderly person," he had sat down to write to his brother. He didn't know what he wanted to say to Matt, but his own getting arrested, and his brother's residence in a training camp for the army, seemed to connect them rather than separate them in Sebastian's mind. When he had gotten out pen and paper, addressed the plain white envelope, and affixed an American flag stamp, he flattened his piece of notebook paper, not knowing how to begin. In the end, he wrote only a line from a book he had been reading in grad school. It was out of print, and a helpful professor had photocopied an old version of it for Sebastian. The book was about the Second World War, written by a German who described himself as an "observer." His name was Friedrich Percyval Reck-Malleczewen, and he had ended up dying in Dachau. Sebastian had not chosen a passage from Reck-Malleczewen that dealt directly with armed conflict. Instead, twenty-nine-year-old Sebastian had copied out: "I have now lived more than fifty years, have been forced to descend into certain dark places, and I have emerged with one piece of wisdom: no harm that I have ever done has not caused me pain later on, if it took decades."

The letter was there in the bottom of the Tupperware, creased and stained as if it had been read many times. Sebastian was ashamed to see it now. He didn't know what he had meant by it then, if it had been a warning, or an admonition, or an invitation. Now, he felt that it was preposterous that he had chosen that passage for his little brother, and that he had tried to pass on the hard-won wisdom of a much older man. But Sebastian remembered that time in his life. Leaving jail, feeling his bruised ribs, returning to his cold apartment. He had felt old then.

He was more morally certain then than he was now. He thought about that protest, the one at which he had suffered his only arrest, all the time now that he was walking a picket line with the other striking projectionists at the small, independent theater where had been working full-time since he dropped out of graduate school.

He put his brother's belongings back where he had found them, and fell face-down on the bed. "I'm sorry," he mumbled into the pillow. He prostrate himself for as long as he could bear, but it was hot in Matt's room, and he could not, after several minutes, focus on his grief.

He found himself thinking of Evey. They had met shortly after he was arrested. They married seven months later, in the Somerville Town Hall, in the middle of March. Now, they had been married for slightly longer than two years, and he was afraid that they were sliding toward trouble. He could not yet envision what the trouble would be, what it would look or feel like, but he felt it coming like fishermen felt the air pressure drop and, without looking at their barometers, knew they had to get off the water for the day. He knew there were other, probably more helpful ways to think about this new part of his relationship, this feeling of dis-ease, but he couldn't do it. *Maybe*, he thought, *I should pray*. "Our Father," he began. And that was a far as he could get. His voice drifted off and Sebastian was overcome with a feeling of indifference and inadequacy.

He got up and left his brother's room, leaving the door ajar. He went to the bathroom and washed his face. Then Sebastian snuck past his mother in the living room and began the long walk to the Palais Royal. He didn't know what tonight was going to be like, or what any day for the rest of his life was going to be like, but he could foresee that he would be too drunk to drive home.

CHAPTER FOUR

There were three worn wooden steps leading up to a wide porch and the door to the bar, which, Evey thought, did not look like the door to a bar at all, but more like an ordinary door to someone's ordinary house, painted a peeling dark blue. Evey knew there were other Palais Royales in the world, probably grand places with historic pretensions, and little settees, and big bands. But the Palais Royale in Ilium had no illusions and certainly no pretensions. It was said that the building was originally a whorehouse, one of the first in Maine. The few, small windows and the wide porches and balconies in front and back were offered as evidence. What Evey knew for sure was that the Palais Royale was, in historic town memory, a hotel. She had seen pictures of the hotel, never palatial, in the Ilium Historical Society, which was housed on the top floor of the public library. And the second story of the Palais Royale had operated as a low-rent rooming house when Evey was a child. It had been a terrifying and fascinating place as she grew up, both because it was such an unusual establishment in a small town with white-washed homes and few apartment buildings and no hotels, and because all its inhabitants had seemed to have some imperfection or affliction. Missing limbs—arms or fingers or a leg below the knee—had been common among the men living there, and those who were outwardly whole had still seemed in need of something, wanting or lacking in some way. Evey stared at two small, wavy-glassed, darkened windows above her as she finished her cigarette. She guessed that, despite Maine law, she could still smoke inside the Palais Royale, but she was stalling for time. She was aware of Stan standing silent behind her, still in his chauffer uniform but without his little cap. He had told Evey that the Palais Royale would be closing forever tomorrow.

As she reached out for the knob, she had several thoughts in quick succession or maybe simultaneously: that the bar might seem smaller and outgrown like a childhood home, though Evey had last been there not as a child but as a twenty-two-year-old; that she hated it when things were over; and that if it was the last night the Palais would be open everyone would be there, and oh, god, that meant maybe her ex-husband James would be there. She tossed her cigarette away without looking, in what she hoped was a reasonable approximation of carelessness. As she turned the doorknob, Stan asked, "Should I wait?"

"Oh for Chrissake, Stan," Evey said. "Shut up. Come in and have a drink."

The inside of the bar was exactly as Evey remembered it. The bar itself was almost inappropriately lustrous, looking polished and well-worn with care. It was perpetually gloaming inside, and there were, famously, forty-two portraits of Elvis hanging on the walls. Young people in the area regarded this as an ironic conceit, and attended the Palais the way they wore tee-shirts manufactured to look old or offensive. Evey knew, though, that the portraits—some oils, others sketches, and of course the ubiquitous velvets—were in earnest. She had been told a long time ago by the bartender, the owner's daughter, that they belonged to her father and had been there for as long as anyone could remember. The owner's daughter, Evey remembered that her name was Karen, was behind the bar now, leaning over to talk to a man who was drinking alone. Before Evey could sit down,

Karen asked her, "What can I get you?" And, still standing, Evey answered, "Double shot, Jim Beam, please." Evey leaned against the bar. Stan was still hovering behind her, and had not been asked what he would like to drink. "Stop hovering, Stan," Evey said without turning around. Immediately after saying that, she knew it was unfair. She also knew that she would say many unfair things that night, and that it was going to be a long night.

Stan didn't say anything, but he sat down on the stool next to Evey, and leaned both arms on the top of the bar. The bartender gave him a little nod, and brought him a beer without asking. Evey sat silently next to him, and imagined what Sebastian was doing at that moment. She imagined that he had taken his mother by the arm and led her away from the open grave. His mother was not demonstrative, and that would make it worse. Her silence, the rare tears dripping from her eyes, would be awful in their smallness. Evey imagined Sebastian opening the passenger-side door of their Nissan Sentra for his mother when he had walked her to the car. Closing it behind her when she had gotten in, and once he was behind the wheel and before he turned the key, reaching over and fastening her seatbelt across her shoulder and over her lap.

When Evey pictured him, he was not wearing his funeral suit. He was, in her mind, wearing the pink tee-shirt he had on when she met him. Somehow, the color of his shirt had made him look more masculine. The short sleeves showed off Sebastian's strong arms. His head, she had thought when she saw him, was perfectly round. His face had a clean, strong tan. He was just starting to get lines around his eyes, which he squeezed shut in laughter or thought.

Sebastian and Evey had both grown up a parent short. His father had disappeared, and her mother had died when she was four. Evey tried to imagine buckling her father into a seatbelt if she needed to, but she couldn't picture it. She tried to imagine what Sebastian would say to his mother, but only heard low, whispered conversation or the ridiculous rush of air through all the open windows of their car. But she could imagine that now, after a short ride and a walk up the driveway that would have seemed long, Sebastian would be sitting opposite his mother in the ancient wing-backs in the living room, loosening his tie. His mother would be staring straight ahead at the ancient, silent cabinet television.

Evey signaled the bartender for another drink. It was early yet, and she knew she couldn't keep doing double-shots all night, so she ordered a Jack and Coke. Karen said, "I'll set you up," and brought it to her quickly, in a glass that was damp and warm from the dishwasher. Evey sat and sipped slowly at it, not looking at Stan. Evey thought again of her father, wishing she could stop these thoughts. She had been angry with her father lately, until Matt's death supplanted the smaller hurts of her life, and until Matt's funeral had caused Evey's father to be, as usual, wonderful, and had caused Evey to accept that from him. Evey's father was most often described as a good man. Evey knew that people said he was a good man, Richard, for raising her after her mother died. And she hated that idea that being a father somehow made a person exemplary. As if it would have been okay, or at least understandable, if he had run off and left her after her mother's death—because he was a man, and men did things like this, it was to be expected; or because she was a black child, dark-skinned like her mother. When Evey, as a child, was being taken to the pool at the YMCA, or the library, her little mitten swallowed by her father's large glove, strangers often asked Richard if she was adopted. He never failed to be indignant about that question. "No," he would say, his benign face clouding, "she is my daughter. And what about yours?" he would ask, pointing to an identical miniature of a curious woman who looked like uncooked dough. "Did you get her from Guatemala?" he would ask. White ladies were taken aback, often speechless, when he did that. Every time this scene was repeated, Evey's heart would swell with pride—for her father, who was such a good and clever man, and for herself, who was loved by him.

Richard was good at everything. He could fry Evey an egg for her breakfast every morning and never break the yolk. He taught her how to shuck a clam, paint the outside of a house, whistle a tune, string a tennis racquet, use a bottle opener, and snap her fingers by the time she was ten. He was sensitive about her difference in the town, too. Every year in February, Richard would make sure the school system celebrated Black History Month. "Racism is not a problem *black* people have to deal with," Richard would say each year as the kick-off speaker in the gymnasium, looking solemnly out at the assembled students. "It is important for *all* of us to know our heritage, to know where we come from. All people originally come from Africa." Some little kid would always nudge Evey from behind and say, "Hey, isn't that your dad?"

Evey had always thought of herself as black, not as *mixed*, which sounded like a term for dog breeding, or *biracial*, which was clunky and didn't seemed to apply. She had thought of herself as black, but growing up, she would not have said she had experienced racial discrimination. She knew that there had been awkward moments with the ladies at the YMCA, or when she went to a friend's house for a sleepover, and the mother inexplicably asked, "Do your people eat pork? I bought you some chicken, if that makes you more comfortable." Surely, she had received strange looks from time to time, but, she always thought that was because she was *different* in Illium, or even, when she was older, because she was beautiful, not because she was black, precisely. Her race, she had always thought when she was growing up, was just like Anthony Pagoli's harelip, or Karen being Jewish, or James being a punk rocker. When Evey had moved to Boston and seen other black people close up, and together in groups, her first thought had been: *I'm not that kind of black person.* It had been years until she knew enough to be ashamed of that thought, and longer still before she was angry. It was similar to the time she had said, at a party in Somerville, that when she was a child, the other kids had called her "Oreo" for her entire fifth-grade year. She had been sitting around, late, in someone's triple-decker, swapping stories of terrible schools or nightmare parents, little traumas everyone was nursing along with their PBRs, to try to tell each other something about themselves—where they came from and how they got there. Evey said: "They used to call me Oreo," and there was a collective intake of breath. "You know—black on the outside, white on the inside." A black man on the couch opposite her had laughed, and the only other black person in the room, a woman with her straightened hair done up in huge curls, had shot him a scathing look. The white woman to Evey's left asked, "Did they get in trouble when you told an adult?" And Evey had been stunned. She recovered herself quickly and said, "They didn't know what they were doing. I don't think those kids knew whether they were insulting me or complimenting me." But what had shocked Evey in that moment was not that she had never told on the kids, but that it had never, in all the intervening years, occurred to her that she should have, or could have; that there was anything to tell. When Evey had said that her classmates didn't know what they were doing, she had only told part of the truth. She hadn't known, either, at the time, whether she should regard the name as an insult or a compliment. She had secretly suspected it was just a statement of fact.

Still, Evey was taken aback when she called Richard three weeks ago and told him that she had discovered her heritage, only to hear his tight-lipped anger over the phone. What Evey had found was the other half of her family, in Alabama. There was a craze at this time among her friends in Boston for genealogy. Evey had been curious, and felt for the first time curiously bereft of half a family. She had taken the little information she knew about her mother's family—her father had told her they had cut off contact after her parents' marriage—and looked them up. Evey had been astounded to get a woman with a wavery drawl on the other end of the telephone: her grandmother. The conversation had not been as awkward or uncertain as Evey had assumed it would be. The first thing her grandmother had said was, "I remember your mother's bridal shower. I don't remember where we had it, though. Maybe the Grange. You ask your father, I bet he knows." And then later, "You should come visit us sometime. We do wear shoes in Alabama, you know. Sometimes." Her grandmother had an explosive, smokey laugh. Evey was excited when she got off the phone. She had promised to call her grandmother back, and as soon as she hung up with her new-found relative, she had called the only relative she was ever close to, her father. "Do you remember," she had asked Richard, "where mom's bridal shower was?" It had been a shock to hear him say in response, "I don't remember, Evey. I don't like thinking about all that. It was a long time ago, and that was a difficult time. I don't have to drag all that back up." And then, "Have you been going to the gym lately? The last time I saw you I thought you looked like you might want to go to the gym."

"I weigh a hundred and thirty-five pounds, Dad," she replied.

"I know. But you're not very big, you know. You don't want to carry extra weight around. It's not good for your heart. And women lose bone density if they don't do weight-bearing exercise." She had hung up on him for the first time in her life. He didn't call back, and Evey found herself waiting for something—she didn't know what—before she contacted her grandmother again.

And the worst part was that she didn't feel that she was allowed to still be angry with him. Not now that Matt had died, and Richard had come to the funeral, steady and strong and unbending as usual. Evey couldn't be angry with her father anyway. She needed him. She needed to ask him for money. She needed to ask him for close to three-thousand dollars.

Evey loathed the thought of asking anyone for cash, but especially her father. And not just because she wanted to be angry with him right now. The Kiss family had never lacked for money, but Richard had always made it clear that he and Evey were going to slough off as much economic privilege as possible, in order to make a stand for justice and equality in America. Evey had worked her first job, stabbing lobsters in the back of the neck to make baked stuffed for tourists at the restaurant Ocean Farms, when she was fourteen. By the time she was fifteen, her father stopped buying her school clothes. It wasn't that Evey ever lacked anything she really needed or wanted, it was just that she was discouraged from wanting too much. Now that she was an adult, Richard seemed to have lost faith in his social experiment. Evey knew he would give her the money, but she also knew how he would look at her when she asked for it. And it was almost worth it not to pay the rent this month, not to know where her groceries were coming from while Sebastian was on strike, to not have to see that look her father would give her. Almost.

"So, um," Stan said to Evey. "You've been away."

Evey shifted on her bar stool so that she was looking at Stan dead-on. "I live away, Stan. I haven't been away. I'm not from here anymore. It's just where I grew up."

"I know. I mean, you live in Boston?"

"Somerville. It's one of the most densely populated cities in America." Evey spent a lot of time sitting on her front stoop in Somerville smoking cigarettes. She had a view of the closely spaced triple-deckers across from her. She was concerned that all this closeness was making her vision and her thoughts myopic.

"I mean, what do you do?" Stan said. Before Evey could answer, he added, "I mean, what do you really do all day? So many people, you know, have jobs and they'll tell you their job title, and you have no idea what it's like to go into work and accomplish that, accomplish whatever they do all day. No one ever tells you, when you ask that question, what it's like to be them."

"I'm not sure most people know what it's like to be themselves, Stan," Evey said. "I work at a coffee shop."

"But what is that like, is what I mean," Stan said.

Evey thought of asking Stan for money. She thought of really explaining her life to him, playing on his sympathies, ending with *I need three-thousand dollars.* It had not escaped her notice that he said he made a ton of money. She was desperate for the cash. Sebastian didn't have any money coming in since the strike started, and Evey needed, at minimum, three-thousand dollars to cover rent and food, electricity and phone bills for the next two months. She could ask Stan, she thought. But she couldn't be obligated to him, to this person who was right now a stranger. She wanted to keep the people from her past in her past, and if she asked for money, this night would not simply be an odd moment of discontinuity in her life—it would mean that someone from her past had entered her present, *real* life. Instead, she said, "Harvard students come in and say ridiculous things. They're wrong more often than you would think. I get there at seven-thirty in the morning. First I have to grind some beans and put up the specials on the chalkboard. I get to pick the music we listen to. Anyway, I'll quit when I can find something better." All of a sudden, Evey wanted very much to quit her job. She thought about Angela, thought about the text message Angela had sent earlier in the day, checking in, that she had never answered. How when she had received that message it was both a relief and a responsibility. It had placed her.

"Wait, you're going to quit?" Stan lifted his glass of beer to his lips, concealing the bottom half of his face, as he swallowed the sentence.

Evey thought about this question. Then she thought about a radio program she has listened to once. It was about amnesia. About how what the host of the segment had called "real amnesia, the kind you see in the movies," is incredibly rare. It almost never happens that a person, through some trauma, can't remember anything about himself or his life. Evey thought about what happened to James, her first husband. How, because he had an undiagnosed tumor in his chest, he lost his short term memory for a couple days. Her father told her that James could remember his name, and who his friends and family were. He had asked for her. But he didn't know from minute to minute where he was or what he was doing. At first, he knew there was a problem. Evey's father had told her that James had called his doctor. But when the receptionist answered, he couldn't remember why he had called.

On the radio show, the producer said he thought that even though the kind of self-negating, ego-destroying amnesia during which a person's past is obliterated almost never happens (if it occurs at all), we persist in making movies and soap-operas about it because it fulfills some primal human desire. He said everyone loves the idea of a clean slate.

But Evey thought he was wrong. Even the fantasy of perfect amnesia doesn't really provide a clean slate for the amnesiac. Even if a person can't remember his past, he still has to live with its fallout, its consequences—he would still be marooned in the middle of his life. The fantasy, Evey thought, is really this: when we forget ourselves, it enables us to admit what we all suspect anyway: that we do not know who we are. We are terrible judges of our own character and our place in the world and the effect we have on others. It is not up to us, Evey thinks, to define ourselves. We can re-imagine our lives as many times as we want and still never get to the heart of who we are. If Evey were to lose her memory of her past, she would feel relieved. She would be relieved of the obligation to try to weigh one remembered detail of her life against the next, to try to sort through her life to attempt to identify the salient details. In those movies about amnesiacs, she thinks, the main character often embarks on some high adventure, during the course of which he is shown by others who he truly is. And that, Evey thinks, is why the disease is so fascinating and appealing. We long to abdicate the understanding of self, and to admit that we are not in control of our identity. We want someone else to tell us who we are and what our life means.

Stan put his glass down. "Evey?"

"I'm not sure if going back to the coffee shop is a good idea. Maybe I need a change. We all need to change our lives sometimes, right?"

"Yeah. But how do you know when it's the right time?"

"What?" Evey distractedly shaped the straw from her drink into a pretzel. She tried to focus on her job. Slicing lemons with a dull knife for the tea drinks, running the dishwasher and running it and running it and running it all day, cleaning the iced coffee machines, which had a tendency to develop mold after two or three days. She had already told Stan too much about Angela. Angela was small and chubby, with dark hair and blue eyes and tattoos up and down both beautiful, pale, rounded arms. Evey was thinking of the night shift, how every once in a while when she and Angela worked together they would fill their opaque to-go cups with red wine. By nine-thirty every move they made behind the counter would radiate sexual energy and they would touch each other's thighs below the level of the counter. By eleven-fifteen the store would be clean and the two of them would have pushed the lemons out of the way on the countertop. She wondered if it is the things we do, our job titles and our actions, that defined us. If we wrote out all our statistics: Five-six, brown hair, brown eyes, manager of Great Bean, wife of Sebastian, lover of Angela, would that be who exactly we are?

"Why do you work there?" Stan asked.

"What do you mean? It's a job. I work there because I have to have a job."

"But not there. Not if you don't want to. Weren't you going to be a chef? I always thought your dad would help you open a restaurant and you'd be one of those celebrity chefs."

"Come on, Stan. There are, like, twenty celebrity chefs in the country. I like to cook. There's a difference." Evey looked down at her hands. They were strong hands, with long fingers and square nails, unpolished. When she was a teenager and had worked at Ocean Farms, her hands had always been raw and covered in tiny cuts from picking lobster meat from shells.

"I don't know," said Stan, "I just thought. I mean, you could work somewhere else. And you could go to school, if you wanted."

"I don't want to be one of those awkward adults sitting in the back of the classroom with a bunch of eighteen-year-olds. Can you see me at a keg party?"

"I know. It's just that, if I were you, I wouldn't do anything I didn't want to do."

"I don't know what I want to do. I just want to make my life like a story that has a beginning, a middle, and an end, you know? Like it makes sense when you look at the whole thing cover to cover." Evey thought that what she wanted to do was something beautiful. She wished that she still played the piano, or was a gardener, or flew small planes. "I used to really be somebody, though, didn't I?" she said.

"What?"

Evey looked at herself in the mirror behind the bar. She

looked like a serious person, but maybe it was just her cheekbones, high and arched like a Russian model. She wanted so many things, she thought. To make her marriage work, because she loved her husband, to be able to pay her rent, to do something beautiful every day. But, she thought, that is what unhappiness is: the gap between what one wants and what one has.

"This is what I do," Stan said. "I work at the Shop n' Save, in the deli section, slicing cheese food product for old ladies who want a quarter pound 'and slice it thin.' But a year ago, I had saved up around five-thousand dollars. Which really, if you do the math, means that you can only play the small games, the three-to-six dollar games. So I started playing little poker games online, two or three games at a time. You have to play online because it's so much faster that you can really make money, and anyway, there's overhead involved in getting to a casino from here. So I double my bankroll after playing a couple hundred hours. Which sounds great, right? And actually, I'm living at my dad's place, so it is great. But that's the thing about playing poker for a living. I can make five thousand dollars in a day now, but it's got to be just another day at work, because I know I'll lose some some other day, so it just goes into the bank. So anyway, I sit in my room in the basement and play poker on that awesome new computer I got for myself, and then in the afternoon I come here and I drink beers until I can't look at Karen anymore and then I go home. Oh, and I work at the deli on Tuesdays, Thursdays, Fridays, and Saturdays."

"Who do you drink with?" Evey asked. She wasn't intending to listen to Stan answer this question. She was, she realized as she felt a few beads of sweat break out along her hairline, changing her mind. She was making up her mind right now to ask Stan for money. He had a lot of money, Evey figured. And he liked her a lot. She needed to find a way tonight to make these facts work together.

"By myself, or with some guys from the deli section. Do you remember James Presley?"

"Oh shit," Evey said. And now she knew what Stan had been leading up to. Of course he knew that she remembered James Presley. Evey Kiss and James Presley had been married for three years, what seemed to Evey like a long time ago.

They had been married when Evey was nineteen. Evey wasn't sure if she was more angry that Stan had been apparently waiting to drop this fact of his friendship on her, or that she would not be able to bring up the money she needed just yet.

"James doesn't know this," Stan said, "but I have a picture of you. This isn't creepy, is it?" he said. "I have this picture of you on some field trip when we were in Mrs. Sanborn's class, and you're looking into a tidal pool. I keep it to remember that we were just kids. When everything happened, and everything even that we did in our early twenties, we were just kids. That's what you look like in that picture, just like a child."

"What the fuck do you mean, Stan?"

"Nothing. I just mean that sometimes I think the adults around us, when we were kids, they gave too much weight to everything. Remember when we were twelve and we broke into that cabin?"

"What? No. I don't remember breaking into anything." Evey took another sip of her drink.

Stan looked shocked. "You must remember that. We smashed the window out of Mr. Carlisle's old summer cabin on the lake one night. We must have only been eleven or twelve years old. I think we were sort of playing house, but we were too old to just play house. When we got inside, we just sat around for a while, until James and that kid he used to hang out with, Calvin Fischer, found Mr. Carlisle's golf clubs. They smashed the fuck out of the television, and they would have done anything you could put a club through, but the rest of us panicked. You really don't remember this?"

Evey was sitting very still and staring straight into the mirrored behind the bar.

"And then the police came around to all our houses. I always thought that if we had been kids ten or fifteen years earlier, telling our parents would have been the worst thing anyone would have done. We would have had private, child-sized punishments. But they told us we were going to end up in the Youth Center. And even then, James and Calvin decided to keep your name out of it. The two of them made some kind of deal and told a story to the police. That was a very adult decision. Calvin went away for three months and he was never the same again. James always had a thing for you, even when we were kids." Stan finished the rest of his beer in one swallow and chased it with Jack and Coke. "James is a good guy, Evey."

"I know. James is a good guy. So you decided to try to fuck his ex-wife? Was that of your own initiative, or was that another deal James made behind the scenes, for my benefit? Fuck you. Is he going to show up here later?"

"Evey, I didn't try to *fuck* you."

"That's funny, because it kind of seemed that way."

"Everyone will be here tonight."

"Let's not talk about this ever again. Let's not talk, Stan," Evey said. She had felt fine a moment ago, or as fine as she could be on a night like this. She had known that no one she knew would be coming to the bar for at least a half-hour; she had been beginning to feel her drink. When Stan had started talking, she had wanted to say, *I remember that*, and reminisce. But this was not a story she wanted to hear. She could feel the back of her scalp prickling. She could feel that she was holding her glass much too tightly.

CHAPTER FIVE

Karen Amato was trying to serve drinks without thinking of her uncle. Every time she set a glass down and remembered that the Palais was closing tonight forever and it was her own uncle's fault, she experienced the electricity of anger anew. Right now, though, she was succeeding in looking two customers straight in the face and thinking only about what they would momentarily order. She knew Stan and remembered Evey. When she turned around to pour Evey's double shot, she tried to remember what she had once known about Evey. Karen seemed to remember watching some relationship between Evey and a boy dissolve over many evenings. It was like that sometimes with the patrons, if they were the kind of regulars who were always there, but didn't talk to the bartender too much. Karen never directly knew anything about their lives, but would observe them drinking beers with the same boy every night for months and then cocktails with a group of friends, and then just some of the friends, and eventually beer again with just the boy, and then shots alone, and sometimes after that, with another boy.

Karen moved over to that side of the bar and gave Evey the double shot she had asked for before she even sat down. Karen was glad of the excuse to extricate herself from conversation with Happy Bankovic, who always sat at the other end of the bar next to the payphone. Evey had downed the shot before Karen could place the beer Stan always ordered on the bar in front of him. She glanced up at Stan, who was tall, and then down at Evey, and thought that this was going to be a long night. She looked over the now-empty shot glass. Evey sat down awkwardly on a stool next to Stan, who remained standing. "What do you want tonight, honey?" Karen asked Evey. Evey smiled at her. She looked, Karen thought, thankful.

"I'll have a Jack and Coke."

"I'll set you up." Karen moved to get the drink. Karen scooped ice out of the machine, jiggered out a shot of Jack and filled the rest with Coke. When she set it in front of Evey, Evey gave her another grateful smile. Stan was still sipping his Bass, seated now. She liked Stan, really, but her impulse had always been to avoid him when possible. He looked like a kids who'd had his plastic lunch box stomped on more than once at the playground. And now, as an adult, Karen thought, Stan was the kind of man who would probably get cancer. He would get cancer and when he did he would consider it a great tragedy in his life. It would be a great tragedy, Karen thought, but the bigger tragedy would be that Stan would not see that this was inevitable, not because Stan was a smoker, but because Stan was a man who invited tragedy into his life by not doing anything; by waiting every moment for some great thing to come and tell him what to do and how to behave.

"I'll have one of those too," he said, pointing to Evey's mixed drink.

"With your beer?" Karen asked.

"With the beer."

"Could have told me before, you know." She caught sight of Evey as she turned away from the bar. Evey looked desperate, but there was something Karen found irresistible about her. Certainly she was beautiful, but that wasn't it. She looked as if she was in need of something. Karen had to turn away. And in that exact moment, it occurred to her why she hated the kids, the other kids, the young kids, Happy's two smiling children, so much. Karen had been staring at young people from behind this bar for as long as she could remember, and she had never felt young herself. But she didn't want to consider all that at the moment.

As she filled another glass with ice, Karen thought about the economy of movement required when there was a rush at the bar. She was going to miss these movements between the front and back, and the stage right and left of the space behind the bar. She was thinking of her own point of view—the way most of the things she had seen and thought and most of her interactions were from this perspective, on her feet and separated from the crowd by the old oak bar her father used to polish every Sunday evening. She had been standing there since she was fourteen. She remembered bartending for the first time that summer after she finished the eighth grade, and how she had been hustled out the back door when the health inspector showed up, and again for the liquor board inspection. Karen almost couldn't believe that tonight was the last night she would do each endless thing and make each practiced movement here. She couldn't really understand yet what it would be like not to pour drinks, measure shots, twirl backwards to reach for the liqueurs, pop the tops off beers, and throw the chip packets at the old men. It wasn't that she loved being a bartender, or that bartending at the Palais Royale was a way of continuing to love her father now that he was gone, although both those things were true. It was more that she could not separate these nightly acts from her sense of self. She could not imagine what tomorrow was going to be like for her. Would it feel the same as a day off, and then would the next day and the day after that feel the same until she could no longer remember that she once couldn't imagine not being at the Palais Royale?

Happy had been watching Karen while pretending to watch the ice melt in his plastic cup, and Karen knew it. Happy and Karen had been having an affair for the last three years. *Okay*, Karen thought, *they weren't* having an affair. *It was just that no one knew about it. And they wouldn't.* Karen could tell that he was trying to see her around the sides of his cup. She had heard from someone that women have much better peripheral vision than men, and that that is the real reason that men have a reputation for leering. Women, she had heard, ogle just as often, but it is less apparent.

Karen wasn't entirely sure why she couldn't tell anyone about Happy. Maybe it was because he was thirteen years older than her. Or because Happy had two kids that he loved and Karen didn't want. She couldn't be responsible for all those freckles, the report cards and the endless Bacitracin they would need. Or because Karen's mother was a Catholic, and when Karen was fifteen her mother told her that the moment she had sex she was on her own, she was no longer a child and she wouldn't need a mother. She had said that if Karen became the kind of girl who couldn't have a church wedding in good conscience, she would not be a part of the family—certainly Happy wasn't the first person Karen had slept with out of wedlock, but those words or her mother's came back to her with alarming frequency, and made her shy of telling anyone of her relationship. Or maybe it was because Karen was sure that this thing with Happy, whatever it was, wouldn't last. But she wasn't sure she could think that way anymore. She wasn't sure what to think now, but she knew something had to change. As soon as Karen turned away from Stan, Happy leaned over the bar and waved his whole arm at her, like he was hailing a taxi. Karen wished he didn't always sit at that side of the bar, where all the veterans and schizophrenics sat. "So is today supposed to be the day you agree to marry me?" he said, with his face stuck half-way under the beer taps.

"You have to ask first, Happy. Have you planned a wedding?" She felt a churning in her large intestine.

"That's not fair, you know my cat has been sick." Happy laughed and looked at the schizophrenics at the tables behind him for laughs too, to make his joke sound more like a joke. It was true Happy had a cat, and he was always teasing that where he came from, in Yugoslavia, when it used to be Yugoslavia, the cats were better. After a joke like this, Karen would normally start singing something from the jukebox—maybe something by Sam Cooke. But she wasn't in the mood, and anyway no one ever laughed at their jokes. Karen looked around the bar and thought that either everyone was sick of the joke that the two of them would never be a couple and that they were very funny people, or else everyone knew that these things that they were only pretending to say to each other were real, that they probably said these things to each other and meant them after the bar closed. It was a small town, so it was probably the latter. In the past, Karen hadn't cared that the comedy routine between her and Happy, which had been going on for two of the last three years of their relationship, wasn't funny to anyone else. In the past, that had been part of the charm. But tonight, she was starting to think that there was something sick about continuing to laugh at the same jokes that no one else found funny. So that's what she said: "It's not funny, Happy." She said, "You should never have gotten that cat. Why do people think it's a good idea to get these things for their children? They die, and then the children cry and they will never get over it. When they're grown and adults and living in Denver they will wake up in the middle of the night some night and they will think of Fluffy and they'll realize that you could have saved her if you had spent the money at the vet and they will be sad and they will be angry with you. There is enough in the world, Happy, that can make your children hate you. You don't have to go looking for things."

"You trying to make me change my name tonight, Karen?" Happy said, and he was looking back down at his drink again. "I'm not changing my name tonight. I'm Happy tonight, Karen."

"Why tonight, of all nights?"

And then it was time for one the guys at the tables behind Happy to make a joke. The man looked at Karen and then gestured at the empty seat beside him, "Another beer for my friend here," he said. This did get a laugh. The other three men at the tables around him laughed uproariously. Karen knew that they were all aware they were collectively referred to as "the schizophrenics." They used to make Karen sad, the fact that they were so glad to be looked at, to be known, that they didn't care by what name they were known. The fact that they really were mentally ill used to make Karen depressed, years ago. Eventually she had stopped feeling bad for them and the real annoyance she allowed herself for other customers had taken over. She started to hate them for the drink straws they chewed up and left all over the tables, and the fact that they couldn't leave the sugar packets alone. They would tear the tops off all the sugars and pour the contents in huge piles on the tables. Sometimes they used it for sand art. On really bad days they dribbled their drinks into the piles and left a sticky saturation for her to clean up. At some point, Karen stopped feeling one way or another about them.

Karen popped the cap off a Miller and brought it out to the man's table. His name was Baird.

Karen's stomach was killing her. She had serious intestinal problems whenever she ate dairy, but she continued to do so anyway. That day she had cheese fries for lunch. She was trying to hold the gas in, and she could hear an audible churning in her gut.

It was only six-thirty.

•

"Stan," said Karen, easing herself out from behind the bar. "Watch the place for me for a minute, will you?" She handed him a bar towel and said, "And don't give the schizophrenics anything hard. Just beer." Stan nodded, and Karen walked toward the door, knowing that Happy would follow her, seeing, out of the corner of her eye, Happy sliding in and out of her shadow.

Karen Amato had decided the time had come to make a decision. Standing outside the Palais Royale, with the sun edging its way down toward the tree line and Happy silhouetted against the door to the bar, Karen wished that she had taken a shower this morning. She could still smell Happy on her skin from the night before and she was nauseated. She brought her hands up to her face to cover her eyes for a moment, wishing she could instead smell the damp earth she had dug her fingers into two nights before. It was what had happened between two nights ago and now that would end it all, that had to end it all.

Two nights ago, Happy had stayed at the bar until she had closed it. She hadn't asked him where his kids were. Happy could usually get a neighbor or a parent of one of their friends to take the kids for a night. He was a widower, and that engendered an unquestioning sympathy from women acquaintances that made Karen vaguely squeamish. All those PTA ladies would do anything for him, and frequently did. That night, after she swept out the front room, cleaned the taps, and turned on the dishwasher behind the bar, she had told Happy that she wanted to visit her father's grave. She had felt strange, leaving her father's bar to go see her father. The Palais Royale had been her father Rocky's creation, and it still looked exactly as it had it when he was alive. He hadn't so much designed it, or decorated it, as he had just allowed his favorite things to accumulate in the bar. This was why the Palais Royale was still dominated by forty-two pictures of Elvis—Karen could trace their outlines in her mind. She had the frames and each Elvis brushstroke memorized. When Rocky died two months ago Karen had considered renaming the place "Rocky's" in his honor, but had thought better of it. The Palais Royale was a better testament to the quietly grand aspirations and accomplishments of her father's life.

Last night, she and Happy had climbed into the cab of his truck, and it had backfired when he started it. Happy had driven to the cemetery and when they got there, Karen thought that Happy was exactly the kind of man you wanted to visit a gravesite with. He was one of those people who was prepared for this kind of conventional tragedy. They sat by Rocky's big granite slab for a long time in the dark, Karen tearing handfuls of new grass out of the ground and shredding the blades.

Karen did not go to the cemetery because she believed that this was the place where she could speak to her father. She could not believe that dead, Rocky was any more present there than he was anywhere else. Although Karen didn't believe in god, didn't believe in an afterlife, she couldn't shake the very emotional wish that her father was not gone. Sometimes, she felt that he was watching her. But she often felt his presence as an intrusion rather than a comfort. When she felt this, she immediately felt guilty; her father had been an easy-going man in life, and almost fastidious about her privacy. She couldn't help feeling that if he was looking down on her daily life, they would both be embarrassed.

At the gravesite, she had sat by his stone, feeling comfort emanate from its dead, solid mass. Happy had put his arms around her, where she sat. She could feel his breathing, and the slight unsteadiness in his small arms. As he pressed his face against the back of her head, Karen had what she knew alcoholics call a moment of clarity. There was a rare moment when she knew what she really wanted right there in the cemetery. She wanted Happy to do something wrong. She wanted him to move his hand from around her waist and bring it up to her breast, right there amidst her grief. She wanted him to be inappropriate and unpleasant, so that she would have the opportunity to be angry with him. She knew what was coming in the near future: their relationship was coming to a point where something had to change. And she wanted to be the one who was wronged. Karen knew that sadness, anger, hurt, were things that she could bare, and could bare alone, but guilt would be much, much harder. She willed his hand to move to caress her. She thought so strongly of the feeling of his hand on her breast that she couldn't believe Happy couldn't know what she wanted, or wouldn't obey. She thought about what she wanted so hard that her longing for him to do something wrong turned into just longing. She stood up, pulling Happy with her. She walked around the headstone until the two of them were behind it, where she felt somehow concealed, and pulled Happy to the ground. Leaving her shirt buttoned to the throat, she wrenched her pants down to her ankles and pulled him on top of her. She was breathing hard, and she wanted Happy. She wanted to have sex like a long scream.

But Happy had never been an angry man, and under his hand, which moved softly over Karen's bared right leg, all the tension went out of her pose. Karen's legs fell open, into a simple invitation. She closed her eyes, and Happy made love with her behind the headstone, slowly, sadly, painlessly.

Happy was the kind of man Karen wanted to visit a cemetery with, but he was not the kind of man with whom she wanted to have the discussion she knew she needed to have today. Maybe, she thought, this was because in the face of death there was no action that could be taken, and this discussion, this decision they were going to have to come to about their relationship, about *them*, would have to require some act, some change. She could never fight properly with Happy. "Happy," she said. "It has to stop." It was a shock to Karen, to have said these words aloud. *It has to stop, it has to stop*—these were the words that had lain between them in bed for three years. The words that had been on the tip of her tongue while she was licking the inside of Happy's arm, the phrase in his eyes when he looked at her by the light of her bedside lamp. But she could always see, in his eyes, that he was holding back. They had both put this phrase away for another time, a thousand times. They had been saving these words, always holding off for one more day before they said them, the way new lovers will think, in a surge of emotion, *I love you*, knowing that they will eventually say it out loud, but knowing that this is not the time, not yet. "It's wrong, and it has to stop," said Karen.

Happy walked to the front of the porch and sat down heavily on the steps. He took a folded handkerchief from his pocket and slowly turned the small square into a larger rectangle. "I am afraid you will stop this, yes," he said. "But do not say this, that it is wrong. It is not wrong. It has to stop, Karen. But do not be morally outrageous."

At another time, Karen would have corrected his English. At other times, she had found his handkerchief endearing. But at the moment he had pulled out his handkerchief, Karen had felt a surge of rage pulse up behind her eyes. She knew that there were much seamier things people did than whatever she was doing with Happy. She knew saying it was wrong was an overstatement. But it felt, well, not right. She wanted to scream at him, ask him if he was preparing to dab at his eyes to dispel the tears she knew he wouldn't shed over this, but she knew that it was beside the point. "So is that it?" she asked. "Is it over? What do we do?"

"We will do," Happy said slowly, "whatever you want."

"Don't make this my fault," Karen said. "I am not going to be the one who makes the decision, the one who always *does* things. We're in this together."

Happy was not looking at Karen, but Karen imagined

he could feel her hostility, a miasma of anger like the stink of yesterday's vodka on a drunk. Karen had always imagined that when this time came and this relationship had to end, that her mother would be the one who was angry. She had often pictured her mother finding out about this relationship, about the lies she had created to cover for it, about her embarrassment at living so deeply in the shadow of her mother. Despair, sadness, longing, Karen had expected from herself. But not this undeniable rage.

Karen watched as Happy crumpled his handkerchief in his hand, and suddenly she did feel an ache behind her eyes and deep in her throat, as if she would cry. She sat there remembering another time. For a moment, she could almost breath in that other time—of the two of them, each with a hand covering the other's mouth, moving together late at night in Happy's bedroom, after the children were asleep, the fingers of his free hand desperately feeling each of her ribs as if he were memorizing them—of him and her, covered in crumbs, eating toast half-supine in her huge bed in the middle of a school day.

When Happy didn't immediately speak, Karen said softly, "You motherfucker." She hadn't realized it until that exact moment, but she had been looking for a scene. She had wanted shouting and pain and tears, and instead she got what she had always had: Happy, sitting quietly on the stoop of the Palais Royale.

"Okay," said Happy. "You want I should do something that hurts me? This hurts me, Karen. But still I do not know what to do." The sun was turning the tops of the trees a blazing orange. Karen could hear the jukebox kick in with an old Beatles song inside. Happy carefully re-folded his handkerchief and stuffed it into the side pocket of his slacks.

She could not explain why she never figured out a respectable way to love Happy, if she loved Happy. And now she could not find a respectable way to break it off. If her mother had know about the relationship, how would Karen explain it? And how could she ever explain its dissolution? She could not imagine saying to her mother, "It was the children's fault. I could not care for the children." She knew she would have to say: "It was my fault." She could not be who she thought she needed to be in order to let Happy love her. She felt weak, and that weakness was all around her.

"I have responsibilities," she said, and she got up and walked to the door of the bar. She did not look back as she closed the door behind her.

Later, it would seem to Karen that this moment, as she yanked the bar towel back out of Stan's hand and took her place behind the bar, was the last moment for a long time in which she felt so certain. Stan, at a stool facing her, looked miserable. Despite herself, Karen was somewhat contented with the little drama she had pulled from her moment with Happy, somewhat sure of herself in her anger at him. That she was in the wrong, she was sure of. But she had been wrong for a long time. And now, she had been hurt. He had let her leave because he did not love her. Her own assuredness of emotion would come to seem good and true in the excited uncertainty of the months to come. But she didn't know that now, and after she polished the bar with a few hard strokes, she turned and caught her reflection in the mirror.

She looked, she thought, substantial. Karen was an odd looking woman—almost six feet tall—who towered over Happy when they stood together. She was solid. Not chubby. She only looked as if her bones were large and steady. And she was so pale that her hair was almost white and her eyebrows nonexistent. She had inherited her father's height, but not his coloring. She sometimes joked that she fluoresced, but she wasn't in a joking mood now. Instead, in that instant that she looked at herself in the mirror before she turned around and went back to work, she was seeing her white skin and remembering how it had all begun with Happy.

When Karen had graduated from high school her mother had tried to get her to start classes at the community college. And Karen could have done that. She had never minded school, and many of her friends had gone off to take night classes in criminal justice or moved out of state to study early childhood education and attend parties and meet with professors during office hours. But Karen had always been her father's child. She had grown up in the bar, and when the time came to make a decision she hadn't been able to do it and had opted instead to wait out the troubled longing and confusion she was experiencing by doing what she had always done: wiping down the bar, mopping the floor at night, setting up the glasses and filling them with beer, liquor, mixers. Her father had expressed concern when she had announced her plan, saying that for him, the bar had been a second chance at a successful and fulfilled life, and that he didn't think it was a suitable place for a first chance. But he hadn't pressed the issue, and it had seemed to Karen then that he was a little bit proud of her wanting to do a thing like that. It had been his idea that she take a suite of rooms upstairs. The clientele of the hotel part of the Palais Royale, really a single-room occupancy, hadn't been any better then than it was now, and Karen's mother had objected loudly and for years.

Karen had loved it, though. The room was her own, the biggest in the hotel. It was in the back, and through three floor-to-ceiling windows, she had a view of the Royale River. She had her own bathroom and a little alcove with a desk. She had embellished it with curtains and prints from her own photography hobby. One of the things she liked about her decorating scheme was that the photographs changed every couple weeks as she took new ones and matted the best. Though she had never really considered taking photographs professionally, she still sometimes poured over art books. She loved especially the conflict photography, and part of her felt disappointed that she had no war, or protest crushed by police, or Ku Klux Klan activity to document in Illium. She tried to imbue the portraits she captured with as much anxiety as she could, and she would wait for signs of trouble as she agitated the developer tray in the darkroom her father had built her in the basement of the Palais.

If someone had told Karen six years ago that she would be working at the Palais and living above in the company of the schizophrenics, she would have believed them, a little sadly. She would have been immediately defensive if anyone had hinted that it was a circumscribed life, or that there were so many options she was neglecting to take. Karen would have said to someone, in fact said to herself frequently in those days, that the most awful life she could imagine was the life that most of those girls who went off to college or moved out of state eventually ended up living: nursing babies or husbands or hangovers in identical duplexes. Karen would have said that her life was never boring. She worked until two in the morning, so she could never become one of those women who spent evenings at home, eating solitary microwavable brownies. And the entertainment of the customers was show enough that she never felt the need to own a television.

Karen had believed in the calm good fortune of her life for a long time. Longer, maybe, than most nineteen-year-olds. But at some point after her twenty-first birthday, when her father had invited the entire town for free drinks at the Palais in celebration of the day that would make it possible for Karen to be a patron at the family business, Karen had started to feel that possibly something was wrong. Sometimes, when she got drunk with a friend who was home for the holidays, or had a few too many with the customers, she would start to cry when the last person had left the Palais. Her long frame arched over the mop, she would feel the muscles in her back contract when she pushed the mop into the corners under the tables. The sight of all the stools and chairs atop the tables, their legs in the air, would overwhelm her.

It was a night like that, a night when she had been dipping into the porter between setting them up for customers, that Happy, a regular for several months, had offered to help her clean up when she shut down. He was thirty-six, had a dead wife and two kids and his own half of a duplex on the outskirts of town. He had a matte-blue, one-ton flatbed, and he said he couldn't drive it home just yet, so he would like to help her with sweeping for an hour or two. Karen wasn't sure why she didn't just call him the one cab that patrolled Illium. He had made a real mess of restocking the sugar packets in the holders on the tables, talking all the while in his imperfect English about the Yugoslavia he had left behind when the army came to knock on his door and invite his mother to give him up for his second year of compulsory service. He had not been at home, because he had been, at the time, in jail for refusing to pay a bribe to an officer who had stopped him for speeding.

Karen remembered thinking that Happy, whose name was a literal translation of the meaning of his given name in Serbo-Croatian, was probably comparing her to his wife the whole time he was staring at her skirt and pretending to focus on the sugar packets. Though Karen had never seen a photograph of Happy's wife, it made her feel beautiful to imagine Happy sizing up her own forearms and high forehead. She was inexplicably certain that if she and the dead wife were standing side by side, she would be the desirable one, and she would be more desirable in comparison than she would ever be on her own. And for this, she felt guilty. *What kind of fucked-up person*, she had always asked herself, *needs to be better than the dead?* Her needs in relation to Happy had always seemed monstrous to her.

They had had a kind of sex Karen had never had before that night. Frightened, desperate sex standing up in the bathroom of the bar. Sex that made her forget about absolutely everything. Sex that made her cry out with sounds she didn't recognize, as if she were speaking in tongues. And when Happy put his hand over her mouth, fearing perhaps that the boarders at the Palais would hear them and talk, she had put her hand over Happy's mouth too. She had bit down on his fingers until she tasted blood.

And after, lying next to him in her bed upstairs, she had immediately envisioned him forgetting his deceased wife, coming for her, loving her above everything. She had imagined her own long, white hair spread out on a different pillow in a halo around her head, next to his. It was the next morning when she learned that he had children. They had been at a sleepover at the neighbor's house the night before, and Happy had to leave her that morning to pick them up. Then, she thought of Happy leaving his children, coming for her, loving her above everything. It was the most selfish thought she had ever entertained in her life.

It didn't stop there, although it had been immediately apparent to both of them that this was a bad idea. She met Happy at his house several nights a week after the kids had gone to bed, skulking into his bedroom and holding her breath when she got up to use the bathroom. In the summers, the children went to Serbia to stay with Happy's mother and Karen was left alone for a month with her lover and her guilt and her revulsion at herself. She could never tell anyone about her relationship, because she could never reconcile this problem with the children. She wanted to love them. She wanted to let Happy love her. But it was a bad idea in Karen's bar, it was a bad idea in Happy's bed, the children just down the hall, and it had been a bad idea when Happy had finally brought Karen to his gym after it was closed for the night. Karen was surprised when she found out what Happy did for a living. He was a small man with a beautiful face. His nose had been crushed to one side, but his ears and brow were perfect, and his eyes were a blue that was more often seen in the eyes of infants. Happy was the proprietor of a training gym a couple of towns away. It was called Happy Family Boxing Club. Karen had laughed out loud when she heard the name. Happy looked hurt. "What is funny?" he asked.

"Nothing," Karen replied. "It's just that, well, Happy Family *Boxing*?" She looked at him, bemused, by the light of the speedometer. It had come out that the name of the gym was originally "Happy's Family Boxing," because Happy wanted to train not just boxers, but children and adults in the sport of pugilism for fun and for exercise. The sign painter had left off the apostrophe, and the nuance had been lost on Happy in his pride of ownership. It had not conjured for him, as it undoubtedly conjured for others, the image of happy families, perhaps dressed in the formal garb of middle-class 1950's Americans, beating the crap out of each other—Junior tossing a right hook in the direction of his immaculately made-up mother who was still clutching the handle of a vacuum cleaner.

In his truck on the way to Happy Family Boxing Club one night in that first month, Karen had asked how such a small and beautiful man could be a boxer. "But I am not boxer," he had explained, "I am training the other boxers." And then, when Karen looked confused, Happy had told her a long story. After the World Amateur Boxing Championships had been held in Belgrade in 1978, there was a craze in Yugoslavia for pugilism. There was something about the uncommon sport of violence divorced from its natural causes of hatred and anger and fear that resonated with people in the country, communists or otherwise (now, Happy told her, when he phoned his mother, who had been content to weather the real violence in Serbia all these years, she said to him, "Under Tito, we said that we are all the same, and we are all equal. That was a lie. But after Tito, when we stopped lying, we started killing each other"). Happy had trained to be a fighter as a boy, and kept it up at university despite the fact that it had become apparent, by the time he was twelve, that he had no natural talent and would only ever be a mediocre flyweight. He had founded Happy Family Boxing Club after coming to America when he had eventually saved up enough money painting houses and bussing tables and fixing cars. Now, he rarely trained real fighters, but his establishment was kept financially afloat—barely—by parents who brought their boys, and recently some girls, for self-defense classes, discipline, and slimming down.

Karen had been amused by the gym. She had had to work hard to contain a smirk when she looked around at the old-fashioned and shabby equipment, had felt laughter welling up in her when Happy laid her down on the mats in the ring to make love to her.

Once, Karen had gone to Happy Family Boxing Club to look for Happy on her day off. She had left the other bartender, Clarisse, wiping tables and keeping an eye on the taps. Karen had wanted to surprise Happy with a new photograph. It was of him, his narrow, hairless chest naked, his boxing gloves tied together and hanging just bellow his right and left collar bone. It was a black and white, and the gloves looked silver. In the photograph, his face was tilted up at an imaginary sun. He looked, Karen had thought, triumphant. He looked like a fourteen-year-old boy who had managed, for one night, to fool the world into treating him like an adult. He looked, Karen thought, perfect. She had matted and framed the photograph herself, then wrapped it in tissue paper. She carried it into the boxing club in front of her like it was a birthday cake, aflame with candles.

Happy was ringside, watching two small boys jab at each other with enormous gloves. The children's heads were swaddled in protective foam helmets. "Is a combat sport!" Happy yelled. "Do not be afraid of him! There is no fear in boxing!" He didn't notice Karen. "You are participating," yelled Happy at one of the boys, "in a ancient Greek right! You are boys! And you acting like ninnies! Ninnies!"

One of the boys stopped, mid-punch, and turned completely around. Karen thought he showed a good deal of agility. "Dad! No one says 'ninny.'"

"You fight!" yelled Happy. "And I talk! Do not be afraid of that boy!"

"Yeah," said his son. "Only, what *is* a ninny?" And then the other child, bored in the ring, sucker punched him on the neck and he went down.

Karen was immobilized by the sight of the child. Deciding not to be noticed after all, she brought her photograph to the back of the gym, to the room where Happy had a small office. The office contained a filing cabinet, a small desk and desk chair. The only thing on the desk was an old rotating fan. She had propped the picture against the fan and left.

Now, Karen looked away from the mirror and took stock of the bar. The dishwasher was full, so she kicked shut the door and watched it chug into action. The schizophrenics were in their place in the corner, mumbling at each other and themselves. The door to the bar opened, the heat of the summer expelling not Happy, but Karen's mother.

Karen's mother was named Sarah, and she looked both shrunken and unnecessarily meaty when she was in close proximity to her daughter. She was short, with an embarrassingly large bosom, and oversized hands and feet. She had the otherworldly paleness that Karen had inherited, but it made her look more like a creature from space than an angel. She didn't spend much time in the bar. Now that Rocky was dead, Sarah had increased her hours working as a lifeguard at the YMCA pool in town. "I'm not going to stay," she said to Karen, "I just wanted to bring you your mail." She pushed a large white envelope from Apollo College onto the bar. Karen knew what was in the envelope. It was information her mother had requested on her behalf about a two-year associate degree in Dental Technology.

"Thanks, Mom," she said.

"You're welcome. And you can stop by the house tomorrow, after you've looked it over, to use the computer to fill out the application."

"It's not a real college, Mom. I don't think they reject anyone. I'm sure I can handwrite it." Karen took the envelope from the bar and placed it on a high shelf behind her with the dusty bottles of more obscure liquors.

"That's ridiculous, Karen. You have skills—you know how to be professional—now use them. And I thought we could go to your father's grave tomorrow," she said. She wouldn't say that it would be the appropriate time to visit because it would be the day after his bar closed for good. But Karen knew this was what her mother was thinking, and it somehow touched her.

"Okay, Ma. You want a drink?" It was one of the endearing features of their relationship as mother and adult child that Sarah hated it when Karen called her "Ma" and that Karen always, inadvertently, used this term when she meant to show great love or deference to her mother.

"No, thank you," Sarah said, studying her daughter's face. Sarah looked like she was restraining herself from offering additional maternal advice. She looked around the bar. "Karen," she said, "your father loved this place; it made him who he was for the last twenty-five years of his life. I know you have always loved it at much as he did." *But*, Karen could see she almost said, and then hesitated. "Have a good time tonight, and don't burn the place down."

Karen nodded. For some reason, she glanced back at the packet from the college. She hadn't objected when her mother had come to her with the idea of going to school to be a dental hygienist. It was a good career, and it wouldn't take too much schooling before Karen could start making money that way. The part of her mother's plan that she really objected to, and that she hadn't found a way around yet, was her mother's assumption that Karen would return to her parent's house to live while she completed her associate's degree. There was also her distaste at the idea of sticking her fingers into someone's open mouth, but she knew that this was ridiculous. She shuddered, though, looking at the envelope, as though she had in fact just been forced to insert her index finger behind someone's molar.

"It's probably going to be a late night," she told her mother. "I'll come by the house tomorrow in the afternoon."

"Sure." Her mother looked around the inside of the Palais Royale, examining each unchanged feature. Karen watched as Sarah closed her eyes and took a deep breath. Then, she leaned up and kissed her daughter lightly on the cheek. The bar was only half-full. Karen's gaze fell on Evey, who was shifting uncomfortably on her bar stool. Karen decided she would do something that night to help this woman. She had no idea what.

CHAPTER SIX

It was four in the afternoon and Ryan Wilson had to concentrate. He had a job to do today, and really, when he thought about it, today was no different than any other day. From where he sat in the boom truck, Ryan assessed the patch of ground in front of him. The grass looked dry enough, but he knew it was loamy and soft underneath. Yesterday it had rained hard, and now the skies were swept clean. The air was like a child's face after his mother had roughly swiped a wet washcloth across, removing all evidence of the day's trouble before bed. The ground, though, had absorbed a lot of water, and the muck beneath the grass could be real trouble. At least on this job, he could pull the truck right up next to the gravesite. There were days when Ryan had to get out the hand cart and wheel his heavy burden to the plot, and it seemed that those paths he navigated in other cemeteries were always narrow, and never straight, and almost always up a hill. This morning, he had set up the tripod with some difficulty, but the legs had held, and he had lowered the weighty vault into the hole successfully. This afternoon, there was only the cap left to be settled into place.

Ryan was a boom truck operator for a molded concrete company. It was a small company, based in South Portland, and there were only two boom trucks and drivers. Lowell, the other guy, preferred to do stairs and pavers and things like that. Lowell hated the cemetery gigs, but Ryan liked these best. On days like today it was Ryan's job to get up early in the morning, load a larger-than-man-sized concrete vault onto the truck with the winch and the boom, and bring it to the place where the recently deceased would soon be put into the ground. After the dead was lowered into the ground and the mourners had left, it was Ryan's job to put the cap on the vault before the landscaping crew covered the whole mess with dirt and sod. All coffins placed in the ground at public cemeteries went into one of these vaults. Most people, Ryan had found, didn't know this about burials. When he talked to other young people about his job, he could see the look of fascination and doubt cross their faces—most were reassured to think of the bodies of loved ones, and perhaps someday their own body, secure in these dry and cool encasements. Every once in a while, Ryan talked to someone who looked horrified. Usually they turned out to be claustrophobic, or maybe an environmentalist who suddenly realized that none of us would be allowed to decay, to return to the earth after death, that dust was not in fact to dust anymore, and ashes, well, that was a different story. None of the people who looked so alarmed when Ryan spoke of his job at a bar or on nights when his roommate had girls over to the house to smoke pot and listen to music or play video games and drink, knew anyone who had recently died.

But Ryan was happy to take the cemetery duty and leave the pavers to Lowell. Ryan found that when he was installing stairs, for instance, at some plumber's ranch-style, or a lawyer's McMansion, there was a lot more supervision and therefore a lot more trouble. The contractors at these places always had really specific ideas about how and when and where everything was supposed to be done, and they were always in the way. It was worse, though, when the homeowner was herself in charge. People returned things, people wanted things moved, people were concerned that everything was a half-inch off. And people were always too close to the truck. But out at the cemeteries, it was just Ryan and the funeral director and the dead. Maine law said that the funeral director on every job had to stay until the cap was placed on the vault in the grave, and most of the time they did. Ryan knew most of the funeral directors in Maine these days, and they were mostly young men, mostly nice guys. Some of them just wanted to get out of there as quickly as possible, to go out drinking for the night or take a girlfriend to the movies. Many of them cared about their jobs, especially the older men who were approaching retirement, and felt that it was their duty to see the deceased out of this world, to watch until their fate had been finally sealed with a solid barrier between their coffin and the sky above, covered with concrete and then with earth. One guy up in The County told Ryan every time he was there that personally, the whole thing creeped him out and he was going to be cremated when he went, to avoid a visit from Ryan and his cold sepulchers. Ryan had looked that word up when he got home, stored it in his vocabulary, turned it over frequently in his mind.

He knew the names of all the funeral directors and remembered who he liked to work with and who he wished he could avoid. But he didn't often know the names of the dead. He did today, though, and Ryan thought of Matt with a shock of discomfort he tried to suppress by again checking out the terrain. The ground in front of his windshield gave up no new secretes. Just beyond his plane of focus was the hole into which Matt's body had been lowered, and then there was the headstone. Ryan did not shift his gaze to these things. He had noticed earlier how cheap Matt's coffin was.

Normally, after he lowered the vault into the hole, Ryan would fold up his tripod and take all his supplies back to the truck before driving a respectful distance from the fresh grave and disappearing while the family mourned graveside. Sometimes he drove his massive truck into the town, people on the streets stopping to look as he throttled down on the hills. He would hit a Subway or a Burger King for lunch. If the funeral was promised to be short, and the family was only going to attend the burial briefly, he would sit in the truck somewhere in the cemetery out of sight and read a book. Today, though he was starving and had a paperback copy of *Jarhead* his girlfriend had given him wedged between the seats in the cab, he had stayed at the cemetery. He had parked out of sight and waited in the cab during the time of the church funeral, eating nothing, reading nothing, staring mostly ahead.

When the family and friends of Matt Hulot had made their quiet way to his headstone where Kevin, the funeral director, was already standing, Ryan slipped in at the back of the crowd. Ryan knew Matt from the bars downtown. They went to the same trivia night at Rosie's on Wednesdays, and though they had never been close, Ryan had felt a weight in his stomach since he had heard about the death. Standing there with Matt's loved ones, Ryan had felt a wave of uncertainty pass over him. It was always harder to do the funerals of young people, and this had been a particularly difficult day for him.

Now, sitting in his truck, he couldn't explain to himself what he was feeling, but it was maybe like anxiety. Whatever it was, the combination of emotion and hunger was making him light-headed. When Matt's loved ones left the cemetery, Ryan, not wanting to stand out, had pretended to leave too. He followed the crowd toward the parked cars, and then looped silently around to where he had parked the truck. He had been sitting there ever since, waiting for something, he was not sure what, before he got to work again.

•

Ryan let himself out of the truck and allowed the door to fall shut softly behind him. He looked over at the grave. Kevin was supposed to have removed the chrome frame for lowering the coffin into the hole already, and rolled up the Astroturf around the site in preparation for Ryan to lower the lid onto the vault. He had not, and he was nowhere in sight. "Damn," Ryan swore softly, then looked around to see if he could find Kevin. "Kevin?" he called. "Where are you?" There was no answer. He decided to secure the vault lid to the chains hanging from the boom, and then worry about Kevin. Ryan scuttled onto the back of the truck and got to work. He secured the lid and then started up the winch. When he threw the controls, the machine sounded like it was straining. He brought it to a complete stop to check it out, but when he looked, the winch appeared the same as it always did. He checked the head and the drive brackets, and everything looked fine, so he stared it up again, shifting the assembly into movement.

When he first heard the noise and felt the crash, he thought for sure he had fallen to the ground, the impact was that great. But then he heard Kevin's voice yell, "What the fuck, man?" and he recollected himself. Ryan was still standing on the side of the truck, and the concrete cap had slipped off of the chains that were supposed to hold it while he used the winch to lower it toward the grave. Kevin had emerged with one of the landscapers from behind a backhoe three graves away.

"I'm okay," Ryan said weakly. Then he looked at the concrete vault cap, which had cracked in two, a jagged but clean line down the middle of it. "Fuck," he said. He must not have secured it properly. It happened sometimes, he knew, but never before to him. The vault cap was ruined.

"What did you do that for?" Kevin asked. Kevin was in his twenties, too, and he and Ryan had worked together before. Kevin always stayed until the cap had been placed, but he also liked to make jokes with Ryan and sometimes try to share a little weed. Ryan never smoked on the job.

"What do you mean, Kevin? I fucked it up. Slipped. Cracked."

"Shit man, hard day," said the landscaper, who was standing next to Kevin.

Kevin surveilled the scene and then gestured at Ryan with a smoldering joint.

"Nah, man," said Ryan. "I have to go back to town to get a new cap now."

Kevin took the joint to his own lips and took a drag. After a moment of reflection he said, "Wait, though. That'll take you a long time."

"You haven't even cleaned up here," Ryan said. "At least this bullshit will give you time."

"Look, it's been a long day." Kevin kicked the dirt in front of him with the toe of a shiny black lace-up. "Did you know Matt?"

"I did, actually," said Ryan.

"Yeah," said the landscaper, "Everyone knew Matt."

"He was a good guy." Kevin passed the join to the landscaper.

Ryan thought about the last conversation he had with Matt. Three weeks ago they had both been early for trivia night, alone at tables with beers before the rest of the group that made up their respective teams arrived. They had started talking about work, and then quickly about their girlfriends. Or, in Matt's case, ex-girlfriend. He had been in the market, Ryan guessed. Ryan had found himself admitting to Matt how much he loved Catherine, his own girlfriend of six months. He was able to talk to Matt without embarrassment. That was what he remembered most.

Kevin walked over to Matt's grave, still open and ringed by the chrome lift. He sat down cross-legged beside the headstone and started pulling up handfuls of grass. It came out not in single blades but in hanks, the new sod still flexible and thin under

Kevin's fingers. Ryan watched him and didn't know what to do. He jumped down from the bed of the truck and stood awkwardly, staring. When the landscaper handed him the roach of the joint, he accepted and took a hot, quick drag. Then, not knowing what to do with the butt, he held it in his hand and let it smolder to death. After a moment, Ryan went to join Kevin. "Are you okay?" he asked quietly. He crouched down.

"I've never done one for someone I knew," Kevin said. "It's fucking me up. I didn't think it would, but it is."

"Okay," Ryan said.

The landscaper came to join them, pulling a flat little bottle of vodka from his back pocket. He twisted off the cap with a satisfying sound and nudged it toward Kevin.

"Shit," said Ryan. "Starting early. Who are you anyway?"

"Joe," said the landscaper. And that was all he said.

Ryan felt like this, whatever it was that the three of them were doing, would take awhile. He didn't want a drink, necessarily, but he wanted to be here. He felt right for the first time all day. The grave would wait, he thought. It could wait all night.

CHAPTER SEVEN

From Stan's point of view, things were not getting better. In fact, everything seemed to have decidedly taken a turn for the worse. Evey was still sitting next to him on a bar stool, and he could still in the gloom just make out the top of her thigh where her dress rode up a bit, but she was looking straight ahead with an expression of unparalleled fury. She had refused to look at Stan for the last three minutes and twenty-six seconds. He was counting down the silence, hoping it would evaporate into nothing and that later he wouldn't remember the calculation or this exercise in enumeration. But he was hoping this with an increasing feeling of desperation. He should not have told her about James. Or he should have told her differently.

People kept coming into the bar. When Stan arrived there had been four middle-aged guys sitting at a corner table. Everyone called them The Schizophrenics. And that skinny guy with the funny name down at the end of the bar, always talking to Karen. And a woman Stan didn't recognize, sitting in a booth by herself. Now, there were probably thirty people inside, and the door kept banging open to admit another small grouping. It looked like everyone in the town was going to come out for the last night of the Palais Royale. Stan had just spotted the guys from produce at Stop n' Shop, but he didn't feel like talking to them right now, and so far they seemed not to notice him. He wondered if it was because he was wearing the uniform. Someone had turned up the volume on the jukebox. Someone he recognized from school walked in.

And then Evey got up, pushing abruptly away from the bar and leaving her stool ajar when she walked off. Stan quickly took off his cap and placed it protectively on her seat, so he was sure it would be there for her when she got back.

She was gone for just a second, and Stan was convinced that she was on her way back to sit next to him. Then she was gone for a minute, and he was sure she was in the bathroom. Stan wasn't entirely clear on what women did in the bathrooms in bars, but he thought there were probably a considerable number of things that went on there. He sipped at his drink, staring. The thought of Evey earlier in the back of the limo jolted through him. She had liked him for a moment there, had confided in him. What had gone wrong? He should have told her earlier about James. He could not come up with a way to make this better, to not know James or to protect all three of them from their pasts. When he raised his head and looked around again he felt like he was surfacing from a pond.

"This is what I will remember," Stan heard someone say. When he looked over to the end of the bar, he realized that it was the guy who was always chatting up the bartender. Stan had heard it said that they were having an affair. He had never paid much attention to the man, though.

"Hey," Stan said. "What's your name, anyway?" As soon as he said it, he blushed. It was not like him to shout out to strangers, or to speak with confidence in his voice like that. But suddenly, he really wanted to know the man's name.

"My name is Happy," Happy said.

"What kind of name is that?" Stan was leaning into the space along the bar that stretched between them. There were three empty chairs in that space, but Stan didn't want to get up, and Happy looked stuck where he was.

"It's my name. It's from Yugoslavia." Happy did not ask Stan what his name was.

Stan did not ask Happy what there was to be so happy about. Instead, he said, "You look kind of pissed off. Come have a drink with me." He motioned for Happy to take the seat next to him, on the other side of the one he was saving for Evey, and then he waved at Karen to get them another round, though Stan still had more than half a Jack and Coke getting warm in a glass that was attached to his cupped right hand. Karen ignored him. Happy slid down to the seat beside Stan and sat in it. And then Stan didn't know what to say. He wasn't a curious person by nature. But he thought that Happy looked exactly the way Stan felt. "Okay, then," he said after a moment. "Tell me one thing about yourself."

"I am not pissed off," Happy said, elucidating every word carefully. "I am a little sad. I maybe am in love with a person who is not loving me."

"That's hard, then."

"And what about you? What would you be telling me about yourself?" Happy didn't look at Stan when he asked this.

Stan was at a loss. What did he know about himself? "Once," he said, starting to talk before he knew what he would say, "I saved a person's life."

"That is commendable."

"When I was a kid, I pushed a kid named Adam out of the way of a car. We were standing by the road with our bikes. The weird thing is, I never really liked that kid."

"You know they say this, right?" said Happy.

"What?"

"That if you save someone's life you are dependable for it."

Karen turned around quickly and stared hard at Happy. "Don't you talk to him!" she said.

Stan jumped in his seat. "I'm...I'm sorry," he stammered. Stan hated being yelled at more than anything. He didn't understand why Karen looked so upset, her lips pressed together so tightly that her pale skin was the shade of soap around her mouth.

"Not you, Stan," Karen said, dismissing him with a tilt of her head. "Happy, I don't want you to say anything." Her words were short and clean, like they had been hammered into a rock. "I don't want you to say another word."

Happy looked stricken. Stan said, "Look. What's going on here? What's the deal between you two?"

Then Happy and Karen both turned their eyes to Stan. They had identical expressions on their faces, of incredulity tinged with dislike, as if someone had just done something improper in front of a roomful of children. It was the expression Stan thought would be appropriate if he had just bitten Happy lightly on the nose, rather than asked a question. They stared at Stan too long, and Stan stared past them, not looking at anything, until he caught his own reflection in the circular mirror behind the bar. The mirror was ringed with Christmas lights encased in a clear tube. Stan thought he looked very young, sitting there in his uniform jacket, uncomfortable under this lasting gaze. His hair was his mother's hair, blond and ranging over the planes of his face, stretching toward his cheeks. "Look," he said again, finally. He blushed deeply and hotly when he started to speak. "I know what's going on. I'm sorry I asked. But you can't do it this way. No one wants to be angry tonight." Stan didn't know what he was saying. He only knew he was caught in the middle of something and he didn't want it to be unpleasant. Stan felt that he was always caught in the middle of something, and it was usually something he hadn't done himself, and he could never figure out how he had gotten to that point. "Happy?"

Happy said nothing.

"That's your name, right?" Stan asked, looking at Happy's frozen face.

"Yes, it is my name," Happy said slowly.

"It will be fine. If you're just nice to her, it will be fine. I promise."

Karen leaned in close to Stan and said, "I'm not sure you're qualified to make that statement."

"So I'm not," Stan said. "But isn't it reassuring? Don't you think that if we all think that, then we can make it true?"

"You maybe should not drink for a while," Happy said to Stan.

Stan said, "No. I think I'll have a double." He was looking at Karen.

"Shut up, Stan," she said.

It was true that when Stan was eight years old he pushed Adam McKinley out of the way of an onrushing car. Stan remembered the driver of the car, though she never stopped. He was sure she was entirely unaware of the danger that had so briefly been averted. It was a Toyota Tercel, Stan remembered it that clearly. The woman inside had been hurried, speeding with her windows down and something softly playing on the radio, her hair a huge mass of blonde curls, whipped around by all that wind. She never swerved or slowed. Adam had been eating penny candy, pulling whole handfuls of it out of a paper sack, and he was unwrapping a sticky root beer barrel and walking his bike. The barrel, the bike, the position of his hands—it was a confusion of barely balanced parts, loosely strung together by this child, and Stan, next to him, always more cautious, had waited on the curb, pausing a moment while Adam wandered into the road. When Adam had stepped down, that's when Stan saw the car, and he could picture, even as a child, what would happen to Adam's body in a moment. He had no experience with accidents of this magnitude, but Stan remembered now that even at eight years old he thought, *I don't want to be the kid who sees his friend get his by a car.* He had lunged toward Adam, his own bike clattering to the ground in a mess of pedals and chain, handle bars wrapped in blue hockey tape, and grabbed Adam around the waist, pulling him back onto the sidewalk. They fell down there together, Adam's body atop Stan's, and the bag of candy exploded, butterscotches and peppermints, Tootsie Rolls and root beer barrels arcing through the air like so many lost jewels. Adam had yelled, "What the hell?" When Stan rolled off, Adam had said, "I saw it coming." And then he wheeled his bike away and didn't talk to Stan for four days. When they came together again, to throw rotten apples at each other in the orchard behind Adam's house, neither child mentioned the car. It was like it never happened.

Now, in the bar, Stan wanted his say. He felt like he was always biting his tongue, never saying the one important thing. Happy was still beside him, but turned around on his bar stool, watching the door and the ever increasing crowd. Karen had not brought either of them a fresh drink. Stan wanted to say something to Happy, about how stupid he could see that he and Karen were being, about how it didn't have to be this hard to love someone. But he couldn't think of the right words.

Evey came back to the bar, moving as carefully as if she were holding an egg balanced on a teaspoon. She stood next to him. "Stan," she said. "Come with me for a minute."

Stan put down his drink and looked carefully at Evey. He shrugged and stood up. Evey led Stan through the bar. Elsewhere, the talk was of what would happen to the Palais Royale tomorrow, when it changed ownership. Elsewhere, the talk was of the price of lobsters, how it was a good season and the price was high, but if you knew Rusty you could still buy them down off the dock for three dollars a pound. Elsewhere, the talk was of the war, and a recent newspaper article in the *Press Herald* by some nut job who said we were going about it all wrong. Elsewhere, the talk was of the Thomas family who had put a giant CB antenna on the top of their house two days ago. Evey walked Stan to the women's bathroom.

Stan was uncertain, facing the door to the women's bathroom. It was a room with a single toilet, no stalls, and a sink and blow-dryer. Evey looked up into his worried face and laughed. "Come on," she said, and pulled him into the bathroom. Stan wasn't sure why he was there, but as Evey closed the door behind them, he suddenly felt like he couldn't get enough air into his lungs. The bathroom was painted entirely black, like the inside of a theater. The toilet and the sink were old and cracked; they looked like they might crumble. But the mirror above the sink was ringed with lights and looked like a vanity mirror in the dressing room of a starlet. Stan looked into the basin of the sink and remembered the time when he was six years old and he lost one of his front baby teeth. His mother had come into the bathroom of their house where Stan was twisting his tooth finally out. She had offered to wash his tooth off for him. While she was washing it, it had accidentally slipped down the drain, and Stan had cried until he was hysterical and his mother had offered, shamed, to write a note to the tooth fairy explaining what had happened.

Stan looked into Evey's face in the mirror and focused on her lips, wet where she had licked them and slightly cracked at the edges. He pressed himself against the edge of the sink and felt himself get an erection. Evey looked at Stan in the mirror and then firmly turned him around to face her. Stan closed his eyes and then opened them again.

From her purse, she brought out her eyeliner pencil, her

mascara, and a tube of lipstick. "Hold still," she said. "I want you to do something for me."

"Anything," said Stan.

Evey pulled the top off the eyeliner. "Look up," she said to Stan. He flinched when she put her fingers on either side of his eye. She pulled the skin taught and drew the pencil along the lower rim of his eyelid, using just as much pressure as she could without hurting him. She pressed down a bit harder when she did his other eye, and Stan had to tense all his muscles not to cry out. He wasn't sure why he was letting her do this. Next, she uncapped her mascara. The color was brown-black and much darker than Stan's blond eyelashes. She held the brush parallel to Stan's face. He didn't blink. She rolled the brush slightly as she stroked it upward on the underside of his lashes. Stan had often wanted to be a woman. Not like this—he didn't have fantasies of wearing women's panties or dressing in high heels. He had never applied his mother's blush when she was out at the grocery store. But he had looked at women, his mother most often, and thought how useful they were. Stan wanted to stand in the kitchen and rinse out a dish. He wanted to bake a cake and then take a shower and cover himself lightly in powder. He wanted to wash a child's face. These were things, in Stan's mind, that women did, and that they did competently. He wanted that ease, that sense of purpose. Evey did two coats on each set of lashes, less and lighter on the lower lashes. She told him to make a fish face as she uncapped the lipstick.

Stan was staring at Evey like he was going to cry. But his lips were still pursed expectantly. She drew the color over his mouth.

"Stan," Evey said. "I'm sorry I kissed you in the limo. It wasn't about you." When she was done, she snapped the top back on the lipstick and kissed Stan on the forehead.

"Don't do that," he said.

"What?"

"Kiss me on the forehead. Like we're friends. Like none of it matters."

"Stan," Evey said. "Listen," she said to him. "Did you see Amanda Lacroix come in the bar?"

"Yes."

"I remember her from when I was little. I want to tell you something," Evey said. "You're probably a good person. You probably have dreams and ambitions and love in your life. But I could never want you. You're like Amanda back there. You're part of an alternate reality. I don't live here. I don't live like this. You don't want me either. Or you shouldn't. Look, Stan. I forgive you. Or wait, no. I'm sorry. I'm sorry I kissed you in the limo, or you kissed me. Or whatever. It's not about you."

"That's stupid, Evey," Stan said. Then he closed his long-lashed eyes. "Can we not talk about this? Can I want you for just a moment? Just for tonight?"

She turned him back around to face the mirror with the same firm, quick pressure on his arm above the elbow that she had used to turn him to face her. They looked at themselves, and each other, Evey's head by Stan's shoulder, looking at themselves full in the face.

Stan blinked at himself in the lights. He smiled. "I can't wear this out there," he said, gesturing to the door.

"Of course you can," said Evey. "Come on." She took Stan by the hand and walked him out of the bathroom and back to the bar.

CHAPTER EIGHT

As Evey and Stan sat back down at the bar, James Presley walked in. Evey didn't initially see him approach from behind her, and when he put his hand on the bar next to her glass, she noticed the curve of his ring finger, a pale elongated comma that made her jump. She clutched her glass protectively and brought it back to her lips without turning around. Out of the corner of her eye then, Evey could see that James was looking at her carefully. But he spoke to Stan: "You look good, Stan."

Stan brought his fingers up to his face nervously, and Evey saw his embarrassment at what she had done to him. He said nothing, but smudged the lipstick a little around the corners of his mouth.

"It's been a long time," Evey said to James, as evenly as she could manage.

"I'll have a gin," James said to Karen, "and tonic."

Evey turned to face James. He had dark marks under his eyes and his hair was very dark—he had dyed it so black it looked blue in the light of the bar. He had always had the half moons under his eyes, and they had always looked exactly like someone had pressed their thumbs into his face. But Evey had never seen him with his hair dyed. She had been told by her father that James had lost all his hair from chemo and that when it grew back it had been prematurely gray. He was, absurdly, wearing a tee-shirt with a kitten on it. Evey noticed these details, but couldn't focus on James as a whole, couldn't get an impression of who he had become or what she thought of him. It was overwhelming, seeing him standing there. And she had to look away.

James rescued her. "I'm sorry for your loss," he said.

There was, Evey thought, always that to say. She had hated hearing it at first because the phrase had seemed both so terribly inadequate to the situation and so outsized in its ritual repetition, almost as if she were not the kind of person to whom a thing like that should be said. But she appreciated it now; she understood why this is a thing that is said, a small elision that made it possible to some day say other things.

"How's your life, Evey?" James asked. He looked, Evey thought hopefully, like he might sincerely want to know. Evey quickly drank down the rest of her Jack and Coke and motioned frantically at Karen, not sure she could wait until Karen brought James' drink before she had another one. She was starting to feel drunk, a feeling that welled up inside her skull and threatened to spill over and engulf her brain.

Evey weighed her options: *I'm happy. I'm thinking about quitting my job. Still in love with my husband after three years. Regretful of so many things. Afraid sometimes for no reason. Having an affair with a woman who I can't stop thinking about. Unable to complain.* "I'm pregnant," she said. It was a lie. James stared at her.

Karen leaned over the bar with James's drink and asked, "What the fuck happened to your face, Stan?"

Stan reached up to touch his mouth again, and his whole body slumped. It occurred to Evey that Stan was the kind of person who was prepared to be made fun of, but who was always disappointed nonetheless when it happened. "I don't know," he said. But then he straightened his shoulders and stopped picking at his lipstick. "Evey did it. Not bad, right?"

Karen snorted and put down James's drink. James took it and swallowed an alarming amount. Evey said, "I think I'm going to throw up." She moved quickly toward the bathroom. She did throw up then, into the old, stained toilet. Just a little liquid came out, but she felt much better. Washing her face at the sink, she thought first of how many people had thrown up in that toilet over the years, how many folks had found their way down this particular avenue of human desperation to heaving into that bowl. Her forehead tingled, and she pushed back another surge of nausea and the knowledge that she would have to return to her ex-husband, and whatever it was that she couldn't put her finger on that was so unresolved about her relationship with him that it turned her stomach, made her fingers shake when she held them out. Then it occurred to her that James would really think she was pregnant, taking her sickness as additional evidence. She laughed a little bit, looking at herself in the mirror. Evey had always hated and often remarked on the fact that in films and on television when a woman threw up it could only mean one of two things: she was pregnant or bulimic. As if, in the shorthand world of fiction, women never got drunk or had the flu. Evey herself hadn't thrown up in maybe a year. But as a young person, she had thrown up when she was nervous or upset, even when she was under pressure. The year her mother died, she had been sent home from school by the nurse fifteen separate days for being sick in the girls' room. She wondered to herself if she should tell James that she was not, in fact, expecting. But then, what exactly did he deserve to know about her life anyway?

She looked through her purse for the tube of lipstick she had just used on Stan, but instead found her phone. She felt an enormous surge of reassurance at its weight in her hand. She flipped it open and typed: "Nothing in my life makes sense in this context." She sent it to Angela. She squeezed the phone in her hand, wanting suddenly and ferociously to feel the buzz of Angela's response. Nothing.

•

When Evey returned, James was still standing in more or less the same position she had left him, and Stan was there, and Sebastian had arrived. *Fuck,* Evey thought, *what if James congratulated Sebastian on becoming a father?* She wasn't sure how she would explain such an outrageous and unnecessary lie to her husband. But as she approached the little group she could hear them talking about the Palais Royale, about the weather, about nothing. They were talking as if nothing was amiss, and nothing was odd about their little grouping. Evey was momentarily incredulous: *how could they stand there, having a conversation, as if this was just one of those things that happened in life? Like it was totally expected for one's ex-husband to talk to one's husband on the day his brother had been buried.* Then she thought, *there must be something wrong with me. What do I expect them to do? This must be my problem. This is, obviously, just one of those things that happens in life.* The fact that she was emotionally, and it appeared, physically unprepared for a meeting of her ex-husband and her current husband, and some limo driver with whom she had gone to grade school, seemed on examination to be a minor point. This was going to be just fine, obviously. Tonight was just going to happen, *and it is going to be just fine,* Evey thought, *whether I want it to be or not.*

Sebastian put his hand on his wife's shoulder and continued asking James questions about the history of the bar. James seemed to know an incredible amount about the history of Illium in general, and this historical site in particular. For example, he knew that the Palais had been designated a historical monument in the town and therefore could not be torn down, despite the rumor flying around, that the place was going to be demolished tomorrow. Rather, James told them, the bar was going to be "refurbished." When Rocky Amato had died, everyone had assumed that he had left the bar to his daughter Karen, and that she would continue bartending and living upstairs. Everyone had assumed that nothing would change. And this, Evey thought, as

James continued to tell the story of the bar and Sebastian and Stan looked on, interested or feigning interest, was precisely the problem with people from small towns. Everyone always assumed that everything would stay the same. The human species, it seemed to her, was poorly adapted to assimilate change. It turned out that the bar had been left instead to Rocky's brother Benny, and he had sold the whole thing to developers. No one, not even James, was sure what would become of the Elvis portraits when the place was "revitalized." Evey, listening, caught herself. She had been engrossed in what James was saying until she looked up for a minute and around at the other people in the bar, and realized she was not in fact interested at all in the words he was speaking, the facts he was bestowing, the affect with which he was delivering his lecture. It was easy to be in thrall of James. But Evey suddenly ascertained, looking at his ridiculous cat tee-shirt, his badly dyed hair, that James was performing "ex-husband," was simply performing "smart guy." And he was performing badly. Evey wasn't sure who James thought his audience was, exactly. She felt her phone vibrate against her in her purse and quickened with the need to see what Angela had said to her. She eased it out of her purse, and angling away from the trio of men, flipped it open. "Oh, sweetheart," she read on the screen.

"Tell me something," she texted back.

As James continued to talk to Sebastian about Illium, Sebastian caught Evey's eye. He had clearly seen, before Evey had, the flaws in James' acting. She could see that Sebastian was asking her silently: *this James? You were married to this man? Is this guy for real?* It was true that James was going on and on about something that in all likelihood he should have known was only of interest to him, and it was true that it was the first time he had met Sebastian, and a normal man, another man, would have thought to pause once in awhile, to ask Sebastian a question or at least check to see if he was listening. At least he wasn't talking about God. Evey had heard that James had experienced a religious conversion after his illness, and the whole idea of it made her suspicious of everything James said. God, she thought, changed the whole context. Evey had forgotten that this was one of James's traits, this heedless talk, this entirely unconscious insistence that what he had to say was the most important and interesting thing that anyone could have uttered at that moment. And it was easy to forget this about James, Evey thought, because when Evey had been with James she was very young, and James had been almost always the most interesting person in the room. Her phone buzzed again in her hand. "I get wet even when you text me," she read from the screen. "How is that even possible?"

"Um, Evey?" Stan whispered in her ear.

Evey closed her phone quickly. "What?" Her eyes were still on Sebastian. She could see him straining not to make a face. She could see that he was on the point of hysteria. Once, they had been invited to a performance by a friend of a friend. It had taken place at PA's Lounge in Somerville, and they had entered with a sense of excitement. They were doing something arty and the fake-wood paneling and cheap beer in cans at the Lounge had given the whole evening a feeling of raciness, of something being done underground, of spontaneity. When the artists had taken the stage, they were so sincere, so without irony, that it was painful. Four young men in various states of undress talking earnestly about their genitals. When one of the men had eaten an entire hardboiled egg, including most of the shell, Sebastian had let out a loud giggle that resounded in the small, credulous audience. When the men asked for people to join them on stage and tell their own stories, Sebastian had leaned over to Evey and whispered, "I haven't seen this many white people in a room in a long time." And when an older audience member had started to recount a long, rambling story about the ritual sexual abuse he had survived in day care in the Eighties, Sebastian had gotten a peculiar look on his face: he was obviously grinding his teeth, and though his features looked calm, Evey had been able to tell that a scream mask was hidden just below the surface of his face. When they had escaped the room and were out in the snowy night, he had started to laugh so hysterically that neither of them had been able to stop, clutching lampposts to keep from tumbling into the street. They had laughed until Evey thought they would both need to be hospitalized.

She noted the same look on Sebastian's face now.

Stan was insistent, his face near Evey's ear. She could smell her own makeup on him. "Can I talk to you?"

"Stan, what do you want to say?"

Sebastian was going to lose it in a minute. Maybe, Evey thought, that would be a good thing. Or at least James was distracting Sebastian from his grief.

Stan leaned even closer, "It's just? Are you really pregnant?"

Evey glanced at James, and then, a little panicky, at Sebastian. "Shut up," she whispered.

Stan breathed into the side of her head: "Maybe we should talk, you know, privately? I mean, the baby, and—"

"Stan," she said, "of all the people in this room, it is probably you who has the least right to be concerned with this. What the fuck do you care?"

"I just thought, you know, with the drinking…and maybe James should…"

A chuckle escaped her throat like a cough. Sebastian gave her a questioning look, now forgetting to even pretend to listen to James. "Evey," he said, and moved away from James. "Stan, what did you—"

Evey didn't wait to hear him finish his sentence. She had to get out of there. To smoke a cigarette. To talk to James. To avoid talking to Sebastian about what she had said or done, or hadn't done. To text Angela. To get James away from her husband.

To get away from Stan, most of all. Evey grabbed James by the hand and pulled him toward the door, calling over her shoulder: "Sebastian, I'll be right back."

Out on the porch of the bar, it was quiet. Half a dozen people were out there smoking, some talking softly to each other, others gazing at the road in front of them or off to the side where the river sparkled a little and moved sluggishly by. The apartment she had shared with James years before was across the street. Evey closed her eyes for a moment. She would have to tell him now that she was not really pregnant, that she didn't know why she had said that. "Evey," James said, "do you have a cigarette?"

Evey looked taken aback. "You can't *smoke*?" she asked.

"Evey, just bum me a cigarette, please," said James.

Now was the time to tell him. She thought momentarily, that he might ask. Surely he would want to know about the baby, her baby. Or at least about what the fuck she was doing in a bar, and about to smoke a cigarette, pregnant and drunk in high heels.

Evey handed him a cigarette, though they both knew that James's gesture was asking for something else altogether. Evey lit his cigarette for him, coming closer to James's face than she had been in a long time.

"You know, I used to go through your stuff," he said. "In the apartment. When you weren't home. I used to look through your journal, your letters. I don't know what I was looking for."

Evey realized she would rather talk about the past than tell James about the baby she was not carrying. "Did you think I was cheating on you?"

"No, not really. Actually, no." James took a drag of his cigarette. Evey mentally put a hat on his head and admired the effect this would have. "I never thought you would cheat on me. I think I was just trying to figure out who you were. I mean, back then. I would have crawled inside your head if I could have."

Evey nodded. She knew what he meant. She realized she had been holding an unlit cigarette in her fist and brought it up to her mouth to light it. She wished she could be somewhere else if she was going to have to have a real conversation with her ex-husband.

"You know," James said, "I understand why you left me."

"Is this some kind of Jesus-induced thing?" Evey asked. Maybe, she thought, he wasn't asking about the putative pregnancy because he had some new godly craze for not *judging*. "Is this where you tell me you forgive me? Because I'm not sure I can handle that, James."

"I'm just saying that I could have made the same mistake. I understand why you left. I just wanted to let you know."

"It wasn't a mistake," Evey said. "I'm sorry for what happened to you, James. But my leaving wasn't a mistake." She wasn't sure that this was true. She had never had a good handle on how regret worked. She was glad, for instance, that she had met Sebastian.

She thought about the night she and Sebastian had gone to Fenway park after it was closed. Sebastian had a friend who worked public relations for the Red Sox, and he had let them into the offices, and then down onto the field at three in the morning once when Evey and Sebastian were first dating. The only other person in the park at that hour had been a worker spraying down the bleacher seats with what looked like a fire hose. The bright lights weren't on, but the field seemed ready to be illuminated at any minute. Evey and Sebastian and his friend had shared a cigarette on top of the Green Monster, commenting that this was one thing you would never otherwise be allowed to do at Fenway. Magical things like that happened, Evey thought, with Sebastian.

"It wasn't a mistake," she repeated. She knew that she regretted not being there for James when he got sick, but she didn't know how to connect this with the gratitude she felt for her present life.

James had finished smoking his cigarette. "Do you have any drugs?" he asked.

"What?" It occurred to Evey, in the long moment she willfully took to allow his words to sink in, that James hadn't avoided asking her whether she was really pregnant for any reason other than the fact that it did not directly relate to him. James was, and always had been, and she supposed, always would be, an entity unto himself, unmoored from anyone else in some essential way. James was simply self-involved.

James looked across the porch at the six or seven other people who were ignoring them.

"Do you have any coke?"

"You can't fucking be serious, James. You had *cancer.*"

"So what am I supposed to do? Spend the rest of my precious fucking life taking care of every minute and being thankful? How long am I supposed to live, anyway? A hundred years? In pristine condition because otherwise I'm just ungrateful. God will tell me when it's time for me to die."

"You can't seriously think like that?"

"Okay. Give me a minute." James walked off down the steps of the porch, and Evey had no idea what to do. She knew what he was going to do. And she knew, from a long time ago, what James would be like when he came back all coked-up.

Evey stood helplessly on the porch, trying not to make eye contact with anyone. James was not gone long, and when he came back and asked her for another cigarette, he held himself very straight. Evey could tell he had gotten what he wanted from some Palais patron, down by the train tracks that ran along the perimeter of the property and where these kinds of deals were informally enacted all night. He looked like he was vibrating inside.

"You know," he said. "I wasn't surprised when I got cancer."

Evey wasn't sure why she was still standing there talking to him.

"I mean, I'm more surprised now. I never thought I would live very long. Maybe into my twenties." James's face was flushed. "I don't know. So then I got sick and I thought, well, this is it then. This is what's going to do it. And when I started reading the Bible and all that, I was obsessed for a while with the Apocrypha. But I survived that too. Or anyway, I don't know. But now that I'm alive, it's like, what am I supposed to do with my life? What am I supposed to do now? Right?"

Evey wanted to back away from James the way she would back away from a dog that was straining at its leash. It wasn't just that he was lost, or euphoric, or morbid. It was that Evey understood what he meant. Evey could identify with what this wreck of her past was saying to her, and it was terrifying. She found that she had backed herself against the outside wall of the Palais. Evey felt the fine fabric of her dress catch a little against the rough shingles. She leaned back and into the wall. "What if life is long?" she said. "What if it's not like everyone says. The days don't go by like a sped-up film, we don't wake up one morning and we're fifty, kids don't grow up in the blink of an eye. What if every moment is an eternity? What if life is long, James?" She looked at this man who she had loved, the dark circles around his eyes, the way he looked hungry.

"What am I supposed to do with all those minutes?" James asked quietly. He wasn't looking at Evey any more, he was looking past her, at the door to the bar.

"I don't know, James," she said. "I don't know what any of us are supposed to do."

James moved toward the door, but Evey didn't follow him. "You coming?" he asked.

Evey shook her head no; she would stay outside for a bit longer. James shrugged and went in.

She was scared of James. Or of herself in proximity to James.

She was scared because it would be so easy to pity him now, or to hate him or laugh him off. But she had loved James once, and she felt she was in a terrible position now: she was too scared to love this broken, ridiculous person now, because to love him would be to wound herself. But it would require her to give away, she thought, a piece of her soul to disrespect something, someone, she had once held so close.

Evey leaned back against the wall and exhaled. She stared at the empty street for a moment, then looked around at the few men and women outside with her. They were not of particular interest, except that Evey tried to see if there was something discernibly different about these folks than the people she would be standing outside a bar with in Boston right now, if she were back home tonight. When one man glanced briefly in her direction, she fumbled in her purse to extract another cigarette. She wanted there to be some indication about her that she was different. Something about her dress, her posture, her purse, that indicated to the people here that she was distinct from them, that she was from away, that she was not a part of this place where she had grown up and which she would never again call home. Of course, she thought, when she had actually lived in Illium, Maine, she had spent a lot of time wishing that she could scrub herself clean of the one mark that made her discernibly different: the color of her skin had always set her apart as not entirely belonging to this place. She was such a rarity then, and now she wanted more than anything to be in control of that difference, to proclaim that she was not, in fact, whatever it was that the people of this town were, was not even what they thought she was. She snapped her phone open and wrote: "I want to lick your pussy." Then, she put it away and considered her unlit cigarette. When she got it lit, Evey stared across the street at the apartment building where she had lived with James for a couple years after she had graduated from high school.

Evey had picked out yellow curtains for the windows in their kitchen, the room that looked out on the street and the hotel. They had married when Evey was nineteen, and only six months out of high school. James was barely a year older. One of her friends in Boston called this first marriage that certain women got themselves into young "playing house," but Evey couldn't think, even now, that what she and James had been doing was play. They were serious people, even at that age. Evey wondered now, trying to peer into the windows of someone else's apartment where used to live, if the only reason she could still believe that she had loved him with a strong, true, adult love, was that it had ended when they were so young. She had not had time to fall out of love with him. They had been married for two years.

After a year and a half of marriage, James had made some new friends. These were friends who would sometimes drive all night to Quebec and get drunk once they got there, returning the next day so that those who worked in the afternoon could get to work hungover and on time. Evey wasn't always invited, but she didn't mind. It was nice, sometimes, to have the time alone, and she trusted James. After a while, though, she started to feel that she didn't know him. Some of those friends he had made listened to music she had never heard of, and read books she had never read, and did drugs she considered dangerous. James began to get forgetful. He would leave for work and then return to pick up his wallet and watch. Occasionally, he would leave for work and come back fifteen minutes later, telling Evey he couldn't remember, once he found himself driving on the town's main road, what he had left the house for. He had grown restless too at night. Lying in bed, he complained to Evey that his skin itched. He couldn't sleep, and he would get out of their bed to read or pace or go for long drives. He always looked distracted. Evey was afraid, and hurt. She felt that his behavior was an excuse, or a metaphor. He was forgetful because he couldn't sleep, and he couldn't sleep because he didn't love her anymore. His physical discomfort mirrored Evey's growing emotional dissatisfaction around her husband. She became honestly worried that he would wake up one morning and ask her who she was, and mean it.

Instead, Evey had woken up one morning and asked herself that question. She didn't think, then, that she was the kind of person who would get married at nineteen. She couldn't reconcile her life with her image of herself, and it only got worse as James scratched and tossed in their bed every night. Once, she was angry with him for not calling to tell her he would be home late, and in response to her harangue, he had thrown a hardcover Bible—a gift from his mother—at her head. He missed. Eventually, Evey had told him she was leaving. When he was, one night, changing a light bulb over the bathroom sink, she told him she wasn't happy. He had looked directly at her and let the bulb go, let it crash into the porcelain basin. Shards of glass had exploded upward from the slick, curved sides, soaring jaggedly into the room, cutting him on his right hand next to his thumb, and nicking her face next to her eye. And she had thought at that moment only: now I know what happens when you drop a light bulb in a sink. The next morning, James didn't seem to remember that she was leaving him. He was surprised to see her packing suitcases and plastic garbage bags full of her things. When he went to work, she finished hauling her stuff to her car and she wrote him a note:

I AM LEAVING. IT IS OVER. NEVER FORGET THAT I LOVED YOU ONCE, AND YOU LOVED ME TOO. MAYBE I WILL ALWAYS LOVE YOU. I LEFT YOU THE COFFEE POT. DON'T FORGET TO TURN IT OFF WHEN YOU LEAVE THE HOUSE. MAYBE YOU SHOULD JUST UNPLUG IT.

Four months later, her father had called her in Boston, at a friend's house where she was staying. James had been hospitalized. The doctors had found a tumor in his chest, on some organ humans didn't even use. Her father couldn't remember what it was called. James was scheduled for surgery that week. Four days later, her father had called Evey back. It was cancer. It was Hodgkin's, which was generally considered one of the most treatable cancers. Evey had wondered what kind of person left her husband while he had cancer. She had wondered how long the cancer had been growing in James. She had wondered if whatever was wrong with her could be described as treatable.

She knew that there were some women who would go back to their husbands if they got that kind of news, because they loved them, or whether or not they loved them. She couldn't do it. She couldn't picture herself nursing someone, and she wasn't sure that James would ever want that from her. When she had sent him divorce papers, she had done it as an act of reprieve for him; she was setting him free. But she had also felt a guilt that had threatened to completely submerge her for almost a year after James had sent back the papers with his signature in all the appropriate places. She had bobbed back to the surface of her life. She had been, thankfully, young and buoyant then. But she would never stop feeling guilty for any of this.

She did think now, though, of another note she had once left for James. Before that last missive, long before, on the way out of the house some Thursday afternoon, she had written on the back of a bank receipt she stuck to the fridge with a magnet:

I ATE ALL THE PASTA. I WAS HUNGRY. I'M SORRY. LET'S HAVE LOTS OF SEX WHEN I GET HOME.

At least, she thought now, she had once been the kind of person who would write a thing like that.

Later, in Boston, she had heard that James had lost all his hair to chemo therapy, but that he had survived. She had heard that when his hair grew back, it grew in gray. She had heard that James had become religious when he had recovered. She knew she was supposed to think of it as remission, a reprieve, rather than recovery.

CHAPTER NINE

Sebastian looked at Stan, at a total loss for what to do now that they were left alone. "Who was Evey texting a minute ago?" he asked. Even as he asked it, he knew it didn't make any sense for Stan to have that information. Stan had been introduced to Sebastian when he walked in, and of course he knew him as the limousine driver. He knew that Evey had gone to school with Stan when they were children, and although Sebastian was aware that the two of them hadn't seen each other in years, didn't mean anything to each other, he had felt since he arrived at the Palais Royale that he was just catching up, that there was something going on between Stan and his wife that he wasn't fully a part of. And he supposed that was true. After all, these people, his wife included, had grown up here, had history in every crosswalk and bar stool, and were living this moment on top of all those others. For him, this was just happening, for the first time. He wished things didn't feel real. He thought people said that sometimes: *things haven't felt real since my brother died.* And maybe he had felt that for a moment at his mother's house, for some moments since Tuesday, but right now he was entirely aware of what was happening to him. Everything felt brightly, ridiculously, real, like the moment after a film he was projecting in a test run slipped suddenly into focus after he stopped its juddering with an adjustment. Reality felt like the bright bath of light from the lens on the screen: beautiful, oppressive, omnipresent, inescapable.

"Um," said Stan. "I don't know. I didn't see."

Sebastian saw Stan's face in the focus of a film's tight shot. He was wearing makeup, and Sebastian could not fathom why. There was a spray of eye shadow, a smudge of lipstick on his mouth. Maybe dark eyeliner. The scattering of acne on his jaw seemed unbearably precious. "My wife lies," he said to Stan. He looked down then, nudged the tattered cuticle of one thumbnail up with the other. "I heard what you said to her."

"I didn't mean anything," Stan said. "I mean, we didn't do anything."

"What, Stan?"

They still stood, protectively hovering about the chairs that Evey and James had vacated. Stan hid his face behind his cup of booze. He started to mumble something, but Sebastian wasn't listening.

"Shit," he said. "Shit, Stan. What did you do? Did my wife try to fuck you, then? Is that what you're saying? Because if she did, you should know." Sebastian didn't want to say what he knew he would say next, but he didn't think he could stop himself. "You're not the only one. It almost never means anything."

Sebastian watched as Stan's face went through quick contortions. First, what looked like shock (his lips stretched tightly over his teeth), then maybe shame (his eyes tightened into themselves), and then something Sebastian recognized for certain. Stan's chin went up just a touch and he looked a little like he was holding something on the tip of his nose. Sebastian recognized the gesture because he had made it many times: it was a move of self-protection, of willful inability to see something clearly; it was the emotional equivalent of pulling the shades to protect the upholstery. And Sebastian had known for a long time that Evey engendered this in people. Maybe, he thought, that was what love was: the fortitude to overlook things in others so as to not get hurt yourself.

Sebastian wondered if Stan loved Evey. "I don't care what happened, Stan," he said. "It's not what I was talking about."

He felt hugely fond of Stan just then. Of Stan's bumbling, of his honesty, or, more than that, Stan's ability to elicit Sebastian's own honesty. It was true that his wife lied often. She was lying about having an affair with her friend Angela from work. If she wasn't actually sleeping with Angela, there was something about that relationship that Evey didn't feel she could tell Sebastian. She came home every Tuesday and took a shower, talking with a pointed lightness about Angela, about the shift, just talking ceaselessly. Sebastian knew that Angela was not Evey's first affair. He had long ago decided that in what he was certain was the long arc of their relationship, it wasn't important that she had kissed a friend of friend in the bathroom of the darkened bar when they were all drunk after a play, or that at brunch in Arlington one Sunday Sebastian's professor had put his hand on Evey's knee under the breakfast table, and she had let him move it up her thigh. But this, this thing with Angela. This bothered Sebastian in a way he could barely tolerate. It made him feel desperate and powerless and teary. It wasn't that they had sex, if they even had sex. It wasn't that Sebastian was concerned Evey might love this woman. He didn't think she did, and anyway, he wasn't afraid of love or non-exclusivity. It wasn't the dishonesty. It was the *way* Evey lied about Angela. The skittering talk when she got home, Evey's need for normalcy. The desire, just below the surface of monologues on milk delivery or muffin sales, to keep it close to her, for Evey to keep her secrets. Sebastian didn't know how much longer he could keep Evey's secrets for her, and he didn't know how much longer he could live this life, with this painful and mysterious frustrating love. He looked again at Stan, who was waiting expectantly for him to speak.

"I heard what you said to her, before she went outside with

James. She's not pregnant."

"Oh." Stan sat down in Evey's empty chair, and angled it away from the bar to continue looking at Sebastian. "Look, I don't know anything about Evey's life. About your life. I'm sorry. I just wanted to talk to her some more."

"It's okay," he said to Stan.

He knew Evey wasn't pregnant. But, fuck. What if Evey were pregnant? Sebastian tried to remember the last time he had noticed a used tampon in the bathroom waste basket. It didn't make any sense. She was on birth control; he sometimes picked it up from the CVS for her. And he was sure she didn't want a kid, or at least not now. For that, at least, he was glad. Sebastian had dated someone before Evey, a woman named Martha, when he was Tufts. It had been his longest relationship before his marriage, and in fact, he still hadn't been with Evey for as long as he had been with Martha. Martha had wanted a child. She knew and Sebastian knew, even at the time, that that would be a bad idea. Sebastian didn't know if he ever wanted a child, or if he wanted a child with Martha, but he was sure that he didn't want the two of them to have a child a year out of college, living in a lead-paint third-floor walk-up in Medford, neither of them with real jobs. He didn't want to have a child while he was still the kind of person who had never bought a new couch. Martha had called him a snob, pointed out that children didn't care about that stuff, that sixteen year olds in the projects down the street routinely had children, and that his attitude condemned all those babies and parents to lives of misery and struggle. He had never known what to say to that, and had hated that on some level he thought she was right. But he didn't want to have a child now, either. And then it occurred to him, in a rush of panic that made the melted ice in his drink tremble together, that Evey had been drinking down whiskey like lemonade all night. She must be on her fourth or fifth drink. He couldn't possibly be married to someone so careless, *could he?* No. No, there was no way she was pregnant. Sebastian thought with sadness that since his life with Martha, when he had refused to even think about children because he hadn't felt like an adult, he had not so much moved up in the world. Or anyway, he still didn't own a new couch. In fact, he had less of almost everything now than he had in college. If he didn't come up with some money soon, he was facing the first month of his life in which he wouldn't be able to pay rent. Sebastian knew rationally that he and Evey wouldn't get evicted for one month's late payment, but it made him feel shaky to think that he might not be able to provide such a simple thing as shelter for himself. He pushed the thought of money out of his mind. He had been successfully pushing this thought away for months now.

Stan said, "I'm sorry for your loss, Sebastian."

And Sebastian started, the cup almost slipping from his hand. He set his drink carefully down on the bar. "Did you know my brother, Stan?" he asked.

Stan looked uncomfortable. In fact, Sebastian thought, Stan looked like a child. Sebastian was thinking of a little boy in a Finnish film he had seen recently, standing at a kitchen counter, twisting himself from side to side, with one foot atop the other, trying to get his mother's attention. Perhaps it wasn't Stan's posture so much as it was his too-red lips that called the image to mind.

"Not well," Stan said. "I mean, not like you did." He took a drink. "I'm sorry, that's a stupid thing to say, he was your brother. I knew him around town," Stan said.

"I don't know how well I knew him," Sebastian said. And suddenly, he was incredibly angry at Evey. He resented her in that moment more than he had ever resented her, for making him think of her, for making him forget, even for a second tonight, to mourn for his beautiful brother. He had hated Evey before, there had been moments in his relationship with her during which he had wished her to disappear, or wished she would just stop whatever it was she was doing that made him feel so crazy. But he had never resented her like this before. Sebastian wanted to think about his brother. And he wanted that thought to supersede any other, especially any thought of his not-pregnant wife. "You know what I wish I had? Or, I'm glad I don't have it, but I can't stop thinking about it?"

Stan seemed to relax a little into the conversation. He looked into Sebastian's face. "What?"

"All that video footage. I wish I had a film of my brother." Sebastian took a drink. "Matt said that in the army, everyone had a video camera, or a camera phone, or something."

"I never thought of that."

"He said that when this whole thing was over, there was going to be some real incriminating shit out there. He told me once that he had some stuff on his computer that could put them all in jail."

Stan's eyes widened.

"Not stuff that he did, necessarily," Sebastian said quickly. "But all sorts of stuff that went on. I think he meant, you know, when we think about the atrocities of war, we think about civilians getting killed, we think about guys mowing down women in burqas while they're waving a white flag. But that's not it, not the really bad thing. I mean, mistakes happen, and those mistakes, I think, are made by generals and stuff, are made by the guys who order the missile strikes. What he had footage of was the day-to-day stuff that they all participated in. Round ups, detainments, casual brutality. Matt hated the whole way the war was conducted, the fact that it was part of the culture to dehumanize people, that you had to dominate to survive. But anyway, he said he had all this footage. And that, when someone was KIA, it was the custom to take any recorders off the body before anything happened to it. To protect, I guess, the dead soldier. I can't stop thinking about all that."

"Jesus," Stan said. "You could—I mean, his computer must still be at the house?" He paused for a minute. "You know," he said, "you know, Sebastian. I don't think about any of that."

"What?"

"When I think about war. I don't think about that. I don't think about war."

It had actually never occurred to Sebastian that now that Matt was dead, he could in fact have access whatever footage Matt really had stored on his computer or his phone. The idea made him sick. "I don't think I can do it. I don't think I could ever see my brother that way, as part of something he hated so much."

"How do you see your brother? I mean, how do you like to remember Matt?" Stan asked.

For the first time all day, Sebastian felt he was going to cry. "It's not fair."

"I know," said Stan.

"Not that he died," said Sebastian. "Not even that he died young. Twenty, thirty, sixty years. What's fair? What can be said to be fair? I mean, it's not fair the way I remember him. When I remember him, I think of moments, of specific interactions. I think of him at five years old, running through the water from a hose I'm holding in our yard, or whatever, him in a picture he sent me with the army buddies. But I never saw him, the whole thing. I never saw him shut his locker at the high school. I never saw him in his bed at night, at twelve years old, about to fall asleep. It's not fair to him to remember a moment and to call that *him*, his life, who he was." Sebastian was crying now, and he tried to stop.

Stan didn't look away.

"I have to go. I have to go…to the bathroom," Sebastian

said. "I'll be right back." He wasn't sobbing, but he didn't wipe the tears from his face. He held up his cup. "Can you order me another one of these?"

Walking through the bar, Sebastian realized how many people were now there. He wondered how many of these people had known Matt. He wished he had looked around more at the funeral. He wondered how many of these people Evey knew. If he had felt, earlier in the day, in Matt's room, as if he was in the home of the dead, he now felt just like he was in a place of the *gone*, of the vanished. So many moments, he knew, had passed before this one in this place. And he knew this was true of everywhere, all the time. But here, he was with his wife, the people of her past, the past that happened to someone he was so close to but the past that he was never a part of. He spotted a jukebox in the corner near the bathroom, and stopped in front of it. Peering through the glass, Sebastian began flicking through the cardboard cards. He had no idea how jukeboxes were updated, or who was in charge of the selections at the Palais Royale, but he was impressed with what he found in between the Beatles and Sinatra. He put five dollars in. Something clicked into place in the unfathomable machinery within. Sebastian leaned his forehead against the cool glass of the jukebox.

That was how he was standing when he felt someone nudge him from behind. He turned around. It was a large man, wearing a ratty striped sweater. Sebastian could tell immediately that there was something not quite right about this man. "Yes?" he asked.

He would have been an imposing man because of his size, but he was made somewhat less intimidating by his slump, and the fact that Sebastian could see, once the man angled himself toward Sebastian, that he was balancing a stuffed tiger on his shoulder. The man looked quickly away from Sebastian and focused his attention on the tiger. "Motherfuckers," said the man.

"Um, hi," responded Sebastian.

The man looked a little startled. "Oh, not you," he said, turning his head away from his tiger. "No. You're fine. And you're somebody's son, or husband, aren't you? I'll just bet you are."

Sebastian glanced uncertainly at the stuffed animal.

"I see you're looking at my leopard," the man said. Sebastian shook his head. He was embarrassed, and anyway, it was most certainly a tiger. "I just talk to him when I'm nervous. My sister bought him for me, and it helps. I can go out a lot more now, and when I'm nervous, I just talk to my leopard."

Sebastian started to turn away from the man, the way he would from someone who was talking too loudly, or was obviously drunk and homeless, on the T. It was an instinct from the essentially puritan city in which he lived—not to talk to anyone at all that he didn't know—more than it was a response to the man's obvious mental illness. But then Sebastian realized that this was, in fact, the most innocuous conversation he had had all day. "What's his name?" he asked, nodding toward the tiger.

"Oh, he doesn't have a name," said the man. "He's not real."

"Right. Sorry."

"I have to go to the bathroom," said the man. "And I have to go now."

"Uh-huh."

"But I'm not sure if there's someone in there. The door isn't locked, but sometimes there are people in places where I would rather that they not be. Sometimes, there are people in my room. And I know I'm not supposed to talk about this because I don't know you and you seem like a nice man, and also there are...well, it makes it so that I have a hard time controlling what I say. But I have to go to the bathroom now."

Sebastian stepped away from the jukebox and gestured toward the bathroom, trying to let the man know that he could go first, that if the man thought Sebastian was waiting for the bathroom, he could go first. It worked, and Sebastian wasn't sure why. He watched him, clothed in what he though now was two separate sweaters despite the heat, disappear into the men's room.

He walked back to where he had left Stan, and was met there with his wife and her ex-husband. He was grateful to see that Stan had ordered him another drink, and it was sitting waiting for him on the bar in front of the seat that Evey had not resumed. "How are you?" she asked him. Sebastian wanted to be grateful for her concern, but he couldn't bring himself to say anything. They all drank in silence for what seemed like a long while.

There was a disturbance in the corner, and all four of them turned to look. A man with a fake leg was pacing back and forth in front of the tables in the corner, knocking people's full glasses onto the floor. Some of them shattered, and some of them just spilled and rolled.

Karen was around the bar and to the corner in less than thirty seconds. It was amazing to watch her tall frame closing in on the pacing man. As she reached him and put her hand out to touch his arm and stop him from moving, she was met by a skinny little man who had been sitting at the end of the bar. He put his hand on Karen's arm as she had put hers on the schizophrenic's. Sebastian assumed that they would throw the man out of the bar, but they walked in the other direction from the front door. They walked him gently to a door in the wall near the bar, and ushered him through. Sebastian understood that the man was probably one of those who lived upstairs, and that Karen and the regular were bringing him home. He went willingly enough, as if he didn't need to be removed, just guided.

CHAPTER TEN

Karen was more annoyed that she found herself in the back hallway of the Palais Royale with a full bar of customers on the other side of the swinging door and Happy looking at her expectantly, or solemnly, or with a questioning but unwavering look on his face, than she was that she had had to take Baird the schizo out of her bar. She released Baird's arm and pointed to the stairs that would take him up to his room. Baird was missing his left leg below the knee. He had been in Vietnam, and he probably wasn't really schizophrenic. He was drunk, though, and he tottered his way up the wide staircase, holding tight to the banister. "Thanks!" he shouted back at them from the top of the stairs, and then he disappeared.

"Don't look at me that way," Karen said to Happy.

"I look this way because I think that we are not done with what we have to say to each other, Karen."

"I can't stand this. It will never be over with you, will it?" Karen felt her stomach begin to cramp. "You only live in the past. You don't know how to make a future for us, or even a future without us."

"This is not fair, Karen."

"You've lived here for how long? Your English is still all fucked up. You don't learn because you don't live here. You live in your head, and your head is only ever on what happened a year ago, or ten years ago. Do you know how many times you've told me about having the mumps when you were ten?" Karen wanted to loosen her belt. She felt the pressure of her bloated stomach against her waistband. She should have had something different for lunch. And stress made her feel physically ill.

It was dark in the hallway. Karen noticed that two of the five bulbs in the chintzy chandelier above them had burned out. She realized that it would no longer be her responsibility to change them.

"This is not true. I have my childrens. They grow up here, and they know nothing. That is what it is to be American. Not to know any past. The future! The future! You sound like Sascha. *What will we do tomorrow?* he asks me when I put him in the bed. How can anyone sleep in this country, thinking about that thing that not has happened yet?" Happy was looking steadily into Karen's eyes. But his body was shaking, like he was freezing.

Karen said, "it's not fair to make this about your children. It's not about your children."

"When you have children it is always about them. I will not lose them. You want me to say—what? You should be my wife? I say you should be my wife. But I cannot misplace my children, Karen."

It was, she knew, unfair. It was about the children, even for her. It was about the fact that they would never be her children, that his house would never be her house, that his family would never be hers. Karen's stomach was killing her. At that moment, she wanted not to be having this conversation, and not so much for all the reasons she never wanted to have this conversation. Her desire to be alone in the bathroom had overwhelmed all her other emotions. She sounded resigned when she said, "I can't do this now." She started to turn back to the bar, but stopped herself. She looked at Happy. "Okay," she said. "Say you will marry me."

Happy looked like he was going to cry. "I will marry you,

and I want—"

He was speaking slowly, and loudly, but the second clause of his sentence was inaudible over the enormous fart that Karen involuntarily let go of at that moment. She felt a huge surge of relief, covered quickly with shame. To his credit, Happy did not laugh at her. But his face crumpled into such a look of tenderness and longing, that Karen felt her fist clench and her arm draw back to hit him. She could picture hitting him in his teeth, but she didn't. She punched the wall next to his head instead. Karen knew what Happy was smiling about. She often farted after sex. At first, she had gone through a thousand internal contortions in bed trying not to, or trying to be silent. But she always failed, and at some point her flatulence had become a joke between them, though it still embarrassed her. Her whole corporeal existence embarrassed Karen.

Her hand felt bruised from punching the wall, but it was not bleeding. Happy took her rapidly swelling fingers in his own, brought them to his lips and kissed them. Then he pulled her down to sit on the stairs with him. She sat, and leaned against the tiny horse and buggies printed on the stained wallpaper beside her. *He proposed to me*, she thought. Karen knew that this required some reaction from her: if she couldn't do anything about it in this second, she should at least be able to feel something because of his words. But she felt utterly emotionally paralyzed. She thought again *he proposed to me*, and then her mind slid shut.

The door to the bar banged open against the wall, making Karen jump. Maurice, the man with the stuffed tiger, walked quickly into the back hallway. "Baird!" he shouted. "Baird!"

Karen pointed in the direction of the staircase, and Maurice nodded at her. Karen and Happy scooted over to the side of the stair as Maurice approached them. He had one foot on the bottom step when he paused. He looked at Happy like he had just caught sight of him. He looked at Happy as if he was reading a sign attached to Happy's head. "You," said Maurice. "You and me. People like you and me."

Happy nodded at him encouragingly.

"People like you and me are never going to fit in. So what do you think you're doing? We're never going to be normal. Look at yourself! Look at the way you talk! And your pants!"

Happy looked annoyed. Even Karen wondered who this man with a stuffed tiger as part of his wardrobe was to comment on Happy's pants.

"Look at you!" continued Maurice. "And me. You should do something with your life. When you don't have any chance of fitting in, you get to do whatever you want. But you have to do something fantastic. You have to just do something extraordinary."

Happy was astonished.

"I'm going to put a candle on my head. That's what I'm going to do. What are you going to do, motherfucker?" And Maurice ran up the stairs, shouting "Baird! Baird!"

Sitting on the steps in the wake of Maurice's outburst, Karen's brain started working again. Rapidly, her mind clicked through ideas, images really: her saying yes to Happy. Happy crying with joy. No, Happy looking uncertain. Packing her belongings from her room at the Palais into her little car. Moving into Happy's bedroom. That horrible bedspread he had. The kids. The kids. The kids. And then, her mind slowed down. Instead of the future, Karen thought of last night at Happy's house. She wanted now to blame him for letting this whole thing come to a head tonight, on the night of the Palais Royale's closing, when she wanted to think about that and nothing else. But after last night, she too could see that something had to be done, some discussion had or decision made. But it seemed neither of them was able to get it right, to even decide what the decision was or what focus their talk should take. Last night should have been fine, or as okay as any night at Happy's house was. She had been telling herself that this relationship was unusual, sure, but it was fine, for so long, had been repressing the thought that this was not okay, that last night had hit her like a physical push; she felt the way she had when she had fallen through the wall of the shower once, when she was a child, the rot-softened sheetrock collapsing behind the tiles when she leaned against it one morning.

She had worked yesterday, but not too late. She closed up the bar before midnight, turning the music to an unbearable decibel and flicking on the full overheads to quash any desire the remaining regulars might have to stay. She had wanted to get out of there. And she did, leaving the mopping for the morning and running only one last load of dishes. The streets were cool and dark and unpeopled as Karen drove to the west side of town, where the houses were mostly small duplexes and sagging ranches. Happy lived in a small development that ended in a cul de sac, and Karen pulled her Corolla off into a public parking spot out of the pool of light cast by a street lamp. Happy had not left the outside lights on for her. She walked quickly to the side door and slid the key out from where it was hidden beneath a loose piece of vinyl siding. The key turned silently in the lock and she let herself in. The lights were on in the empty kitchen, and in the hallway. She edged past the darkened living room and the doors to the children's rooms. She could see the light below the door to Happy's bedroom and she hesitated before going in. Standing in the darkened hallway with the glow of a low-watt bulb spilling just before her feet, Karen was scared and excited. She had been doing this for a year now, and she was still always scared and excited. There was a peculiar feeling she associated with these anticipatory moments, as if a honeycomb had been broken open, flooding her chest with a golden ooze, before a million bees thrummed onto the sticky sensation of happiness.

She turned the knob and slid into Happy's bedroom. He was sitting on his bed, a queen-sized that seemed small compared to the vastness of her old king in the hotel room, which was covered as usual with a hideous purple bedspread, threaded through with little stitches of silver thread that were always working themselves loose and poking her when she wrapped herself in the blanket. Happy was wearing slacks, cinched at the waist with an unfashionable shinny black belt, and had no shirt on. Propped against a series of stiff pillows, he was reading a copy of *Modern Pugilist* by the lamplight. He looked up and said nothing, but a grin stretched across his face. Karen lay down beside him fully clothed.

"Let us get you out of those," Happy said, already tugging on her pleated skirt.

"Not so fast," she said, leaning toward him for a kiss.

"Fast! Fast! Be the American person. It is patriotic in your country to rush around," Happy said, dodging out of the way of Karen's mouth.

Karen went entirely limp, letting her limbs sink into the too-soft mattress. Happy undid each tiny button on her blouse, and peeled her arms out of the shirt one at a time. Then he went to work on the hook and eye above the zipper of her skirt, fumbling with the tiny catch. Karen made no move to help him, or to resist. His incompetency with her clothing turned her on, and feeling the quick awkward movements of his fingers on her hip made her wet. He finally unhooked the tiny metal piece and his fingers slipped and splayed onto her pale belly. She looked at his hand; she thought of men gutting fish on the Illium town landing. Happy clumsily worked her skirt down and off her ankles, and then carefully drew back the hem of her underwear. Every time he touched her, she thought she had never wanted anything as much as she wanted this. *Every time*, she thought, and this feeling had not slackened in the last year. She gasped for air, and moved her body against his, and then she heard something, and went rigid. "Happy," she whispered urgently.

But he didn't stop what he was doing, he just buried his face in her neck. She was sure she heard something in the hall. The slap of small feet on ugly linoleum. When the door opened, Karen scrambled onto her knees.

The boy, Happy's son, was standing in the doorway, his face molded into confusion and loathing.

"Fuck," Karen said quietly. She covered her face with her hands. *Fuck*, she thought, *fuck fuck fuck. Don't move*, she thought. I *am an adult. I am the adult here.*

"Fuck," said the boy. "What the fuck, Dad?"

Karen could see nothing of the scene from behind her clenched fingers. She could feel the air hitting every inch of her exposed skin, and hunched herself over. She heard Happy say, "Sascha! You are watching your language! Do not speak that way."

"Fuck you, Dad. I can say whatever I want. The *toilet* is running again, and what are you *doing*? You can't do things like this in our house and not tell me. I'm thirteen."

"You are twelve for another week. And I can do what I want. I'm sorry, son." Karen could feel the mattress give, as Happy left the bed to approach his son.

"This is so fucked, Dad."

Happy crossed the room, and Karen lost track of what was going on for a moment, sunk in despair and loathing: for herself, for Happy, for the unfortunate child. She heard the door close and she pulled on her clothing. It was not okay. For the first time, she could not think of a way to make any of this okay. This moment would never be undone, and what she had done, what she was doing, what she had been doing for the last year, was irreversibly disgusting. She opened the bedroom door and took note of the light on in the kitchen. She bolted. "Karen!" she heard Happy call, as she made it to the front door of the duplex. She sprinted to her car and started the engine. It was all she could do not to yank the wheel and upend her Corolla and herself in the stream on the way out of the development. She wanted to drown herself; no, more than that, she wanted nothing to have ever happened to her, ever.

It came to Karen now, sitting on the dusty steps, that the reason they were having so much trouble with this conversation was probably because Karen had built everything in her relationship with Happy to a roaring crescendo, had elevated her mixed emotions and little troubles to the height of great tragedy, of impossible confusion. And that really, it was all nothing. What had happened with the child last night, she knew now, could be seen as just one of those things that happened. She could tell that story to a friend, if she had any friends, and they could laugh at the awkwardness. That's all it was: awkward. Not tragic or terrible. But that was her problem, Karen thought, *nothing for me is just uncomfortable. I can't just let things go. And,* she thought, *I can't let anything go because I can't just accept things. Like, okay, there are people who aren't so* mortified *all the time.* It occurred to her that she had not asked Happy what he felt about last night, had not even asked him what he had said to Sascha after she had fled.

"What happened after I left?" she said. She didn't want to know, not really, but it occurred to her that Happy might provide a new way for her to think about this whole thing. "Last night. What happened?"

Happy said, "I told him not to swear. Is a bad habit and encourages imprecise thinking."

"Happy!" she said. She could hear the plaintive, incredulous note in her voice, and she hated it. "It's not a fucking joke," she said.

"Is not so serious either."

She knew what he really meant. What he meant, what he hadn't said out loud, but she knew he had thought, and she had thought, over and over again, was just this: that just because their relationship had started in secrecy and pain did not necessarily mean that it had to end that way. There was always the possibility that they could just decide to be normal people. That Karen could tell her mother, "Oh, I met this man." That they could take the children to the park, have dinner together in a restaurant, make small talk with people over a shopping cart filled with ice cream and deli meats. And that was where Karen's mind always slammed to a stop. Because here was the hard thing: she didn't know if she could do it. She wanted that normalcy, that familiarity, that full life. But then she didn't. She could not stomach those children. She sometimes thought that she just hated those children. The actual children, she wasn't sure about, children in general, maybe, but Happy's children, the fact of them, she hated.

"I love you," Happy said.

"Fine. Whatever." Karen leaned back, felt the stairs press into her back. "Isn't love supposed to make people happy?"

"That is a ridiculous idea. Is probably American, too."

Karen wanted to scream.

CHAPTER ELEVEN

Stan watched the door to the back closely, waiting for Karen to return. Several people in the bar had noticed Karen's extended absence. Stan asked Amanda Lacroix what she wanted to drink, and as he fished a High Life from the fridge, he felt panic rise in his chest. He could not do this fast enough. There was a surge at the bar, and his panic was not just at his own ineptitude, his own inability, again, to rise to a challenge; it was real panic: he could feel the restlessness bordering on alarm from the crowd of tipsy patrons, afraid that they would not get their next drink fast enough to keep a buzz going. He put the beer down on the bar, and asked Amanda for two dollars and fifty cents. He had sloshed a little foam out in front of the bottle. When he took an order from a man for a Jäger shot, he had to turn around for the shot glasses. People started jostling, even pushing toward the taps to serve themselves. One man edged around the side of the bar, and behind Stan's back, grabbed a liquor bottle from the shelf next to Stan before he could be stopped. People started pushing one another behind the bar, and Stan felt his control slipping—the separation between him in back of the bar, and the crowd, which was supposed to stay on the other side, had been breached. Someone else reached for a plastic jug of bottom-shelf rum. There was a sound of a bottle breaking. There were more than a couple people crowded around the more obscure liqueurs. "Stop it!" he yelled. No one listened to him. One of the schizophrenics in the corner was pointing at Stan and snickering. Stan came around the bar. He wasn't sure if he should just give in or run for Karen. Instead, he got up on a bar stool and hoisted himself to a standing position on the bar. "Don't push!" he said. "YOU HAVE TO BE NICE TO EACH OTHER," he said.

The back door opened behind him, and a Stan saw out of the corner of his eye that Karen was making her lithe way through the crowd. He wished that he could have done this one thing for her, kept her bar safe. But Karen didn't look angry, or even surprised. In the midst of all this chaos, Karen somehow looked distracted. He thought, for a moment, that she looked beautiful. Stan glanced away from her again and back to the scene that was unfolding before him.

"YOU HAVE TO PUT THAT DOWN," Stan screamed at a woman who had picked up a huge, novelty martini glass from behind the bar. And then, there was a hush. Stan thought for a moment that he had finally said something right, finally made himself clear. But it was just that everyone in the room had noticed the return of Karen, trailed oddly by a slightly deflated-looking Happy. Everyone looked at Karen to see what she would do. She maneuvered around a few of the drunks who were behind her bar, all hips, and grabbed Stan by his pants cuff. "Stan," she said. "Stan, Stan. It's okay." She pulled him back down to safety. And then she said, "I need a drink."

The bar was a pulse of people now, and everyone was drinking for free. Every bartender who had ever worked at the Palais Royale had come out for the last time, to send the bar off. Stan was standing between Evey and Sebastian now, and he fantasized an end to this night: all these passionately drunk men and women setting fire to the Palais Royale and pushing the whole building into the adjacent Royale River. He could imagine it aflame, floating away like an honorable Viking pyre.

Stan watched Evey's wrist as she lifted what was left of her drink to her lips. She went a little cross-eyed trying to keep her eyes on it as she took a sip. Sebastian leaned over and said something in her ear, but Stan couldn't hear what he had said above the throb of voices and music filling the air. He wasn't sure if Evey could have heard, either. Stan remembered seeing a PBS special once where it was reported that there is a certain range of frequency, he thought it was between fifty hertz and fifteen kilohertz, that the human ear can perceive. He remembered hearing that if human hearing were more acute, we would constantly hear the workings of our own bodies, and would go insane.

Evey turned to face Sebastian, and Stan could just barely hear her say, "Do you want to get out of here?" He felt a spasm at the thought that if they walked out of the Palais, he might be left behind. He wondered if his pride would allow him to follow mutely along, uninvited. Beside him, Evey slipped off her bar stool and glided through the crush to the door. Behind her, Sebastian grabbed Stan's arm. Stan felt a rush of gratitude and relief. "Wait," he said to Sebastian, pulling himself away. Sebastian just shrugged at him and followed Evey.

Stan looked back for James, but James was on the other side of the room now, talking to someone Stan didn't recognize. *Probably talking about Jesus*, Stan thought, and then felt ungrateful and ashamed. He tried to signal above the heads of the crowd, but knew it was futile. And he was secretly thrilled to be out there with Sebastian and Evey, leaving behind James and all these people. He slid behind the bar, nodding at Karen. She only glanced at him before pouring something for another customer. Stan yanked a bottle of tequila off a middle shelf, and no one even looked in his direction as he walked out with it. He trotted out to catch up with Sebastian and Evey.

Outside, there were fifteen or twenty more people leaning up against the rail of the Palais Royale's porch, smoking or talking and nodding at the fat moon. Stan thought of trains, and how when he was a teenager, he would go to James' parents' house, so close to the train tracks it seemed as if he could stretch his hand out the window and touch the trains as they ambled by. They would hang out for hours, holed up in James' room smoking pot or watching basketball on the old television set that had a knob missing—they had changed the channels with a pair of pliers. When the freighters rolled through, the noise was so big that they couldn't even really say they heard them. Everything in the house shook, and everyone in it just stopped, frozen inside this encompassing noise. The first time Stan was there when a train went by he experienced it as a physical shock. But it happened so frequently that James' family couldn't have said at any given moment whether a train had just gone by or not; three seconds after it was gone and they had resumed whatever activity they were absorbed in when the boxcars approached. The crowd inside the Palais was like that now, Stan thought. He could only really hear how loud it was inside—the talking and the music—from out here on the porch, with enough distance from it to make sense of the sound. He stood for a moment, watching Evey: the way her dress moved around her like water, her perfect arm. He could see the muscles under her dark skin move as she rummaged in her handbag for a pack of cigarettes. "Can I have one of those?" he asked her as she withdrew her hand from her purse. Evey fished a cigarette out of the pack and put it in her mouth and lit it. Stan looked away, swinging the bottle of tequila at his side. But Evey took a drag and then handed the cigarette to Stan. The intimacy of the act, and his fumbling, made one whole side of his face burn. Sebastian turned away. Stan remembered a class he had had with Evey in high school. She had sat behind him, and he felt her there, hovering, looking beyond him, concentrating on her desk, even though he couldn't see her.

The night was hot, and had not gotten much cooler when the sun went down. Despite the heat, Stan was still wearing his uniform jacket, and had mashed his cap back onto his head when he left the bar. He fingered the inside of his rayon jacket, lined with something that might have been silk. Sebastian turned back at to him and asked, "Can you drive?" It was Stan's favorite question. He loved the sound of that, loved the possibilities that rolled out before him when he got in his car. He was always the one who stayed a little bit sober, so that he could make movement through whatever night or afternoon possible, and he had never seen the irony of his disdain for his father's profession in this. He nodded now. Took a drag of his cigarette. He pulled the keys to the limo, on an Altman's Livery keychain, out of his jacket pocket, and stepped off the porch. Evey and Sebastian followed him, and he felt purposeful.

He unlocked the limo and got in behind the wheel, leaving the other two to open their own doors this time. *Dereliction of duty*, he immediately thought, and then hated himself for it. Sebastian climbed into the back and shut the door precisely. Through the glass of the passenger side window, Stan could see Evey hesitate. She looked toward her husband, threw her cigarette to the ground, and got into the front seat. She immediately turned around to look at Sebastian. The glass was down between the front and the back, and Stan followed her gaze. Sebastian looked diminished amidst the plush leather and dim lighting. He glanced at Stan. "Where should we go?" he asked.

Evey answered before Stan could. "Let's just drive." Stan was sweating, and he turned on the air conditioner when he started the engine, though it weakly blew tepid air at them. He pulled out of the parking lot and away from the crowd in front of the bar, and pointed the car toward Route One. They crawled along silently, trawling the streets of the town.

"Roll down the windows," Sebastian said. Stan complied, wondering if Sebastian was going to throw up. They had all had a lot to drink, and though Stan was not drunk, he was pretty sure he was the only one, and even he could feel the alcohol making things around the edges of his vision wobble. Stan could see Sebastian in the side view, hanging his head out the passenger window. They were driving along the fast part of Route One now, and Stan could smell the ocean and the fish as the wind whipped around the car. They drove for a long while in silence, passing a bakery and taking a small bridge at speed. Their headlights glanced off a set of high gates in front of them to the right before the light got caught in the bushes and was overcome by shadow.

"Wait!" said Evey. "Wait. Go back." Stan looked sideways at her, surprised, but didn't ask why. He slowed down and moved the big car onto the shoulder. There was no other traffic on the road.

He backed up. "Where am I going?"

"Stop at the park."

Stan pulled the car in beside the tall gates and shut down the engine. The three of them sat in the warm air, listening to the car ticking.

Evey got out of the car, and Stan sat still, clutching the steering wheel, as she closed her door with a pop. She stood just outside the vehicle, surveying the gates. Slowly, Sebastian left the car too, and after he had walked to her side, Stan joined them, stuffing the key ring back into his pocket. "Let's climb it," Evey nodded toward the gates. The gilt sign in the middle read Park Wild Kingdom. Stan saw Sebastian smile. It was the first time he had seen the man smile all night, but Evey missed it, her head turned determinedly to the gates. Stan smiled too. Because he knew what Sebastian had just noticed. Because he suddenly remembered that Sebastian would not have been here before.

The sign was backwards. Of course, it should have read Wild Kingdom Park. "Park Wild Kingdom," he said.

"This is a pathetic attempt at Six Flags," Evey said. They were words that everyone who grew up in the area had said over and over again, a groove worn into their brains from this commonplace thought. Sebastian exhaled. Stan knew this. Evey knew this. Sebastian, here for the first time, must know this. Even tourists in the height of summer knew this. And suddenly they were all grinning wildly, stupidly, uncontrollably at each other. Grinning until their jaws hurt and their temples felt tight and it seemed as if their eyes would squinch up into nothing, because Stan and Evey had said these exact things over and over again growing up and Sebastian could imagine Matt repeating these phrases a hundred times, and it felt good to all of them to say them now. It felt as if they were saying these things over and over and over again.

"Come on," said Evey.

"I've never done this," said Stan. He thought maybe this was a thing that kids who grew up in Illium did, breaking into Park Wild Kingdom at night. Maybe it was something he had missed. And suddenly Stan thought of how little he knew about Evey and Sebastian. He thought about the fact that they would not be friends after this night. He looked over at Sebastian and felt entirely out of place.

"Me neither," said Evey, and removed her high heels. She threw them over the fence to the other side, one at a time. Stan didn't hear them land. He thought of deep wells. Evey squirmed up the fence, and Stan watched her dress stretch over her breasts, and then the hem inch up over her calves, beyond the hollows at the back of her knees, and catch perfectly on the back of her thighs, below the roundness of her ass. She swung one leg over, and then the other, and dropped to the ground. She landed hard, falling to her knees, but got up immediately. Stan couldn't bear to watch Sebastian climb the fence, so he turned around and went back to the car. He opened the passenger door and felt around on the floor until he had the bottle of tequila he had swiped. He closed the door behind him, and tuned back toward the gates. But then, he turned again quickly and went to the back of the limo. He slid in, and reached for the cut glass bottle of cognac. Returning to the fence, he passed them both through the bars to Sebastian, who was waiting now with Evey on the other side. Sebastian accepted the bottle silently, but with a hint of another smile. Stan hesitated before approaching the fence. "Come on, my man," Sebastian said, and screwed off the top of the tequila. Stan could feel the desperation sloughing off him, dripping groundward like hot sweat. Every muscle in his body tensed, ready to be embarrassed. He did not think he could climb that fence. Images of before-the-battle scenes in patriotic movies flashed in his mind. Stan vaulted himself toward the middle of the fence and got the bars in a death grip. He pulled his long body slowly to the top, and looked down on Evey and Sebastian. He swung a leg over and hesitated, thinking he would fall, before he managed the other side of the fence. Inside the park it was dark. It smelled like elephant.

Stan followed Sebastian, who was following Evey to the lion cage. He began to scratch the back of his neck, hard. The massive lion was asleep. Stan matched his breathing to that of the lion. He pretended for a moment that he was the giant animal.

"Wait," said Sebastian. "Why are you wearing makeup?" He was drinking the cognac now, and his gaze was fixed on the side of Stan's face.

"Evey? I mean. I'm not. Or, yes I am. It's… It's just a little lipstick. Shit. Just forget it." Stan watched the lion, trying to pick out individual strands in its mane. He remembered once, in the elementary school, being called down to the office to take his ear infection medication. The nurse couldn't find his bubblegum flavored Ceclor, so she called Stan's mother at home. He remembered the nurse's long long fingernails, pasted with rhinestones, on her fingers gripping the receiver. Stan could have told the nurse his father had gotten him ready for school that morning. He could have said that his father had forgotten to pack the bottle along with Stan's lunch. But he didn't say anything. The nurse spoke with Stan's mother, who must have checked the fridge and found it there. He could hear his mother vaguely cursing his father in the background. Stan remembered running out of the office, running out of the school into the rain in his jean jacket and pretending he was a rock.

Sebastian began to shout at the lion to try to wake it up. Stan picked up the largest stick he could find.

"What do you think its name is?" Evey asked no one in particular. Stan wished he, and not Sebastian, had the bottle of tequila. *Ichabod Crane*, thought Stan. *Willy Wonka.* "We should call him Pal," he said. He reached for the bottle from Sebastian. Sebastian handed him the tequila, but kept the cognac. *No we shouldn't*, he thought, *we should call him Stone Philips.* He poured as much tequila into his throat as he could, and sputtered a little once he tipped the neck back up. He started to move his fingers rhythmically, tapping out his own inadvertent Morse Code on his thigh.

Evey wandered away from the lion cage. Stan could feel the alcohol burn through his limbs. He looked, bewildered, at the bottle in his hand. He squinted his eyes and splashed more tequila into his mouth. Stan watched Evey's dress as she walked away. Watched her roll her bare shoulders back. He followed her. Evey pulled out a cigarette and lit it. "Can I bum another one?" asked Stan. His voice was louder than he meant. Evey turned around to give him another Camel. She looked past Stan to where Sebastian was still standing. "Sebastian?"

"It's okay," he called back. "I'm just…"

And Evey kept walking toward the back of the park and the elephant. Stan pursued her slowly. The park was not large, but it seemed so in the dark. It had always been a bit dingy, but was worse for wear since Stan had last visited when he was a child. He remembered that there was a duck pond and a few more cages in the direction that Sebastian was going. There was a dark expanse off to the right, too, that held the rides. He remembered a teacup ride, a roller coaster, and some giant swings. If he wasn't mistaken, they were on the midway, where the cages of the most popular animals were. If they kept going straight they would get to the concessions. Stan had already lost sight of Sebastian, and he felt uneasy at their group being separated. The park was probably big enough to lose track of someone for hours at night, he thought. Evey stopped in front of the monkeys. "They look sad," Stan said. He was still holding an unlit cigarette, and fumbled in the pocket of his jacket, and withdrew a pack of matches with gold script on the cover reading Altman's Livery. When he got the cigarette lit, he began quietly inscribing *it's a trap* with his toe in the sand in front of the monkey cage. The monkeys took no notice. He drank more. Evey was walking a border underneath his words, and Stan laughed out loud, drunk now with that last gulp of tequila. Evey took the bottle from him and sipped from it as they ambled toward the roller coaster. The cars were at the bottom of the track, bars still flung open as if just now, twelve-year-olds had abandoned them. Stan screwed up his eyes while Evey mounted the track and swung silently into the roller coaster car, one-handed because of the tequila. He lost his footing twice getting into the car beside Evey. *What,* he thought, *if she closes the safety bar and it gets stuck and we have to wait until morning to get out? Would we be arrested for trespassing?* he thought. He accepted some more tequila. The air was getting soft around him. His lips began to tremble.

"I used to go on this coaster with my dad," Evey said. "It's the largest wooden roller coaster in the country." Evey tilted her head back. "That's what he told me," she added, glancing at Stan.

"My dad is dead." Stan had heard that Jim Morrison told people that. He was drunk, and he couldn't tell if he had spoken aloud or not.

"I'm really sorry, Stan. That's terrible." Stan couldn't remember if he had told her that it was his father who owned the limo company. Altman's Livery, never Altman and Son. *Ninety-five thousand dollars a year*, thought Stan. *Last year. Playing poker.* He didn't think he'd ever make that much again. Stan took the tequila from Evey's dangling left hand, and allowed his fingers to brush the unbearably pink nail of her index finger. He shivered and took another gulp. Then, he leaned his head against the safety bar. It smelled like monkey bars on a playground, innocent sweat on metal. "My dad isn't dead. I don't know why I said that."

She wasn't looking at him.

"Evey," Stan said. "James is not okay."

"I know, Stan."

"I think he's in trouble. I think he's doing a lot of drugs these days. And sometimes I think he wants his old life back."

"Of course he wants his old life back." Every ran her hand along the hem of her dress. "Something terrible happened to him."

Stan thought for a moment. "But, I mean, that's what we all want, right? We all want our old lives back. That's what growing up is."

"Oh god," Evey exhaled. "What a terrible thing to say, Stan. There's nothing I can do for James. And I don't want to be back here. There are things, a lot of things, I'm glad I left behind."

"Did anyone ever tell you you should be a model?" Stan asked.

"I was a model. In Boston. I mean, not really. I did nude classes at the art college. But you don't have to be pretty or anything."

Stan felt himself starting to get an erection. He groaned a little, he hoped quietly. "Did you stop? I mean, being a model?"

"I haven't done it in a while. I feel like I'm getting old. The students look so young. I don't want to be one of those models who's a curiosity, who looks defiant the whole time they're standing up there. I don't want the students to think I'm thinking I'm making some kind of *statement*." Evey's voice was rising. "About age being *beautiful* or something, you know? I don't want to teach anyone any lessons."

"That's ridiculous. You're not old."

"I know. Sebastian says I'm beautiful."

"You've always been beautiful."

"I know. But he says I'm beautiful now." Evey paused and ran her hand over her braids. "I need to be better to him."

They both sat perfectly still. They could hear a car pass by on Route One.

I know I'm beautiful, she had said. *It was so disgusting*, Stan thought, *the way she said that.* And yet it was true. She was the most beautiful person he had ever seen. Stan's vision was spinning with intensifying speed, but he took one more drink despite this. He had a sudden panicked vision of the roller coaster swinging into gear. *And the safety bar isn't down*, he thought wildly. When he had convinced himself that the ride was not moving, he put his hand lightly on Evey's arm. If it were raining, he would pull his uniform jacket over both their heads and kiss her in the quiet, silk-lined darkness. He imagined kissing her on both closed eyelids. He imagined kissing her nipples. Kissing her everywhere he had not kissed her this afternoon in the back of the limo. Stan threw his whole self, his entire graceless frame, face first onto Evey's body. His lips met the nape of her neck and his hips landed against her knees.

Evey gripped the sides of Stan's trousers, where the red

stripe ran down the pants' legs, and lifted him definitively off her. She could hear his breathing.

"I understand," Stan whispered.

CHAPTER TWELVE

Evey was pushed back in her seat, as if the ride had suddenly cantilevered into wild action. She felt something collide with her, and it took her a moment to figure out what had happened. Stan had launched himself at her body, landing with his shoulder pressing into her breasts and knees knocking against her shins. He was holding himself rigid against her. He groped with one hand at her, and his mouth sucked at her neck. She was speechless. And more than anything else, more than shock or anger, more than resignation or revulsion, Evey just felt a jerk of pity, right behind her navel. She gripped the side of his uniform pants and lifted him off of her. He was pliable with drink and defeat. He collapsed into the side of the roller coaster car and whispered, "I understand."

She was still holding a smoldering cigarette, so she stubbed it out on the metal bar. "It's amazing I didn't burn you," she said to Stan.

He looked up at her then, his eyes like the water in the bay before it was whipped up by a storm, and she handed him the bottle of tequila. He took a drink. He removed his cap, and the moon was shining off the high gloss of his white forehead. His lips were still dark from her lipstick, and his eyes were accentuated with black, but his face looked clean, she thought, *scrubbed clean*, though she had noticed earlier that his teeth were bad. Stan was fidgeting in his seat. Evey felt exasperated with him, but mostly because she found him painfully endearing, sitting there, lanky and ashamed in the moonlight. She tossed her cigarette away, admiring the arc it described in the dark. "Come here, Stan," Evey said.

Stan leaned toward her, hat in one hand. When he was very close, she took a tissue from her purse and wiped at his face. Her intention had been kind, but it only smeared the makeup.

She looked into his face for a moment and remembered those afternoons they had spent, not together, but flickering through each other's peripheral vision, as children in the public library after school. She remembered learning how to apply mascara. She had bought some from the beauty aisle in the IGA when she was twelve. Having no mother to teach her what to do with it, Evey could have asked a friend from school. But about physical matters, Evey had always been shy, believing for a long time, since it appeared to her that she was the only black person in Illium, that she must be intrinsically different from her classmates, somehow biologically different from even her sweet, white father. She thought that black people should probably wear different makeup, or at least apply it differently. Evey had felt like a smuggler, bringing a mascara tube the size of a Sharpie into the library with her. She had gone to one of her favorite books in the children's section: *How Things Work*. She was glad that it was kept in the children's section, where she could browse it without getting curious, adult glances. She always thought that it was the most wonderful book there because it helped to bridge the worlds of the young and the adult by detailing things like "how men dress," and "computers," and "sailboats." She had looked up "how to apply makeup," and finding no specific instructions for her race, had followed the white lady in the diagram.

She couldn't look at Stan any longer, and turned from him toward the back of the park.

She lit another cigarette and watched the smoke encircle them like arms. She thought about Matt. She thought of him walking into his mother's house, Sebastian's mother's house, the last time she and Sebastian had come up to visit. Thought of him pulling his baseball cap off his head to wipe the sweat from his forehead. Dressed in jeans and work boots, his bare chest covered in grass clippings. She thought of him in the sunlight walking toward her. She thought of him the way she would most often think of him for the rest of her life.

She had no real ties to Stan, but it had been a long night, and for one delusional and sopping moment, she thought of Stan and Sebastian as her boys, as her men. They were bound tightly together in the instant, in her brain. And then, she was startled back to reality. She had no business thinking about Stan that way, just like he had no business talking to her about James. *But that was the thing*, she thought, *about Stan. He was loyal. So loyal he couldn't let anything go. He would*, she thought, *do anything for me right now*. And Evey knew what she wanted to do. She knew what she needed. It had not escaped her that he had said earlier that he made a fortune, yearly, playing poker. He wasn't bragging, just stating a fact. Evey didn't know anyone who made more than thirty-thousand dollars a year, except her father. And she could never go to her father about this. She could never fail in that particular way. This was the moment she had been waiting for all night. *Stan*, she could say, *can I borrow some money?* She could hear the cadence she would use, the slight lift at the end of the sentence as it left her lips. Or, *do you have any money you could loan me?* Evey's armpits pricked with sweat. If she did this, if she asked this of Stan, she would be crossing a line. She wasn't sure what the line was, or what kind of person it would make her to cross it, but she knew she needed three-thousand dollars, more or less, to get through the next two months. She was thinking of the life she had made with Sebastian, and the cost of that life. She was thinking of the difficult and mundane minutia she would have to accomplish for him in the coming years. She felt, for the first time in a long time, like she might be prepared for the task. *Now*, Evey thought, *now is when I ask.*

"Stan," she said, "can I borrow some money?"

Stan said, "What?"

"I need some money," Evey's face was burning.

Stan shifted his weight and pried his wallet from his back pocket.

"No," Evey said. "Can I have a loan? I need a couple thousand dollars."

For a long time, Stan just looked up at the moon. "No," he said. "I don't have it."

Evey hid her face in her hands, and then they didn't speak. *Thank god*, she thought instantly, *he said no.* She felt that what she had done was incredibly dirty, but that somehow Stan's response had wiped her clean. If Stan had said yes to her plea, or even prevaricated, she would have felt lasting guilt at having conned him, used him, used herself—her beauty and history and sex—to get what she wanted. But his refusal had nullified all that. Now, he was in the position of power, and that was an enormous relief. She was not so culpable anymore. She felt she could cry.

They sat in fraught silence for a moment, while Evey breathed deeply. She lifted her head to speak, but Stan jerked his arm in her direction. "Wait," he said. "Shhh." Stan was swaying in his seat a little, clearly unsteady and drunk. "Do you hear something?"

Evey was uncertain, but she didn't think she had heard anything. "What is it?"

"I don't hear it now. Something crunching maybe. But it was probably nothing."

Evey too could feel everything in her loosening with tequila. She hadn't been this drunk in quite a while. She thought about

Sebastian, who was almost never drunk. One of the first nights they had gone out together they went to a bar in Allston. Riding the Green Line trolley back, Sebastian had sat down on the stairs inside the trolley car, just by the door, and she had been surprised to realize he was tipsy. She had wanted him then, his strength, which was accentuated by these flashes of boyishness, his big hands and broad shoulders, the skin that bunched together at the sides of his eyes. And she had had him. They took the train back to her apartment, where they woke up her roommate shouting because the roommate had forgotten Evey was out and put the chain on the door before she went to bed. When she let them in, Evey and Sebastian had stumbled to her bedroom and fallen on her bed still clothed. They had pulled each other's hair, wrenched pants down around ankles, and then had fucked three times that night.

But she hadn't loved him then. Evey didn't believe in love at first sight. She believed in lust, and then a feeling for someone that grew like debt. She had fallen in love with him only after they moved in together. In Sebastian's apartment, she had fallen in love with the fact that he wore slippers, jeans and a white undershirt when he cooked her breakfast. Fallen in love with him while he broke eggs and flipped hash with a flick of his wrist. She sometimes called him her "last white boy," and he always let her. She had stopped calling him that eventually, but she loved that he had never asked her to. She loved the joke in it, that was also pain. Evey had dated a black man, was dating one when she met Sebastian: Delonn. And despite the fact that when Delonn's cousins had come to visit from Jamaica, and he had sat around stoned, speaking quickly in dialect with them, and laughing when she couldn't understand them, she had felt an enormous relief the whole time she was dating him. When she broke it off with Delonn she was terrified that she was slipping away from some part of herself. But with Sebastian, she had loved going to the Somerville Theater with him, eating popcorn in the projection booth and letting him put his hand down the front of her pants while people sat below them on the other side of the window, rapt, in another world.

And then, as if she had fabricated him with imagined past scenes, he was there. Sebastian, walking back from whatever mystery he had been pondering. *Perhaps*, she thought, *he had found the ostrich*. She hoped he had found the ostrich. No one could grieve in the presence of such a prehistoric, preposterous beast. She took a moment to look at him, still in his button-down, though he had lost the tie and jacket at some point, and his creased suit-pants. Evey thought she should probably feel bad for him –his brother had just died—but all she could think was that he looked *sharp* dressed like that. He looked like someone she wanted to bring to a party.

"I want to go back to the cemetery," Sebastian said.

Evey slumped down where she was sitting. "Sebastian, why?" *He's dead*, she wanted to say.

"You got something better to do?" he asked. He had lost the bottle of cognac somewhere along the way.

Vicious, she thought. He sounded vicious when he said that. Evey did not want to go to the cemetery, maybe ever again. "My mother is buried there," she said. Evey's mother had died when she was four.

Stan stood up next to her. He climbed unsteadily over Evey and balanced for a moment on the roller coaster track, like an acrobat about to leap. Then he fell to the ground feet-first and collapsed briefly to his knees. He steadied himself and rose, stood tall and erect. "Let's go," he said, repositioning his cap on his head.

Evey groaned. "You're too drunk to drive," she said to him.

"I'm not," Stan said. He stood even straighter, but his posture was that of someone trying to regain his sobriety.

"Oh, Sebastian," said Evey.

There was a hollow sound behind them in the dark. And then an uncertain light caught Evey full in the face. She screamed. The light dropped down to the ground, and she could hear someone fumble for it.

More noise of footsteps on the dirt path. "What are you doing here?" came from the darkness. It was a female voice, and Evey was surprised. "Security. What the fuck are you doing in here?"

Sebastian stepped forward, toward the light. The beam swung around, and pointed at his chest. "I'm sorry," he said. "I'm sorry. We're leaving."

"How did you get in here?"

Evey could see the woman now, the outline of a small frame clad in the blue security uniform. The woman was black, and Evey didn't recognize her from childhood. Evey was aware that she had no idea how to relate to this woman. They were both black in a place where being black was entirely anomalous, but there were the obvious differences: of age, and job, and probably of class. Evey still didn't know what it meant to be black in Maine, other than that it was complicated. She felt she should give this woman some kind of nod of solidarity, but the thought also repulsed her; she didn't know this woman, probably had nothing in common with her. Evey didn't want to have any of these thoughts, couldn't sort through them. She dropped her gaze to the ground, felt herself flush with a kind of panic.

Sebastian looked serenely at the guard and said, "That doesn't really matter. We're not doing anything, and we're going to leave, okay?"

"No, man. It's not okay. I have to call the cops. There are animals in here, and insurance. This is my job. You can't be in here." The woman was withdrawing a cell phone from a small holster on her belt. "How the fuck did you get in here?"

Evey's hands started to shake. She looked at Stan, who looked like he was about to bolt. *No*, she thought. *This is not happening. I am not going to jail tonight.* Every part of her body was focused on denying what was happening. Stan shifted in the sand, turning toward the entrance to the park. He dropped the mostly-empty bottle of tequila on the ground.

"Don't you move," the guard said. "I'm calling the cops." She flipped open her phone.

"Look," said Sebastian. "We both want the same thing. We want to leave and you want us gone. We're leaving. We just got a little lost."

"You're not stupid. You guys aren't even kids. How could you think this was a good idea. You cannot be in here!"

"We're not, okay?"

"What did you do in here?"

"It doesn't matter. Nothing. We just sat here."

"This is not okay," the guard said. "You know this isn't normal, right? Nothing about this is normal."

"I know," Sebastian said. "We're just going to leave and then it will be as if we were never here," Sebastian was moving very slowly toward Evey. She reached out her hand to him, but he took her by the upper arm. "We're going to walk out of here now."

The guard looked uncertain and angry. "Okay, okay," she said. "You are too old for this foolishness. Get the fuck out of here and do not ever do this again." The guard pointed her flashlight at the path and indicated that they should get going.

"Yes," said Sebastian. "We won't ever do this again." He pulled Evey with him and walked toward the entrance gates firmly, not looking back. Evey could hear Stan stumbling behind them. The guard was leading the way, periodically looking back to make sure they were all still in line. When they reached the fence, Evey thought she would unlock the gate for them. But instead, the guard just made a disgusted noise and said: "Well, then. You can go out the way you came in, I suppose."

Evey wasn't sure she could climb the fence again. But Sebastian said, "You first," and Evey grasped the bars, still shaking. He put his hands together to make a step for her, and Evey wondered if it hurt when she placed the flat part of one high heel in the hammock of his palms.

The guard walked resolutely away from all three of them.

CHAPTER THIRTEEN

When the guard had let them go, Stan had wanted to run, but had kept pace with Evey and Sebastian. Sebastian seemed to know what he was doing. Stan couldn't believe Sebastian had managed to talk them out of that one. And yet, even though he had stood passively and nervously by while Sebastian had saved them, it was Stan who felt powerful now. He hadn't been afraid. A little nervous, maybe, the way he always was when confronted with a conflict that could turn ugly, but not afraid. He had known in that moment that whatever was coming—jail, or a foot chase, being berated, whatever—he could handle it.

At the fence, Sebastian had helped Evey over, and then extended his hands to Stan, but Stan had shrugged at him and made it over on his own. And now, beside the car with the two of them, he felt like laughing. He did laugh, head back and adam's apple pumping like he was swallowing beer.

"It's not fucking funny!" Evey said. Her voice was pinched and high-pitched.

But Sebastian laughed too, and the two of them were carried away with it. Stan felt like the sound of it was flying out from the two of them, down Route One and to the ocean. "Oh, god," he gasped, and laughed some more. "Yes it is. It is funny!"

Stan saw Sebastian glance at him, and he allowed one more giggle to escape his diaphragm, before he calmed himself down.

"We should get in the car," Sebastian said, "And get out of here."

Stan squared his shoulders and scratched an itch on his chin. He wiped his forehead, and then grabbed the car keys and fitted them into the door lock. When he sat behind the steering wheel he felt like he sank deeply into the chair. Evey, he noticed, got in the back with Sebastian. He sat still for a moment, thinking about what Evey had asked of him, back at the roller coaster. He didn't have the money to loan her, but he didn't feel like he wanted to admit it. And he didn't feel like he had to. He knew that she was using him, and could only imagine that she needed the money for rent, for bills. He didn't know how she would have spent it if he had cut her a check, but he knew why she had asked him. She had asked for the money because she knew he loved her, or was infatuated with her. Because he was an easy mark. And he knew that if he had had it, he would have given her everything. *Maybe*, he thought, *I still will. I could give her a thousand dollars. Maybe it would change her life.* He didn't care that he was a sucker, or that she would never love him. Stan felt for the first time in a long time like he could get a measure of what he could and could not do.

The lipstick on his mouth was sticky and gritty now, and he licked his lips. He turned the key, and when the engine caught it sounded like a roar to him. He was drunk, and he knew it. He had always hated drunk drivers. It was one of the few moral imperatives he had: there are some things you do not do. You do not shoot heroin, and you do not drive drunk. It would be a stupid thing to do, to drive drunk. Just unnecessary, to put yourself and others in that kind of peril. What a stupid fucking thing. But he pulled out onto the road anyway. He drove slowly and could feel the lines in front of him wobble. *There's no one else on the road*, he said to himself. *It's just driving. You've done it a thousand times.* He concentrated on making the steering wheel follow the curves of the road. He could envision the cemetery, where it would be acceptable to crawl along at fifteen miles an hour. It was so *dark* in Illium.

Stan kept the double-yellow snapped into place in his vision, and the one-way, winding paths of the cemetery in his mind. He inched closer and closer to graves. If he had not chosen tunnel-vision as a life preserver, he would have noticed: the bank where his father had brought him to start his first pass-book account, the 7/11 where James had once stolen a six pack of beer while the manager was distracted trying to chase a Luna moth out of the store, the water tower beneath which he had his first kiss, the ice skating rink where he used to play pinball and eat Twizzlers. And behind a stand of pines to his left, unseen but always present, he should have remembered that the Royale River was winding ceaselessly by.

He saw the stone pillars marking the entrance of the cemetery ahead and to his left. He slowed the car to a crawl and made a wide swing at the path. As soon as the back of the car cleared the pillars and he was safely on the cemetery path, Stan stopped the car. He let the engine run, but he didn't want to go any farther. He turned around in his seat. Evey was slumped down, looking disheveled and a little sweaty, and Sebastian was rigid beside her, looking lost in thought. He studied Evey in the moonlight. She was as beautiful as ever. Stan thought she looked superimposed. After she had rebuffed him on the roller coaster, Stan was deeply ashamed. It wasn't that he thought what he had done was wrong. What had he done, after all? He had given it a try. And Stan honestly believed that that was the best we could do in this life: give the things we believe in a try. *Or, okay,* he thought, *it's not that I believed that it could work out with Evey. I think it's important to try for the things that we want,* he said to himself. *No, even the things that we don't want. Because we might end up wanting them,* he thought. Then he thought, *fuck. I'm drunk.*

"Where do we go from here?" Stan asked.

No one answered him, so he shut the engine of the car down.

"Did you know," Stan said, "that this is the only cemetery in Illium?" James Presley had told him this, twice, over drinks (once at the Palais a long time ago, when they had lined up shots to celebrate the end of James' chemotherapy, and then again, two weeks ago, when James and Stan had sat in the back of someone's pickup drinking OE). No one responded to this either, so Stan kept going. "There used to be two. A long time ago, I mean. There were two cemeteries. One was private and one was public. So, like, anyone who lives here whose family goes back to, like, when they were killing Indians, their family has probably always been buried in the private cemetery. Like the Shinks and the Greelys. Do you remember Kevin Greely, Evey? From high school? His family has been here forever. I think he's related to everyone in town."

"I doubt he's related to me," Evey said.

Stan hadn't realized she was listening. Ordinarily, he would have said nothing in response to her comment, but the night and the alcohol freed his tongue. "Come off it, Evey. On your dad's side he could be."

"Probably not me, though," Sebastian said.

"Fair enough. Anyway, when that development went in at Woodside pond, they moved the poor people graves. The public cemetery. Did you know that development didn't go in until the fifties? There was a poor people cemetery here, well, not here, somewhere down near Woodside, until then. They moved all the graves to the private cemetery. Just dug folks up."

The three of them sat in silence for several more minutes. Stan shifted in his seat.

Sebastian said, "Let's go to Mabel's grave first." Evey looked surprised, and it took Stan a minute to realize that this must be her mother's name.

"Do you know where it is?" Stan asked.

"By the east side," said Evey. "Near that horrible obelisk."

Stan navigated them slowly up the past and toward the east side of the cemetery.

"I'm afraid I won't know which one," Evey said quietly. "Oh, wait, no. It's got to be near here." They glided up to the tall, phallic monument of some old veteran. Evey started to get out of the car while it was still running.

"Wait," Stan said. There's a flashlight in the glove box." He fumbled with the catch for a moment, then released the door of the compartment. On top of a small folder of papers there was a half-sized Maglite. He extracted it, turned it on, and got out of the car, pointing the beam irresolutely at Evey. She took it from his hand and began counting rows of headstones. Four away from the obelisk, five graves in, she stopped.

Wait, thought Stan. *What are we doing here?* He suddenly felt sick and silly. He was drunk, at a cemetery, in the middle of the night, with two people he really didn't know very well. He had just escaped from a second-rate closed amusement park. *Wait,* he thought again. He needed a moment to figure something out. He looked at the graves lined up in front of him, and caught his breath. He didn't know what Evey and Sebastian would do, now that they were in the cemetery, but he wasn't sure that he wanted to be a part of it anymore. He wasn't sure he wanted to be here.

"This is it," Evey said

"Wait," said Stan. He wasn't sure what he wanted. He had wanted Evey for so long, and so intensely, that it had simply become the background to his life. Even in the long years when he hadn't seen her, and in the long months when he hadn't thought about her at all, she had been the static in his mind. And tonight, he had wanted simply to be with her, to be a part of things. But now he was a part of things; he was right in the middle of something. It occurred to Stan that back when he was in high school, escaping from Park Wild Kingdom with Evey in the dark would have been the best night of his life. But he wasn't in high school anymore. *This should be exciting,* Stan thought. *But it's not.* The guard who chased them off had said, "This is not normal," and it resonated with him now; she was right. It was not normal for people in their twenties to chase after high school crushes in the dark, to break into amusement parks, to trespass in cemeteries. He didn't feel normal tonight. And suddenly, he wanted to. He wanted to be living his regular life again right now. He had stepped into another story, something entirely separate from his days at the deli, from sitting at the kitchen table with his mother and eating manicotti, from his father's long stares and his love for his brother, and Wednesday nights drinking beer in green bottles and playing trivia. He thought, *just because I'm living in my parents' basement doesn't mean I'm living in the past.* He thought of Evey asking him for money, climbing over the fence, throwing a half-smoked cigarette to the ground. He thought, *what she is doing is juvenile.* He thought, *I don't have to do this any more. I can walk away.*

The headstones in front of him were pinkish-gray in the moonlight. He knew he had family buried here, but he thought they were on the other side of the vast cemetery.

"Stan?" Evey said.

He turned around so he was facing the car. "I have to go," he said. He fought down the bile in his throat, and felt his stomach churn.

"What?" said Evey.

"I have to go right now. I'm going home."

"Stan, you can't leave," Evey said. "How will we get home?"

Stan hesitated for a moment, turned back to face her, but then shut his eyes. He swiveled his head so that when he opened them again he saw the car.

"He can go," said Sebastian from behind him. And then, after a long pause, he said, "We can walk home."

Stan took three resolute steps toward the limo, put his hand on the door handle. "Okay," he said. He looked again at Evey, focused on her face. "Good night, Evey. I'm going home."

Sebastian caught his gaze, and they nodded at each other. Stan walked around to the driver's side door and let himself into the limo. He started the car and drove forward, deeper at first, into the cemetery, and then looped his way out slowly.

He didn't go home. On Main Street, he pulled into the lot of the 7-11. Suddenly, he was ravenously hungry. The door bonged when he pushed it open, and the store was an oasis of fluorescence. He widened his eyes. By the counter, he could see shimmering hotdogs rotating on their metal rods under red salamander lights. Next to this, a cooler held flimsy burritos in plastic wrapping. He selected two, and put them together into the conveniently-provided microwave. He set the time for double what the wrapper instructed. Waiting for his food to heat, Stan listened to the radio and took in the details of the store. Coolers lined the back, with striped orange and green panels above the doors. The front shelves held bags of chips, large ones reclining and small ones hanging from little metal clips. There was an aisle of ancient-looking cleaning supplies, Clorox hiding near Borax, and sponges looking dried-out in plastic wrap. The toilet paper looked more current. Behind the counter, the clerk was reading a novel in front of the cigarette display. Stan could almost feel the fabric of this clerk's poly-knit shirt against his own skin. It was a different color, but the same design, as the polo he wore to work at the deli. Stan was startled when the microwave dinged, but the clerk didn't even look up. He brought the steaming burritos to the counter, juggling them from one hand to the next. The clerk looked up at him, and then, watching him reach into his back pocket for his wallet, waved him off. Stan coked his head, silently asking *really?* The clerk just gave a curt nod and then went back to his paperback. Immediately, Stan felt enormously fortunate. He brought the burritos to the limo, and ate each greasy tube sitting behind the wheel in the light of the store's security lamps.

When he was done, he licked his fingers, and then wiped them on his uniform pants. He balled up the wrappers and stuck them in the glove compartment. The grease in his stomach seemed to be holding him in place. He felt more grounded now. He thought about going home, and then he thought of the bar he had left. James would still be there, and other guys he knew. He wanted to see James. He took one last look around the parking lot, and then headed for the Palais Royale.

CHAPTER FOURTEEN

Sebastian had visited Mabel's grave once, at the beginning of his relationship with Evey. They had come back to Illium then, and it had been an odd feeling because they weren't sure who was showing whom around the town—Illium meant such different things to each of them. Sebastian had forgotten, until now, their visit at that time to the grave of Evey's mother.

When Stan said he was going home, Sebastian understood. For a moment, he wanted to say, "Take me with you!" But he realized how ridiculous that was. They were at the cemetery at his request. There was nowhere for him to go. He didn't want to go back to his mother's silent house, and Boston seemed very far away. As Stan got into his car, Sebastian nodded to him.

Evey was on the ground next to her mother's grave, and Sebastian kneeled beside her. He heard Stan drive away. He wanted to say something to Evey. He wanted to say something about her mother's death, about her pain, about her.

He thought of stories in which men and women survive great hardship. Not just the fiction of his graduate school days, all those emotionally tortured Russians and physically tortured Americans, but nonfiction too, true stories of long lives filled with despair, starvation, privation, *survival*. Sebastian could not understand why some people could survive war, disease, famine, depression, divorce—sometimes all these things—in one lifetime. And yet his brother had been run over by a truck, and died, several hours later, at Maine Medical Center, of his injuries. Evey's mother had died after a routine appendectomy. Once, Sebastian had read a *New York Times* article about a Marine who was injured when he was trapped in a burning tank. At the Army hospital, surgeons had removed the entire back of his skull, which had been crushed, and replaced it with plastic. They had completely reconstructed the man's face with tissue from his thigh, although they had to leave as open holes the places where his nose and ears should have been. This man had survived thirteen surgeries, but Sebastian's brother had begun to bleed to death in the driveway of Anderson Landscaping.

Evey sat fully down on the ground and crossed her legs. Sebastian eased himself down next to her. She clicked off the flashlight but kept it clutched in her hand. They sat in the dark together for a moment. Sebastian felt like he hadn't had a real conversation with Evey in months. He wanted now so much to say something meaningful to his wife. "You know what I'm thinking about?" Sebastian asked.

Evey shook her head.

"Did you read that article in the *Boston Globe* the other day? About the anniversary of the discovery of AIDS?"

"AIDS and I were born on the same year, I think," Evey said.

"I know. I can't remember a time when I wasn't terrified of AIDS," said Sebastian.

"No one is afraid of AIDS anymore," Evey said. "I mean, like, the kids at the coffee shop. When I talk to them, they're like, 'Oh yeah, none of my friends use protection.'"

"How is that possible?" It wasn't working, he thought. He wanted this conversation to be about things that really mattered to them. *No*, he thought with disappointment, *don't make this about the world, about politics, about despair, about the young. Fuck*, he thought. He was chattering meaninglessly when he had wanted to really talk to his wife. He wanted to say: *I am afraid.* He wanted to say: *what are we going to do about the money?* He wanted to say: *what are we going to do?*

"I know. It's like nuclear war," Evey said.

"What?" Sebastian turned his head to look at his wife. He felt like he was seeing her face for the first time all night.

"There's still almost as many nuclear weapons as there were when we were kids, but no one talks about it any more. I remember when I was a kid, every time I saw a grain silo, I thought there was a missile in it."

"Enough nuclear weapons to annihilate the world three times. I can't remember a time when I didn't know that statistic," Sebastian said. "People always talk about how the Cold War was this terrible thing in the fifties. You know, duck and cover."

"Bomb shelters in the backyard."

"Yeah. But I think it was worse for us. Growing up in the eighties, we never thought any of that stuff would save us. The idea was always that we would be totally annihilated, and if we survived, you know, we would wish we were dead. I spent, like, the first ten years of my life waiting to be herded into a bomb shelter, even though I always knew it wouldn't do any good. I always figured that would be it. The whole world gone. That's a fucking lot for a kid to ponder."

"Oh," said Evey. "Yes, I remember getting into a fight with a boyfriend in high school about that. I said that if the bomb went off and I was one of like ten survivors, I'd just kill myself. He got really mad at me, saying that he would want to be around to see a new world take shape or something. Like it was irresponsible to not want to have that adventure, and build up a better society. I couldn't believe he and I were fighting about that."

Sebastian asked, "Do you still feel the same way?"

"Oh, I don't know," said Evey. "I'm not so keen on the idea of wading through melted flesh to try to establish the first new post office or whatever. But as I get older I see the appeal of wanting to live. For a very long time. No matter what."

"I'd do it." Sebastian shifted on the grass. It was cool beneath him. "I'd be one of the pioneers, trying to find other people with a ham radio. Even if part of my face was melted off."

Sebastian looked up at the sky. There was a fat moon overhead, spreading a light that looked too warm for night over everything. He wondered if the moon was setting, or rising, and tried to remember what this had to do with the spinning of the earth. "Tell me again how your mom died?"

"No," said Evey. "Wait. What were you saying about AIDS?"

"Oh, nothing. That article. The one in the *Globe*? Well, do you remember what it was like getting tested for AIDS in the nineties?"

Evey nodded. "I remember one time in high school, a friend of mine had to get tested. She was so scared she made me call the clinic for her and set up the appointment. And then, when we got there, they had to buzz us in, and the lady didn't want me to go in with her. I forget what I said to make her let me in. But I remember reading *Home and Garden* in the waiting room. And when she came out she had gauze stuck to the inside of her elbow. It used to take two weeks for results. She was terrified for two weeks. And they used to make you come back to the clinic to get them, and you had to bring someone with you then. I went back with her."

"I know. I can't believe it used to take two weeks. And we were all so scared. That's the thing. I've probably had five HIV tests in my life."

"I've had six."

"And I've probably never even had an infected partner. That article I read said that the chances of getting the virus from sex even with someone who's already infected, is, like, one percent. One percent! That just floored me."

"What, if you had known that you'd have had a lot more unprotected sex?"

"No. Shut up." Sebastian glanced at Evey to make sure she wasn't pissed off. She smiled at him and made her eyes big. "I'm not saying it would have changed my behavior," he said. "Or that I'm not thankful I was careful. I can't think of a time when I didn't know to use a condom." He was quiet for a moment, remembering. When he and Evey had been dating for three months, they both went to the free clinic in Somerville and got tested for everything together. The HIV test results were ready that day, and when they had gotten the word about everything else (they were clean) a week later, they stopped using condoms for good. "But anyway," he said, "it just made death seem farther away, I guess, when I read that."

"It's worse for women. Sex is this doubly dangerous thing for us." Evey reached out and touched her mother's headstone. She traced the letters of her mother's name:

MABEL (ALLEN) KISS
1954-1984
IN MEMORIUM

Next to the stone, was another, exactly matched in style and size. Sebastian looked more carefully at it when Evey reached her hand to trace the words on this stone, too.

RICHARD ANSEL KISS
1956-
IN MEMORIUM

He started. "I know," said Evey. "It's a little creepy, right? He's had it for a long time, since a couple years after my mom died." Sebastian didn't know what to say. "He told me he did it for me. So when the time came, I wouldn't have to think about the logistics or the expense. Why do parents do shit like that? Things that are supposed to be for their children, that just crush their children." Finally, Evey lay her hand in his palm.

Sebastian did not understand how death could simultaneously be so close, and so far away. He thought maybe other cultures did this better. Maybe in places where everyone cared for the sick, and helped with childbirth, maybe in places where people lived with their grandparents, it was possible to make more sense out of death and its place in life. *But that isn't it either*, he thought. *Even if death has a place in life, sudden, violent death is still not normal.* Matt hadn't died of an illness. And Mabel didn't either. There was no understanding it. Sebastian thought he had read something about pictures of military coffins. The press wasn't allowed to take photos of the war dead. Some anti-war protestors he knew said it was a conspiracy, to keep the American public from understanding the real cost of the war. Some had said, instead, that it was out of respect for the fallen. He didn't know what he thought, and he wasn't sure whether seeing pictures like that would help him understand his brother's death or not. Sebastian thought that as he got older, he had started to understand that the world is a vastly unequal place. He knew that there was great inequity of resources, opportunities, and even rights in the world. And he knew that it was the job of people like him, people who had the education that let them know this and the fortitude to care, to try to do something about it. But it was the great inequality of *luck* in the world that he just could not reconcile himself to. *How is it possible,* he thought *that there is such a terribly inadequate distribution of luck?* He thought about people in refugee camps, who lived their whole lives there and then died there. And people for whom nothing ever seemed to go truly wrong. Or people for whom many things went terribly, and it rolled right off them. Sebastian's grandfather had been a POW in the Second World War, and had survived to smoke a pack a day until he was eighty-seven. Three of his children had preceded him to death. He had seen an earthquake, the invention of the television, three house fires, the inside of one German and two American prisons, had purchased one of the first refrigerators, and maxed-out one of the first credit cards, lost a foot to diabetes, and still, he had been eighty-seven when his heart stopped. He wondered how this could be, what the point was. He wondered how anything anyone did could matter in this context.

Am I really so incapable? Sebastian thought. *On a day like this, are we really two people, two married people, who cannot talk to each other about anything that matters? We are all alone in this,* he thought. "Stan left," he said.

"Where do you think he went?"

"He said he was going home. We'll have to walk," Sebastian said. "How far do you think it is?"

"Why did he have to go?" Evey looked at the ground, and Sebastian traced the contours of her shoulders in the shadowy light.

He took a deep breath. "I don't know. Maybe if I was someone else I would have left too."

"What do you mean? Where does he have to go?"

"Maybe he just couldn't stand to be around us."

Evey rummaged around in her purse until she found a cigarette. She withdrew it carefully, and when she clicked the lighter and her face flared into sight, Sebastian could see that she had her eyes squeezed shut.

He placed his thumb over the soft, exposed under-part of Evey's wrist. He could feel her pulse there, or maybe it was his own. He knew the human thumb has its own pulse. Sebastian had heard that small animals have shorter life-spans than larger ones. He had heard that this is because of their hearts. The heart is designed to last for a certain number of beats. When that numbers is up, the animal dies. And of course, smaller hearts beat faster, so they reach their finish line sooner. Big heart, little heart. He wondered if he was getting the science right, and how accurately life-spans could be predicted if there were no accidents, no suicides, no cancer or meningitis or AIDS, only the number of beats assigned to each person, each animal. Sebastian wished he could believe in his mother's god, or even the liberal-minded Jesus that James had been trying to tell people about back at the bar. But the most he could muster was a bit of superstition regarding predestination. He wondered how many beats his heart had left in it; how many throbs until Evey's stopped, or his mother's, or Stan's.

CHAPTER FIFTEEN

Now, as Evey sat in front of her mother's grave with Sebastian, she wished that she had a flower to lay atop it. She knew she would have to get up soon, let Sebastian lead her to Matt's new grave, but she felt that something was called for here. She needed something to mark this moment for herself. She was, as so often happened, disappointed that she was unprepared.

The grass she was sitting on was cool through her dress, but beneath that, she could feel the lingering warmth in the earth. She withdrew her hand from Sebastian's and clicked the flashlight back on.

"You ready?" Sebastian asked.

"No," she said, "not yet." She ground out her cigarette and tossed it away, toward someone else's grave. Evey opened her purse and pointed the flashlight into the interior. She was looking for something, anything, she could leave with her mother. She found a silver necklace in her purse that Sebastian had given her on their one-year anniversary. She had thought to wear it to the funeral, but forgotten about it. It had a small garnet pendant suspended on the chain. Evey held it up in the light of the flashlight and decided that this would do as a token of her life to give to her mom. She gathered the chain in her left hand and snapped her purse shut again. She turned the flashlight around and tried to use the butt to gouge a small hole in the earth next to her mother's headstone. But pointed upwards, the flashlight sent an erratic, jumping beam at the moon, and Evey couldn't see what she was doing. She felt exhausted and small.

Sebastian took it from her hand, and held it up so she could see the ground. She began to pull up huge hanks of grass, and dig in the earth with her fingers, and it occurred to Evey that she hadn't had her hands in the ground for a long time. One of her fingernails tore off jaggedly from the side, but she kept digging. The dirt on top was hard-packed, but once she had clawed through it, the soil underneath was softer. It took her a long time. Sebastian crouched next to her, silent, keeping the blade of light steady. Evey could hear frogs croaking somewhere far off. She started to sweat a bit, and could feel her chest and forehead flushing. When the hole was a few inches deep and a few inches wide, Evey coiled the necklace into it and left the pendant, with its face toward the deep earth. She scooped loose dirt with the side of her hand into the hole. Sebastian dropped the light and helped her smooth the turf back into place. When they were done, there was a bald spot in the grass marking Evey's gift to her mother.

They slumped back together and looked at their work. Evey's hands were damp and dirty and a line of blood came from her torn fingernail. She wiped them in big strokes on the grass next to her. She examined her fingernail, running the pad of her thumb over the torn edge. It wasn't too bad.

"Do you ever think," Sebastian asked, "what it would be like if we weren't born? I mean, like, what our parents would be like?"

"Yeah. You know, I'm older than my mother was when she had me. Soon, I'll be older than she was when she died." Evey paused, wiped her hands again. "I can't imagine having a child now."

Sebastian looked at her sharply. "You told James you were pregnant. At the bar."

"I know." Evey's voice was soft.

"Why would you lie about that? Why would you lie about anything?"

Evey sighed and lay back on the grass, stretching her arms above her. "I don't know. I just wanted to have something to say to him, I guess. Or maybe I was testing him, trying to see what he would do. It didn't work. It didn't matter, anyway. James is too wrapped up in James to care about anything in my life."

"You know," Sebastian said, "he's an idiot. I'm sorry. I know you loved him. But the whole time we were at the bar I just kept thinking *how could you have been married to this moron?* I mean seriously. That tee-shirt. Jesus."

"Don't be petty."

"No, I'm not. I mean, you were a different person then. "

"No I wasn't!" Evey sat up and looked Sebastian in the eyes. She could feel her voice rising in her chest. "I'm the same fucking person I always was. Or anyway, you don't know. You didn't know me then." She wanted to say, *you don't know me now,* but realized how ridiculous and melodramatic that was. Of course he knew her. He was her husband. She had made him soft-boiled eggs. He brought her coffee in the morning. They had unprotected sex. She knew him. She just couldn't talk to him. Or maybe he couldn't talk to her. "Oh, I don't know," Evey slumped back, leaning on her elbow. "Forget it. I don't know whether I'm the same or different. I don't know why I loved him, or why I didn't love him enough. Fuck it. You think I'm probably different?"

"Of course you are," Sebastian said softly. "We all grow up."

"I guess. I don't feel that different."

"What's going on between you and Angela?"

"Nothing."

Now it was Sebastian's turn to sit very upright and very still. "That's not true, Evey. You don't have to lie to me."

"She's just a friend."

"You hardly ever go out with her." Sebastian didn't move.

Evey could hear him breathing next to her. "I go out with her after work sometimes."

Sebastian didn't say anything.

"Sometimes we have sex at work," Evey said. It sounded wrong to her, untrue. "After we close the shop and lock up. Sometimes when no one is there."

Sebastian looked like he wanted to hit her. "You lick her clit? Put your hands on her big tits? Does she make you come, Evey?"

Evey whispered, "Fuck, Sebastian."

He looked carefully away from her. "I knew, Evey. I knew. Why did you lie to me?"

"I didn't have to lie to you, Sebastian. You already knew, and you never said anything. So it's all the same. It didn't feel like lying."

"We can't keep fucking doing this!" Sebastian said.

"Doing what, Sebastian?"

Sebastian paused. "We should have talked about this. We should have done this a long time ago."

Evey felt defeated and angry. She wasn't ashamed of what she had done, not exactly. But she was mortified by having to say it aloud. She was terrified and trapped. This felt very real to her, and overwhelming. She could feel small sticks and dirt pressing into her arms where she was supporting weight. She felt gritty. "Fine, Sebastian," she said. "We didn't, though. So here's your chance. Let's talk. What do you want to say?"

Sebastian said nothing, and Evey knew he could not formulate a thought to express. When she looked at him, the shadows accentuated the chickenpox scar on his forehead. She knew that she wouldn't be able to say anything if it were her, either. *What was there to say?* she thought. She wasn't afraid that Sebastian was going to leave her. She wasn't afraid of Sebastian.

She was afraid only of herself, of who she had become, of having to make herself real by talking about her life. When she had fucked Angela all those times, she had liked it. But it hadn't seemed a part of her life, it hadn't seemed consequential. She hadn't had to think about the kind of person she was becoming: how each of her actions added up to someone who, if viewed by another, might not look the same way she felt about herself. And she knew that it was terribly unfair for her to ask Sebastian *what do you want to say?* There was no possible answer to that question –or too many answers to pick just one. *But,* she thought, *it's not always about fair.* She wondered what kind of person her mother would have wanted her to become, if her mother had lived. "You asked me," Evey said slowly, "what it would be like if we were never born. You know, my mother died when I was so young. When she was young, and my father was young. I think that if I had never been born, my mother—my father's relationship with my mother—would have just been a thing. You know, a story that he told as he got older, maybe to other kids he would have had with someone else, or maybe to people at dinner some time, about this thing he did when he was young. He married a black woman that he met when he was down South one summer. He married this woman during the Civil Rights years. And then she died. And that was the end of the story."

Mabel was unambiguously the most beautiful woman Richard had ever seen. And she was a good swimmer. They had met at a newly-integrated pool in Cloverdale, Alabama. Richard was traveling in the area, trying to figure out what was going on in the South in these turbulent years of change. He had bought her an ice cream when they had met at the concession just as Mabel was realizing that she had forgotten her purse and didn't have the change to pay for the cone she had just ordered. Mabel had always said she liked Richard's clipped, strangled northern accent. She had also liked that Richard let her pick him up in her car when they went for a date. He had been seventeen. Mabel was twenty at the time, and Richard lied about his age because he didn't think she would go out with a man who was younger than her. It wasn't until the signed and official marriage certificate had arrived in their mail that Mabel realized how young Richard was. Her parents had disapproved of the relationship so strongly, on the basis of race and geography, rather than age, that when she moved to Illium to marry Richard at the end of that summer, she had rarely spoken to them again, and only went home to visit once or twice in all the time they were married. Richard had not seen them, until Mabel's funeral, seven years later. But he always told Evey how happy they had been together all that time. How Mabel had loved being pregnant. How she was so happy, carrying Evey around in her belly, happier than she had ever been. Just twenty-two years old, but proud and comfortable, confident in her family. She had died when Evey was four.

Her mother had died just before Vanessa Lynn Williams became the first African-American to win the Miss America pageant. Her father woke Evey for the eleven o'clock news to watch the segment on William's crowning. Evey remembered sitting on the living room floor in her footie pajamas listening to the closing bars of the news program's song—much more clearly than she remembered her mother's death. Evey knew at the time that her mother had to go to the hospital. Her father had explained to her that her mother would be gone for three days, but that on the second day, Evey could go visit her. Evey was excited. Her friend Crystal had gone to the hospital a couple months before, to have tubes put in her ears. When she had come back, she told of dark purple popsicles in the recovery room, and that the nurses had hooked her Cabbage Patch Kid up to a heart monitor. But Evey had never gone to the hospital. Her father had not come to pick her up from her friend's house on the first night her mother was in the hospital. And when he had come for her on the second day, he had been unshaven. Evey had never seen him with whiskers, and she was frightened. She clung to Mrs. Pierce's legs in her red and white kitchen, not wanting to go with her father. She remembered throwing a tantrum while he tried to get her into the car seat. She remembered fighting in his arms while he opened the car door. Her father did not tell her that her mother was dead. Not right away. She did not remember when she started to understand what had happened: her mother had gone in for a routine appendectomy after experiencing abdominal pain. And there had been a complication with the surgery, from which she had never awoken. Later, Evey understood that her father had sued the doctor. When she was fifteen years old, Evey had found the legal document laying out the terms of the settlement. Attached, was her mother's medical report. And Evey had felt like a thief, reading the words of that report: her mother had died when CO_2 used to inflate her abdomen during surgery had unexpectedly diffused into her arteries, traveling up to her brain, where it blocked the blood flow for long enough that her mother died. It was called an air embolus. The money from the resulting lawsuit was placed in a trust for her, and when she turned eighteen years old she accessed it. It was nine thousand dollars. She was so angry, that day at the bank, that she had wanted to spit on the worn carpet at the customer service desk. She withdrew the entire amount in cash and handed it to James. She didn't want to have anything to do with it. Nine thousand dollars, for a lifetime without a mother. For dresses that never fit because there was no one in the dressing room at Marshals with her. For a family she never knew. For awkward stares at parent night at school. For never knowing who she would have been with the love and guidance of a mother.

Evey didn't remember crying at her mother's funeral, though she must have. What she remembered more clearly than the funeral itself is that her father brought her to this cemetery on the anniversary of her mother's death, when she was seven. Richard had wept, and Evey had been uncomfortable, frightened and ashamed by his tears. She had looked down at her mother's gravestone, and, noticing for the first time Richard's stone next to it, she had screamed. She had screamed and screamed, until her tiny, tortured voice was only short, rhythmic busts of hysterical sound. Richard had thrown her over his shoulder in a fireman's carry and ran back to the car with her.

Sebastian looked up from the ground and into Evey's face. "Are you going to do it again?" he asked.

She knew what he was talking about. Evey thought about the coffee shop. She pictured long lines of customers at the register during a rush, Angela moving behind her in a steady rhythm, filling orders. She thought of Angela laying a hand on her shoulder, then moving it slowly down her arm until she caught her hand in hers. She thought of Angela with her head tipped back and her eyes squeezed closed. Of Angela, hot and soft and solid in her arms.

"I don't know," she said.

CHAPTER SIXTEEN

Sebastian licked his lips. He didn't know what to think about what Evey had said. She had made it difficult, saying that she didn't know if she would sleep with Angela again. He wanted for this all to be over. But at least she had finally admitted the truth. He wanted his grief to ebb, and his uncertainty about his relationship with Evey to be in the past. He wanted to go home and hold his wife, and be loved by her. He wanted not to have to think so much about important things. He didn't know what to do, and he wasn't sure he would know what to do ever again.

He didn't think she would stop seeing Angela, but maybe he was wrong. He knew that she loved him, and that in a day or two they would go home. He knew they wouldn't talk in the car, and then when they got home, they would haul their suitcases up the three flights of stairs in their building, past the walls in the hallway that they had scratched moving in their couch and still hadn't spackled. He knew that they would take showers, and make sandwiches, and that after her shower Evey would pull on a pair of his boxers and one of his thin, white undershirts, and that her nipples would press upward and he would see them, dark and perfect there beneath the fabric. He wanted to know why he wasn't enough. It wasn't the sex, or even the love, if she loved Angela. He didn't care if he couldn't provide enough of those things for his wife; *god knows there's precious little of either in the world,* he thought, *and we should get it anywhere we can.* It was that she lied, and he wasn't enough to hold her truth.

Sebastian had heard people say that before: that when someone has an affair, the sex isn't as bad as the lying. He never understood what they meant before. *So what?* he thought, *people lied.* He didn't feel like his whole life was a lie, or his marriage was a sham—nothing like that. He didn't think Evey had lied about loving him, and she had never denied an affair, or even, probably, told him she was somewhere when she was another place in order to facilitate the affair. He wasn't afraid their friends would find out. No, what bothered him was that she lied about everything. She lied about stupid little things. And she did it all the time. She lied about the foods she liked. She lied to her boss when she needed a day off. She lied about going out to the porch to make a phone call—she'd just sit there, phone closed and clutched in her hand, smoking. She lied about having paid the bills, or having paid them on time. And she had lied to James at the bar earlier. Sebastian thought that this was the worst part. That there life together, their actual, true life just wasn't enough. And she had to fantasize and fabricate, prevaricate and spin one tale on top of another, just to get through the day. She lied not to protect him, or to protect herself from him, but because the simple daily truth of their life together was—*what?* Sebastian thought, *boring? Just not enough for her.* He wished it could just be enough. He wanted to say: *Evey, this is all there is. And it's not fabulous, but it's not that difficult either. Just be here. Just deal. Just live your life.* He thought, *I like my life. And I like Evey's life too.* He just wanted so badly for her to feel the same way. He wanted to ask her: *do you remember the time we went to my boss's cabin, on the lake in New Hampshire? And we drank all that rum and then decided we wanted to roast marshmallows? Remember, Evey, we didn't want to start a campfire, so we tried to roast them over the gas burner and they collapsed all over the stove and we set off the fire alarm? Do you remember? Do you remember?*

This is what he said: "I think that if I was never born, my father's life would be pretty much the same. He had another family before me, you know."

Evey nodded.

"That's the first thing I thought of when I found out that Matt was being shipped out. I thought, if he dies, will our dad come to the funeral? Now I know the answer."

Evey shook her legs out one at a time, trying to get the blood flowing back through them. "You know what I can't imagine though, about not having kids?" She glanced at him quickly, and Sebastian knew she was checking to see if he would stop her, to see if he would bring up her lie to James again. He let it go. "I can't imagine," she said, "what all the *stuff* in our lives is for. I mean, the stuff we save. Like my mother's high school class ring, or old things my dad has kept—his Boy Scouts pocket knife, their marriage announcement from the *Press Herald*. I have that kind of stuff too, in my jewelry box at home. When I was a kid, I used to be, like, in awe of the hidden things I found in my parent's room. I found a box in my dad's closet—my mother's diaphragm was in it. She was dead. I found my grandfather's diploma, and my baby shoes. But it was like I *discovered* that stuff. I used to memorize those items and put them back exactly the same way so my dad wouldn't know I'd found them."

Sebastian knew exactly what she was talking about. It was a trouble with the *proportions* of things. He couldn't tell how much any one thing mattered. *What did it mean*, he thought, *that Evey's mother's class ring outlasted the woman, and would outlast Evey too?* "Do you think," he asked, "that those things are intrinsically interesting, or only because of the people, the children, who find them? Like, we're told to get a class ring as a memento, and mementos are supposed to have this *value*. But if I had one and I put it away in a box and no one ever found it there, it wouldn't matter, right?"

"I know," said Evey.

Sebastian thought of all of his brother's belongings. *What would his mother do with Matt's stuff?* He thought of that tiger mask in Matt's room, and wondered why Matt had saved it. He wondered what would happen to that piece of cardboard now. Would his mother put it away in a box? Leave everything in Matt's room exactly as it was? Would it finally be relegated to the trash? *And what,* he thought, *was Matt's life made up of? What was his life, really?* Sebastian had thought that he wouldn't know what in his own life was important until he was dead. He had thought once that when he died, that would be the end of the story, and so the narrative arc would reveal itself, if not to him, then to whoever he left behind. But it hadn't worked. Matt was dead, and Sebastian still had no way to know what was important in Matt's life, which parts had mattered more, and which less. *Was it the war?* he thought. *What about that? And what about the protests I went to?* He wished he had a historical overview of things. He wished he could tell how much of all this would be remembered as a turning point in his life, or a moment of import in history. He asked Evey, "What dates and names and places from now do you think school kids are going to be taught in sixty or a hundred years?"

"I don't know. Everything's all fucked up." Sebastian could see that she was getting uncomfortable on the ground, bringing one knee and then the other to her chest to stretch out her long legs.

"Do you remember where you were when the Berlin Wall fell?"

"Yeah, I do." Evey sounded surprised. "My dad woke me up. He was big into important moments. I was in bed, and my dad brought me downstairs to watch people on top of the wall, on the news, with sledge hammers."

"I had to write a report," Sebastian said, "on current events for school. I chose the Berlin Wall. And I got really into the research. But this is what I really remember about the fall of the Berlin Wall. I had my report all finished, and I left it on the kitchen counter so I would remember to bring it to school. I remember coming back into the kitchen from somewhere and my mom was on the phone. We had a big, red, rotary phone on the wall. And she was doodling all over my report." He paused. He didn't know why he was talking about any of this. He knew he should be talking about Angela, or Matt. But he couldn't shut up. "Do you ever think," he said, "that it's like a broken promise? When the Wall came down, we thought we'd be okay. We thought maybe we'd get to live past thirty anyway. And now all this war on terror and global warming and fucking getting attacked on our own soil. It's like, we're still not even old enough to be the ones who fucked it all up." Sebastian gasped. He rubbed the back of his hand over his forehead. "I just—" He started to cry. And then he couldn't stop. He was choking on his own breath. "They fucked it up, Evey."

She got up and came around behind him. Sitting on the ground again, she put her arms around him, and pulled him in to her chest.

"They fucked it all up."

"I know," she said.

They sat there for a long time. Sebastian stopped crying, and he was starting to feel stiff. Evey's arms, encircling him, felt like wax. "We should go," he said.

"Do you still want to go to Matt's grave?"

"Just for a minute. Yes. We should." Sebastian moved Evey's

arms away from him and got up. "I want to say goodbye." Once he was standing, the cemetery seemed much darker. When they had been sitting down, he had unconsciously imagined himself ensconced; the little place in front of the grave carved out by the moon and the tiny beam of the Maglite had seemed protected. But now that he had changed his perspective, he felt suddenly the expanse of this place. He was nervous for the first time all night, sobered by the dark and the strangeness of what they were doing. "Let's go," he said.

Evey hesitated, and he realized she did not know in which direction Matt's grave lay. Sebastian looked around him, and thought he knew where to go. He clicked on the light and started forward.

It was so quiet he could hear the wind in the trees. It sounded like people whispering in a large room. He was walking along the main, paved path now, with Evey beside him, passing rows and rows of other people's dead. After a while he said, "I just feel like I let him down."

"Matt? Oh, Sebastian. You didn't let him down. You were a good brother."

"No, I wasn't." Evey grabbed Sebastian's arm and started to say something, but he cut her off. "Evey. I know I wasn't as good a brother to him as I could have been." He walked a little faster. "I remember one time when we were kids, our mother took us to the carnival. He wanted to go on all the rides. I hate those rides. But so I took him on the Scrambler—you remember that one, where there's all these cars on long arms?" He could feel Evey nod beside him. "And the thing starts up, and I'm terrified. And Matt is just sitting there, cool as a cucumber. But I am shitting myself. So I start to talk to myself out loud, to calm myself down. I'm saying 'This is fun. People do this for fun.' And that's when Matt freaked out."

"Sebastian, that's a sweet story. You did something you

hated for your brother."

"I scared the fuck out of him because I couldn't keep my mouth shut. I couldn't protect either of us." Sebastian remembered the look of horror on Matt's face. He remembered realizing that he had made a mistake; that it was he, not the ride, that so frightened Matt.

The air was getting cooler, he thought, the further he walked. And then there he was. He recognized this area of the cemetery, and slowed his gait. "Wait," he said, "here it is." The most shocking thing about Matt's grave was not the newly-torn earth, but the bare top of the casket, which looked rough in the light from the moon and the starts. He was reminded of how cheap the coffin was. His mother had selected a bare-bones box, rough-hewn and lightweight. It fit with her own sense of propriety, and Sebastian wasn't quite sure if it would have fit with Matt's sense of what was right. Probably. The fake grass carpeting the rectangle around the mouth of the hole. The apparatus for raising and lowering the coffin electronically. There was a mound of dirt that looked ready and expectant.

The grave had not yet been filled with earth.

"What the fuck?" asked Sebastian quietly. The two of them were paralyzed by the unexpected sight of the coffin, bare in the night. Sebastian thought that this was simultaneously ominous and shocking and yet somehow comforting to see. No one spoke. Sebastian backed away from the grave. Evey approached the edge. The ground covered by the fake grass was not entirely level, and she started to slip. For a minute, it looked like she would fall into the grave and land on top of the coffin. Sebastian was torn between fear and disgust, and the urge to laugh hysterically. He ran forward to grab Evey by the arm, but when he grabbed her, the high-heel of one of her shoes sunk into the sod. There was a moment when they fell toward the open grave. Everything seemed to slow down. Sebastian could feel his body tipping forward, and he wanted to wheel his arms at his sides like a cartoon figure who has just realized he has run over the edge of a cliff and kept going into the void of air above a long drop. Instead, he pinned Evey's arms to her sides, and with an enormous effort, he lunged to the left and brought them both safely to rest on the Astroturf. From where they lay, Sebastian could see each individual short fake blade of grass. Evey started to laugh. She laughed so hard tears slipped down her cheeks, and she was hiccupping. It was a laugh she was not in control of, and at some point, Sebastian was no longer sure if she was laughing or crying.

She pushed him off of her. "Jesus," she said. "Let's get out of here. This is no place to be, in our state."

"This is no place for anyone," said Sebastian when he got his breath back. "Why haven't they filled in the grave? Earth to earth, and all that." He looked up and down the length of the coffin. "This is ridiculous," said Sebastian. "I don't want to leave him here like this."

"Shit," Evey said.

"What are we going to do?" he said.

But Evey wasn't looking at him. "Shut up," she said. "I hear someone."

CHAPTER SEVENTEEN

At some point it was all too much for Karen. There were too many people the bar, more than she had ever seen there at once, come to share in this moment of her life, and it felt as if the temperature in the room was ten degrees warmer than normal. She didn't pause to notice all the ex-bartenders at the bar serving drinks in her absence. She didn't stop to see the chief of police, or the entire volunteer fire department taking shots of Jägermeister. She didn't hear her mother call her name. With so many people in the bar the light looked like a strobe. Happy was leaning against the wall beside her. She turned around to Happy and said, "You stay here," and then she walked as quickly as she could without actually jogging to the front door. She turned back to Happy again when she reached the door, remembering something. She didn't have her car keys, and her room upstairs seemed unfathomably far away at the moment. The idea of fighting her way back through the crowd exhausted her, and she knew she'd never make it out if she tried. Despite the decibel level inside, and the fact that Happy had not followed her, he heard her perfectly when she spoke to him across the length of the room. "Throw me your keys," she said. Happy nodded that he had understood. Without moving from his spot, he threw the keys to his truck. They made a perfect arc, just missing the head of the eighth-grade science teacher, and the owner of Handy

Andy's Convenience. They caused a slight wind to disturb the hair on the top of Karen's mother's head as they passed over her. Karen caught the keys easily, paused to wonder why her mother was back in the bar, and then walked directly out into the night. The porch was almost as crowded as the bar had been, and the night was hemmed in by the cigarette smoke creating a skin around the porch.

Karen got into Happy's truck, painted on the doors with the logo of Happy Family Boxing Club. When she started it and it backfired, the sound was like a shot. A huge cheer went up from the porch at the noise. She had to get out of there—to leave her own party behind. She didn't want to be a part of her own life right now. She wanted to let go on her own, not to see the bar feted and mourned by people who could not understand what it meant to her. She knew that she should be worried about leaving the bar. She knew the till might get robbed, she knew there could be an accident or an incident, she knew that her own room could be broken into. But she just didn't care. The business was gone, and she couldn't think of a single thing from her life that needed to remain unscathed. If the whole thing had disappeared it would have been a relief. She could feel herself peeling away from the bar and her life there, reaching into some new space.

She didn't know where to go, until it occurred to her the it would be quiet and cool at the cemetery. She thought it was fitting on this night to go to her father's grave. She had some things she needed to say to herself, maybe to her father, and that was as good a place as any to do it. She headed there in the big truck, already picturing the serene silence. Silence, she thought, was exactly what she wanted.

Karen dragged the big truck around the turn and into the cemetery and brought it to a stop next to the row of graves where her father was buried. She jumped down from the cab and latched the door behind her. Karen wished it were fall. It seemed wrong to her to visit a cemetery when it was warm out. Death was ridiculous in the face of the hopeless optimism of New England summer. She sat on the ground in front of her father's headstone, right over the spot where he lay and so close that if she leaned her head forward it would have touched the stone.

Though Karen was not religious, she believed in miracles. Raised a Catholic, the politics and pomp of it had never appealed to her, but she was primed for a miracle of the Jesus-in-the-Cinnamon-Toast-Crunch variety. In her family, one had to be. Her parents' meeting had always been described to her as a miracle. At the time they met, her father Rocky had been down on his luck, living in crumbling apartment building slowly losing his job because he was quickly drinking himself to death. Karen's mother had been attending a teacher's college and living cheaply but much more neatly in the apartment upstairs from Rocky. She had changed his whole life one day, when Rocky was kneeling in front of the toilet throwing up his breakfast and Sarah had literally fallen into his life. The plumbing in that building was bad and Sarah's bathtub leaked constantly. Years of bath run-off had weakened the floorboards and that morning, as Sarah was shampooing her long, white-blond hair, the floor had finally given way and she had careened through the floor in her bathtub, coming to rest next to Rocky like a Mary-on-the-half-shell statue embedded in someone's lawn. He had looked up from his own vomit long enough to realize that Sarah was not an angel, though she may have represented divine intervention, and that she was unhurt though terrified, and that he needed to do something about his life. This is the story that Sarah and Rocky told. They told it to everyone who asked, and many people who didn't. Karen was almost twenty before she realized that this could not possibly have happened. She imagined that Sarah had knocked on Rocky's door and asked him to finally fix the bathroom pipes. She imagined it was her father who came up with the embellishment. She could not imagine why her mother went along with it.

Karen reached out a hand and touched the stone. It was lukewarm, where she had hoped it would be cool and refreshing. She was angry with her father for leaving the Palais Royale to her uncle Benny. Benny was an abhorrent man, always slinking around in custom-embroidered track suits. He owned two Chinese restaurants that were entirely staffed by illegal Mexican immigrants. One of the restaurants had burned down last year under circumstances that were suspicious enough to warrant an investigation by the fire marshal, but not suspicious enough that Benny couldn't eventually collect a large sum in insurance money. For Karen's birthday every year, Benny had given her a collectible Barbie doll. Karen thought that Benny never saw a thing for what it was, only for its dollar value. She thought for a moment.

"This is just the way it is," she said to her father. "I know what you were doing, Dad, when you left the bar to Benny. It was a bullshit move. That's such typical parent stuff, giving your children what you think they need instead of what they tell you they want. I'll never forgive you for it. But it's okay, Dad." Karen leaned her forehead against his stone. She wasn't crying. "I don't think family is about forgiveness anyway. Family is about *no matter what*. I'm going to be nicer to Mom."

She wanted to ask her father what she should do about Happy. She wanted to ask if he counted as family, as the kind of person who could not be left, moved-on-from, forgotten. If she had, or should have, the kind of relationship with Happy that in some way was immutable. Karen wished it had been possible to ask her father that when he was still alive. Even now that he was dead, she didn't think she could talk about it aloud. She wasn't sure she wanted to anyway. Maybe it was time, she thought, to stop with things that she couldn't articulate.

It seemed to her that she had lost track of the trajectory of her existence. Other people had been young adults—had gone to school and met new people and learned new skills and had sex and dorm rooms and heated debates. What had she been doing? When Karen thought about the college application her mother had brought to her, she thought of giant incisors, flexible plastic suction tubes, green surgical masks. But maybe, she thought, none of that mattered as much as the opportunity to live the life of a young person that she had never been. Suddenly she could picture herself, textbook clutched to her chest, entering a restaurant she had never been to, pushing a pair of latex gloves into the pocket of a pair of tight jeans and smiling a perfect smile at a classmate as he asked her what she would like to eat.

And then she heard voices, like the tiny, indecipherable whispering of God, telling her what to do. She looked up, and realized her eyes had adjusted to the dark. She listened with every cell in her body. What she heard was conversation. If God was out there, he had debate team. Karen got up and walked slowly toward the sound, scanning the ground for potholes and old graves lying on their backs like loose bricks. She thought those old graves were the most intolerably depressing. She couldn't imagine having all that was left of her be a little block with the word MOTHER or DAUGHTER etched into it. She was getting closer to the voices and was almost able to make out words. She thought she heard someone say "grave robbers." She was starting to think that walking toward unidentified people in a graveyard at midnight was not, actually, a good idea. But she just couldn't picture herself coming to harm at the hands of another person in this place, or in any place in this town. It would be too stupid.

As she got close to the voices, she could see something on the ground. Something was moving, and it was a confusion of incongruous shapes. Her first thought was that they were two teenagers, come to the cemetery after dark to make out. They were moving together on the ground, and Karen stood some distance away, and watched for just a moment. She had done this once, with a boy when she was in high school. Anthony Murphy. She remembered his car, an old Plymouth with a bench seat in the front. They had dated for most of her sophomore year. He took her out sometimes, to the Nickelodeon downtown for half-price films, or to the diner. He sucked on fruit-flavored Lifesavers before kissing her in the front seat of the Plymouth. And once, they had come here, and he had gotten her pants off before she made him stop. He had gone to college in Colorado, maybe for psychology.

But these were not high school students. Karen saw one push the other away on the ground, and they were fully-grown people. The one still on the ground was a woman, slight, but definitely adult. And as she raised her head, she caught sight of Karen. Karen saw her sit up and pause, and she stepped closer to the couple. "I'm sorry," she called. "I heard something."

"Hello?" the young woman asked. Karen recognized her from the Palais Royale.

The man pulled himself up off the ground and started to walk toward Karen. "We're not doing anything," he said, and Karen thought she recognized him too.

"No, I'm sorry," Karen repeated. "I was just here to see—my father died. I was at his grave."

The man stopped. "My brother died. Matt. He was buried today."

"I'm so sorry," Karen said. She thought she should leave them in peace, but the strangeness of encountering them at night, in a cemetery, kept her from moving. She thought of Happy's truck, parked back on the main road. She didn't want to leave, didn't know what to say. She pushed her hair off her forehead with her left hand.

"You're the bartender," the man said.

Karen took another step toward the couple and the grave. "Yes."

"You're Karen," the woman said.

Despite the fact that she recognized Evey, Karen was surprised that she knew her name. Not everyone, even those who drank often at the bar, did. She took another step forward.

"I'm Evey," the woman said, and hoisted herself off the ground. Karen could see that she was wearing high heels, and the woman stumbled a little once she was on her feet. She wondered if she was drunk, or it was just the uneven ground. She tried to remember what she had served her earlier. Whiskey, maybe?

Evey said, "We've known each other for a long time, from the bar. But I'm not sure you knew my name. You're the owner's daughter at the Palais Royale, right?"

"Yes," Karen said. "My dad. He's the one who died. Now the bar isn't mine. My uncle, he sold it." Karen walked closer now. She gasped when she saw the open grave. "What are you doing? What happened?" She was startled and confused. It was an appalling sight, the open grave. It was so unexpected. Karen touched the neckline of her tee-shirt.

"It's my brother," Sebastian said. "I'm Sebastian Hulot, Matt's brother."

"What happened to the grave?"

Evey was the one who responded. She said, "We don't know. We found it this way. They never filled it in, or something. We were just going to say goodbye."

Sebastian sank to the ground again next to the grave, and Karen approached him before she knew what she was doing. She knelt next to him, and put a hand on his back. Her hand looked white and cold and large. Sebastian let his head fall into the bowl of his hands. Karen could feel Evey moving around behind them, and finally Evey settled on the other side of Sebastian, sitting cross-legged and extending her dark, thin hand, resting it next to Karen's on Sebastian's back. Karen noticed how far out the bones of Evey's wrists stood.

Sebastian said, "When our dad left, Matt used to crawl into bed with me at night. Not my mother, but me. He would get in under the covers, and he was so much younger than me. So tiny. I used to use him as a weight bar. I would lift him above my head while he held himself flat. He loved that. And he would get in beside me, and he never cried. He would whisper, making me promise over and over again that I wouldn't leave him." He stopped, lifted his head. "I can't do this. I can't leave him here like this."

"We could fill in the grave," said Karen. "Cover him with earth."

Sebastian moved so quickly both women felt a jolt of alarm. He pulled back a corner of the Astroturf and fumbled for a moment, until he found what he was looking for. He flipped a switch—earlier in the day, the funeral director had operated it during the internment discreetly with his foot. The coffin began to rise up out of the grave with a well-lubricated whir. Suspended by straps strung between the silver scaffolding, the casket rose smoothly.

Karen thought of mad scientists, and had a momentary image of Matt sitting up in his coffin, sewn back together with huge, jagged stitches, ready to walk the town with arms stiff out in front of him. But then she looked again, and in the moonlight, thought that it looked as if Matt were rising to heaven.

"Oh Jesus, oh Jesus," moaned Karen. "Oh God," she said, and mumbled a prayer under her breath.

With a click, the mechanism stopped, and the coffin was level with the gravestone. Karen jumped up from her crouch, alarmed at this sudden physical proximity to death. They all took a step backwards.

Sebastian approached the coffin again and lay both hands on it, like he was performing a healing. Then he got into what Karen would describe as a three-point stance at the end of the casket, and started pulling. The coffin was heavy, but it slid towards him. "Help me!" he screamed. No one moved. "This is my brother! Help me." It was apparent that Sebastian wasn't going to stop pulling on the casket, and that as it slipped from the straps, the end would fall to the ground. Karen had a flash of what would happen then. She leapt forward and took a position at the side of the coffin, and Evey did the same. They were like pallbearers in a rewound version of the funeral. They lifted the coffin off its hammock, and out into the night. It was extremely heavy, and the end Evey was holding drooped a bit.

"What are we doing?" Evey panted desperately.

Sebastian looked up at her where she was struggling. "Put it down, put it down on the ground," he said.

They placed it gently on the ground. "We're taking him with us," said Sebastian.

"We don't even have a car, Sebastian. We have to put him back." Evey was trying not to cry.

She wasn't sure why she said it, but Karen said, "I have a truck. I have Happy's truck. It's a flatbed."

"Who's Happy?" Sebastian asked.

Karen looked away. "He's my friend. I have straps. If we can get it on the back, we can take it with us."

"And then?" Evey asked. She was shaking.

Sebastian said, "Something better than this. A proper send-off. We can bring him back, if we have to. But for now, we're taking him with us." He paused for a moment and then said, "I just want to spend a little time with my brother. We can bring him back, but after we spend some time together. We'll bring him back, Evey."

And suddenly, they were all beyond the point when they could have said *stop*, when they could have said *this is crazy*. They were drunk and exhausted and spent. They felt small and failed. And there seemed to be a certain honor, or at least inevitability, to what they were doing. "Okay," said Sebastian. "Go get the truck."

Karen started to walk off. "Wait!" said Sebastian. Karen looked back at him, questioning. "Take this," he said, and threw her the flashlight.

When she left the two of them, she knew what she was doing, what they were doing, was crazy. She didn't even know these people. And this must be something she could go to jail for. She didn't owe these people anything. *But that's the problem*, Karen thought, *I don't owe anyone anything. No, she thought, I'm being stupid. What the fuck am I saying? This is not something I should talk myself into. I am robbing a fucking grave. Owing has nothing to do with it.* She decided she would get into her truck and just leave.

When she found the truck, it looked reassuring in its solid bulk. She climbed into the cab, and just sat there for a moment, breathing in the scent of it: the tang of sweat, the undercurrent of motor oil, and something she couldn't quite place. It smelled familiar. She turned the key, and heard the low throbbing of the diesel engine. She couldn't just leave those two by the grave. She had no idea what would happen to them there, but she realized that she was a part of this. And she couldn't just flee. She drove very slowly back to where she had left them. Karen left the truck running with the headlights on, and hopped down from the cab. "Okay," Karen said.

They all took up their positions next to the coffin. They were working silently now. They hoisted it up and toward the back of the running truck, which in the daylight, was the exact color of the sky before it rained. Karen wasn't sure Evey was strong enough to do this, and she tried to help by shifting her weight a bit. The women were in front, and they managed to get their end of the coffin tilted up toward the bed. They had the angle right, and were just able to support it by leaning it against the tailgate. Karen's fingers ached and her arms were shaking. But the coffin was very, very heavy, and now the weight of it was toward the back. It would be up to Sebastian alone to move it up and into the flatbed. Sebastian let out a low scream, a great yell like something splitting open, and pushed with all his strength until the coffin slid into place in the back of the truck. He jumped up after it. "Where are the straps?" he asked Karen.

She rummaged in the cab for a moment and returned with heavy, nylon straps. She helped Sebastian secure the coffin with them, ratcheting them tightly across. When they were done, they jumped back to the ground. The three of them stood looking at the coffin, sweating. Karen felt like they had accomplished something. Like there was something that had to be done, and they had managed, against all odds, to complete the task. She was afraid, and she could tell that Evey and Sebastian were, too.

CHAPTER EIGHTEEN

When Happy was eighteen, his grandfather died. His grandfather had owned a house, in the north, where it seemed to rain all the time. He had built the house himself, and even after his children had all moved to Belgrade, and his wife and his dog and all his chickens had died, Happy's grandfather continued to live there. The neighbors brought him food and firewood, and they noticed that he had started to collect things. Not just to collect them, but to label them. When his grandfather died, Happy was surprised to find that the house had been left to him. Happy had moved some of his belongings into the little house, and took stock of what was there.

In the attic, Happy found an old, broken accordion, three chairs in need of re-caning, a box of assorted silverware labeled "silverware 1909-1982" in his grandfather's unsteady Cyrillic, and another box with fourteen bottles of shampoo which read "Shampoo. Bought 6/8/86. On sale two for one. Note: I don't use shampoo." On the fuse box in the basement, under the topmost fuse, was a piece of tape with the words: "Changed fuse 3/9/93 after breakfast with Dimitar. Eggs and mushrooms and sausage. Very good." When Happy peeled back some of the labels in the house, he found other labels underneath. So that a mantle above the fireplace might bear the explanation, "make fire in here when cold" and then, if Happy dug a little deeper, "Dimitar placed pictures on mantle 4/27/89. All of grandchildren. Said I was lonely" and below that, "Mila hit head on this corner 7/14/74 after drinking rakia" and finally, "repainted 8/12/71. White. Eggshell finish."

Happy was a little in awe of the house. His grandfather's memory had become entirely external, completely physical. Each chair in his house, each fork, each cracked, yellowed bar of soap bore the palpable, blatant idea of its own story, and of the story of Happy's family. Walking through the rooms, Happy remembered the time his cousin had dropped him on his head when Happy was only an infant. He was reminded of the his first haircut, when his mother sat him on the kitchen counter in his grandfather's house, put a bowl on his head, and cut around it in the shape of a pudding. His uncles and aunts had all stood around and teased him about being afraid. They had cheered when the first lock fell to the floor. He remembered kicking chickens out of his way when he came to visit his grandfather, and the time he and his uncle had slaughtered five of them for Christmas.

When Happy had brought Milinka to this home, she had been afraid. They were at University together, Happy studying Archeology and Milinka Biology. They met in their second year, and Happy, who was a proud homeowner, had sometimes brought his friends all the way from Belgrade to drink rakia and Heineken and sing and watch television in his grandfather's house. Milinka had been raised in the city, and she was unsettled by the noises and darkness around the house. She did not want to make love in a house with so much history; she said she felt like the grandfather was watching them. It was not a simple matter of turning around a photograph of Happy's grandfather in the bedroom. The whole house had become Happy's grandfather, all the moments and uses of his life.

Happy had often wished that he could show Karen his grandfather's house. He wanted her to not be afraid of his past.

He wanted her to see the kind of family he had –a gathering group of people around who did difficult and unpleasant things for each other when there were difficult and unpleasant things to be done. But also a group of people, some related by blood, some not, who shared each other's food and drink, songs and children and arguments. He wanted to show her that this is what his children should have been born into—that his children didn't have to be entirely his (no children really belonged to their parents), and they didn't have to be entirely hers either, if she would have him.

Milinka had believed in family. Milinka had come to believe that Happy was an essentially good man, if sloppy, and that her children would be wonderful boys if they were fed, and read to, and taught how to make Turkish coffee. Happy had loved his wife. She was good-enough looking (smaller and much darker than Karen, with tiny hands and big, full eyebrows she waxed into tapered arrows on her forehead), she was sharp (always good at biology, she also read every piece of fiction she could get her hands on, regardless of quality) and hard working (when they came to America she took care of their children better than he did, and cleaned houses for some rich ladies, and was taking classes at the community college to finish her degree) and she was faithful (had never asked him what he did until two in the morning on days when he went out after he had read a book to the boys).

When she got sick, Happy was scared. He was scared of her pain, and scared of her rage. Milinka was so *angry* that she was sick. Happy hadn't wanted to hear the crushing survival rates for pancreatic cancer. He hadn't wanted to hear about the brutal side effects of Gemcitabine, and that only twenty-five percent of patients could be helped. He didn't want to, but he brought both boys to her, in the hospital, on the day that she died. The three of them, even the tiny Radoslav, held her hands while she passed away. There had been nothing at all wrong with Milinka in life, except that she didn't *really* inspire love in Happy. He had never felt the way about Milinka that he felt about Karen now. There was nothing wrong with Milinka, except that he didn't love her. *So maybe*, he thought, *there is only something wrong with me.*

"If there is something wrong with me," Happy said aloud, "that is a very good news. It is only something I should fix." He had been momentarily stunned by his revelation, but he shook his head and recalled himself to his present situation. He was standing with his back to the bar, hands uselessly at his sides, sweating through his shirt. It was getting late, and there were people all around him. It was not really so strange, he thought, that he should be thinking about his house of memories on the last day of the existence of Karen's bar and Karen's home. None of this remembering or parsing of the past was helping Happy feel better tonight, though. He made his way to the bar for another drink. He ordered a vodka tonic and noticed, out of the corner of his eye, Karen's mother standing near the pinball machine in the corner. He knew her from the bar, and had often seen her. But he had never spoken to her, because Karen had forbidden him to. He ordered and took two shots in quick succession, for confidence. Then, vodka in hand, he weaved through townspeople to Mrs. Amato. She turned slightly to face him when he was shoved against her by a young person, green in the face, trying to get out the door and make it to the bushes before he threw up all over himself.

"I am afraid I love your daughter," Happy said.

"Oh," said Sarah Amato, "and who are you?"

"My name is Happy Bankovic. I am from a country that does not exist anymore. I have two children who I love like fishes love in water. I have a wife who is not the daughter that is yours. I was a boxer at university, but now I only am training others. And I have a huge love for your daughter." Happy realized that the vodka was doing nothing for the complexity of his sentences, but he thought Karen's mother might understand because Happy was pretty sure that her husband had been Italian, and he was pretty sure that there were no Italians in the part of the Illium cemetery that dated back to the seventeen-hundreds. Every American, he thought philosophically, learned to speak English from the beginning.

"I see," said Sarah, who extended her hand to shake Happy's. Happy looked at her incredulously. She was completely sober and he wasn't sure how she could stand it. "You don't live here, do you?" she asked. "You're not one of the men from upstairs? Have all your appendages intact?"

Happy shook Sarah's hand while shaking his head no, and then nodding, yes, yes. He did not tell her that he had lost part of his fourth toe on his right foot playing with an axe when he was twelve.

"Well, then. Does Karen know all this?"

"Yes, Mrs. Amato. Your daughter knows. She maybe understands the thing better than I am understanding. She says is morally outrageous, dot. The story is ended. This she says."

To Happy's immense surprise, Sarah began to laugh. "Yes," she said, "that sounds like Karen. It is morally outrageous." She wiped a tear from her eye. "But you said you have children. Tell me about your children."

"My children are brilliant, what you want to know? They're blond. They American now; want everything. Last year it was Thanksgiving they want. Yes, we eat turkey. Our turkey is dead. I never eat turkey in November in Yugoslavia. Gravy even. And I hate gravy. The whole nine yards. I don't know what it means, but the whole nine yards. It probably has something to do with baseball." Happy could not imagine why he was telling Sarah these things, but he couldn't stop himself. He couldn't stand very straight anymore either. He leaned his ass against the back of a seated schizophrenic.

"You said you have a wife?"

"Yes. My wife." Happy brought his glass to his lips to stifle any further words, but they poured out of him. The first bit of his speech was muffled but he gave in and brought the glass back down. "Mrs. Amato," he said. "She is good woman. Works all day cleaning houses for rich people. And worst part is, in Yugoslavia we thought we were capitalists. Say you have so many rights in America. But what rights, I want to know? In Yugoslavia, big oppression, sure. But we have the right to education and medicine and not save every dollar because we might not have work soon. Freedom of speech. This is not big legislature. Come on, is human right, it can't be take away. Big deal, freedom of speech. You know your freedom of speech no good at night, or at certain volume, or with some people. The last good thing to happen in the world was 1917."

"That seems to be before either of our times, Happy. And what does Karen say?" Happy opened his mouth to explain, but Sarah cut him off. "Forget it. Who cares. But this is just great. Jesus Christ. Adultery. And there's children involved." She laughed a little. "It's okay, Happy. I get it; you're a complicated person. Let me think for a minute."

"Okay, Mrs. Amato."

"Sarah, please. We're practically family."

"What do you think I should do?"

"Does your wife know?"

"What? My—no. My wife is dead."

"Oh Christ, Happy. She's dead." Sarah looked carefully at him. "You have a dead wife. You are not married. So what is the problem?"

Happy looked as Sarah, and he couldn't quite tell if she was laughing or angry. "Karen says, that we should —"

She cut him off: "You know what? Karen is a lot younger than you."

"I know, Mrs. Amato."

"Sarah. Karen is a lot younger than you. And the thing about young people is, they're stupid. They don't know what is right and wrong, they don't know what they want, and they certainly don't know what is good for them." Happy blinked at her. "Your children will hate you, if you marry my daughter. If you get remarried, chances are, those boys will never forgive you for it."

Happy nodded sadly.

Sarah looked away from him, and said quietly, "My child was my whole life, and I don't regret a moment of that. But it doesn't have to be that way, you know. Being forgiven isn't really the point." She touched her hair with her hand. "Do you love my daughter?"

"Yes, Mrs. Sarah."

"Show me your teeth. How do you feel about dental hygiene?"

Happy tried to answer and open his mouth for her at the same time. Sarah pulled his lower jaw down and peered into his mouth. It was dark in the bar, and Happy was glad that the gloom would hide nine silver fillings.

"You think she's beautiful?"

"Almost all of her. Especially her hair and her eyes and her feet. Nice breasts too."

"Would you do hard things for her, even when you think you cannot?"

"I would."

"Then that's what matters. You want my daughter, then hey, I think that works. But it is work. And if you ever cheat on her, I will rip both of your arms off."

CHAPTER NINETEEN

Karen drove them out of the cemetery and through the town with their headlights on low-beam, Evey straddling the gear shift in the middle of the cab, and Sebastian pressed against the door next to her. They wound back down Route One at a funeral pace, the truck and its bier moving through the town. When Karen got close to the Palais Royale, she cut the lights and tried to pull discretely into the dirt yard that abutted the river around the back of the bar. But they had been seen. As she and Sebastian descended from the cab, they were surrounded by people, mostly drunk and grinning, some serious and trying to stay upright. They were greeted as heroes. Patrons shoved beers into their hands, slapped them on the back. James was in the crowd, and disengaged himself and approached the one-ton. Evey was still in the cab of the truck. She could see James's long frame moving toward her with gathering speed. He threw himself onto the hood and scrabbled up against the windshield with enough force that Evey jumped. "What the fuck, James?" she shouted through the closed window.

James roared with laughter. "Got you, didn't I?" he yelled back.

"Get off the hood."

James jumped down from the hood, but walked around to the passenger side. He plastered himself against the window, and

Evey could see his face molded into a grotesquery of joy. "Let me in, Evey," he mouthed. Evey stiffened against the back of the seat. She stopped breathing. "Let me in, Evey," James said again, his mouth stretching each syllable into elongated expression.

Evey pulled the door handle and pressed the door open against James's body, hard. She screamed "Sebastian! Sebastian!" James looked wounded, and he collected himself and backed away. He looked—not hurt, but like a child who has fallen down and started to cry before he realizes he is fine, and then has to inexpertly arrange his body into a posture that will garner just the right amount of sympathy. He turned around and stared into the crowd. Evey stepped out into the night and was instantly surrounded by people.

Two men seized her arms and lifted her into the air. "Sebastian!" she yelled. She was aloft and being supported by many hands. She saw Stan by the porch. "Stan!" she screamed. She looked out and saw each shining face. She saw Sebastian, and she knew with complete certainty that she loved him, and that she would do whatever it took to make a life with him.

People leapt onto the back of the flatbed and poured beer onto the coffin. Someone emptied a bottle of ouzo onto the top of the cab of the flatbed. A hymn rose up, drunken voices singing "Savior when in dust to Thee/ Low we bow the adoring knee" in lopsided harmony.

"Where'd ya get the coffin?" someone yelled from the back porch. It became apparent that the people in the bar thought that this was a symbolic funeral for the Palais Royale. And it was easy to believe. The unvarnished coffin looked like a fake. No one knew that this was Matt's coffin, or that this was anyone's coffin. Or rather, they thought it was the Palais's coffin. It was the body of all of what belonged to all of them, and what they all belonged to. They were burying a part of themselves. Evey, who had been put back down on the ground with a Heineken in her left hand, thought of pictures she had seen in the newspaper of a symbolic funeral held by black religious leaders a month ago, burying once and for all the word "nigger." The coffin had looked huge in the pictures, as if that word had been a giant.

The priest from St. Margaret's was at the Palais, as was the Congregational minister. They were herded out to the truck and asked by the crowd to say a few words over the last resting place of the Palais Royale. Both demurred. Happy pushed through the crowd, holding Karen's mother's hand and bringing her with him. When Karen saw them approach she could picture what tomorrow would look like. She could picture going home to her mother, climbing into her childhood bed and pulling the patchwork quilt up to her mouth. Happy wrapped his arms around Karen from behind. He pointed at the coffin with his chin. "This is not," he whispered into her ear, "what seems it to be, Karen, is it?" Karen shook her head.

The Congregational minister was surrounded. The crowd had started by respectfully asking for Biblical verse to make this a proper funeral, but their request had devolved into shouts of "Speech, speech, speech," as if this solemn occasion were in fact the end of a bachelor party and the minister was the best man.

The minister saw no option. He raised both hands above his head, and the gesture silenced the group that had gathered around him. "Let us pray," he said, out of desperation. The group lowered their heads. Andy of Handy Andy's Convenience Store grabbed the hand of the man next to him, and grunted for him to do the same. They formed a small, connected circle of worshipers, men and women who were not necessarily normally found in a pew on Sunday. The minister wanted to say "He who believeth in me shall never die," but his nerve failed him at the last minute. He settled on "For every thing there is a fixed time, and a time for every purpose under the sun," and then, skipping ahead past the part of the verse he had always felt to be inadequate, he said,

"I have considered the task which God has appointed men to be busied about. He has made everything appropriate to its time, and has put the timeless into their hearts, without men's ever discovering, from beginning to end, the work which God has done. I have recognized that there is nothing better than to be glad and to do well during life. For every man, moreover, to eat and drink and enjoy the fruit of all his labor is a gift of God. I recognize that whatever God does will endure forever; there is no adding to it, or taking from it. Thus has God done that he may be revered." The minister took a huge breath. "Amen." It had worked, the crowd was silenced, some with tears in their eyes, some grinning like they had just been sated.

The Catholic priest shouted from the edge of the crowd, "Blessed be the Father and the Son and Holy Ghost. As it was in the beginning, is now, and ever shall be. World without end. Amen." And all the assembled shouted back, "AMEN."

Evey looked around in the crowd for Sebastian. She was horrified and panicked. But when she found him, he was right up next to the truck, leaning against its metal flank. She was reminded of protests in the street, water cannons, broken bottles, but Sebastian looked calm. He was shaking his head, but he was grinning and crying at the same time. She put her hand on Sebastian's forehead, as if she were checking him for fever. "I wanted to say goodbye to him," Sebastian whispered. "I wanted to say some last words."

"What would you have said to him?" Evey asked.

Sebastian shook his head again. "I don't know," he said. "I never knew what to say to Matt. We were so different." He couldn't speak through his sobs. "But," he said after a minute. "I loved him so much." Sebastian caught his breath and grinned at Evey. "This is better anyway." Someone threw a beer bottle from the back porch. It hit the coffin and shattered, showering them in glass like sharp falling stars.

Evey's father Richard detached himself from the crowd and ran toward them. Glass crunched under his boots. "Evey!" he said.

"It's okay, Dad. We're okay."

Another bottle exploded on the side of the truck.

Stan too ran to Evey's side. He had no words to say. He thought for a moment that he would always love Evey, and that there was very little he could do about it. He also thought: *the world is not made up of Eveys and Jameses. The world is made up of people just like me: human beings who live every day and will have very little to show for it. This is, he thought,* normal. *And there is,* Stan realized for the first time ever, *something noble in this. It is a kind of winning to live a regular life. To have just this—parents and siblings, a few drinking buddies, a small paycheck, maybe a hobby—to show for it, and nothing else.*

Evey grasped Stan's hand, and he let her. Evey could see now that she would go back to her apartment on Anson Street soon, that this night would be over and that other things would happen in her life. She would make Sebastian dinner and they would eat it and watch the Red Sox on their second-hand television.

Suddenly, the crowd parted. The entire volunteer fire department of Illium was coming down the steps of the Palais Royale, carrying a case of 151 between them, like a tiny stretcher. They hoisted the box onto the back of the truck and leapt up after it, the first fireman extending his hand to pull the second up after him, and the second the third, and so on, until they were all on the back of the truck, surrounding the coffin like an honor guard. Evey recognized the first fireman as Anthony Alby, who had been fat and asthmatic as a child. In a strong, carrying voice, he started singing an old Protestant dirge, "Savior when in dust to Thee." The crowd joined in, screaming the words along with him. And the second verse, fewer voices knew this one with as much certainty, but there was still a chorus of people, holding up their bottles, singing to the moon about wants and tears. With each phrase, the firemen poured out more bottles of 151. The fumes were almost overpowering to anyone standing near the truck. When the last line of the song had faded, all the firemen jumped back down to the earth.

It was Sebastian who stuck and threw the match. The fire caught unevenly, moving first around the coffin in a dancing circle. A huge roar went up from those assembled when, with a whoosh, the wood of the cheap, flimsy coffin caught.

"My truck!" Happy whimpered. "My truck."

"It's only a thing," said Karen's mother, grabbing Happy by the upper arm. It was at that moment that Karen knew she would never be satisfied with him, and he would never be satisfied if his children did not love her. And she knew, just then, that she didn't want him anyway. Happy was part of her old life, of the years that seemed now to her like an interlude in her chronology. But she didn't have to tell him that this moment. There would be plenty of time to let him know of her decision, she thought. Tomorrow, she knew now, she would go to her mother's house and fill out the application for Apollo College.

Sebastian put his shoulder to the back of the Happy Family Boxing Club truck and pushed. The crowd, realizing what he meant to do, surged forward. With a huge yell, all moving together, they pushed the vehicle forward. It seemed to hover, for a moment, on the edge of the embankment, before tipping wheels-first into the Royale River. There was a sizzle, but the flames did not go out. The truck with its burning bier floated a ways into the river, and blazing, started to sink.

Though it was Matt who had died, Sebastian saw his own life flash before his eyes. He saw himself being rocked in his mother's arms while she sang to him about it not being long "before another time." He saw himself in the hospital, peering through thick glass at a newborn Matt. He saw himself secretly pouring gin from his mother's liquor cabinet into a glass of Crystal Lite, and standing in the doorway of his college dorm room, and smoking at a party where he noticed a beautiful and languid Evey. He saw himself on his wedding day, and in a jail cell, and making eggs in his apartment in Somerville. He saw himself and saw himself and saw himself until he saw himself standing in the dirt lot facing the Royale River next to the Palais Royale.

This was happening all through the crowd. Stan pictured himself on his first day of school, feeling his He-Man lunchbox slip from his hand. Evey glimpsed her father's gloved hand, holding her mittened one in their back yard, and heard his voice telling her to look up at the Northern Lights. Richard saw himself, tanned and muscled in tiny swim trunks. The Catholic priest remembered his first, unconsummated love. One of the firemen looked across the years into the face of an infant he had pulled from a flaming crib. Happy could see the flowers he had clutched sweatily to hand to Milosevic at a ceremony during his compulsory stint in the Yugoslavian military. Sarah looked again into Karen's huge, round eyes, peering out of her then-five-year-old face and heard her daughter ask, "What color is that flower, Mommy?" Karen thought in still-lives: of the pictures she had taken of people in Illium, looking lost and larger-than-life, frozen for all time behind the register at the Dunkin Donuts, or in the orchard behind the Congregational church, or smoking a cigarette by the side of the highway, or washing a windshield at the Exxon station. Everyone there saw the moments and the things that they thought they had forgotten.

"Jesus," mumbled one of the schizophrenics who had just stumbled out of the bar and down the steps. "It smells like a tragedy out here."

When the truck started to sink, a lanky twenty-one-year old released a long murmur like he was watching satisfying fireworks. And then the fiery one-ton slipped into the river like the sun going down to rest before inevitably climbing its way back up and into the mess of the lot behind the Palais Royale, and the world, in the morning.

ACKNOWLEDGMENTS

Chapter one previously appeared in a slightly different form in *Words and Images*. Part of chapter three previously appeared, in a different form, in *Action Yes! Quarterly*. An excerpt from *Diary of a Man in Despair* by Freidrich Reck-Malleczewen is quoted in this text. Quotes from the Bible are taken from the Oxford University Press Authorized King James Version published in 1997.

I would like to thank Pine Manor College and Atwood's Tavern for the gifts of time and space while I was working on this novel. I would also like to thank the members of the Atwood's Redraft Writers Group, including Jeremy P. Bushnell, Jake Ruiter, Devlin Farmer, Maric Kramer, and Alex Bandazian. I would like to thank all my students for being a distraction and an inspiration. I am immensely grateful to my husband, Scott Thomson, for his love and support, and to my daughter Megan Agnes for teaching me so much. And thank you to all my friends and family for letting me use your stories, your lives, your ideas and your patience; most especially: Amanda Anderson, Zach, Paige, Clementine and PJ Enright, Ali Dunn and Andrew, Madeline, and Althea Rhine, Alex and Isidora Skular, Kyle J. Simonson, Rebecca Prahl, David Godowsky, Patrick Tonks, Emmet Hunter, Dennis Jen and Joshua Gerber, Lewis Riley, Jamie Thomson, Lucy Hutyra and Bob Reeder, Heather Brown and Glenn Willets, Kurt Klopmeier and Krysten Hill, and Hannah Baker-Siroty. Thank you to my family: Margaret Clark, Christine, Michael, Stephanie, and Meghand Curci, and Wayne B. Clark and Lisa Jacobs.

www.ingramcontent.com/pod-product-compliance
Lightning Source LLC
Chambersburg PA
CBHW031945010726
47493CB00007B/2086